THERE FELL A SHADOW

Andrew Klavan, a former newspaper and radio
reporter, is a two-time winner of the Edgar
Award, one for *The Rain*, the third of the Keith
Peterson titles. Under his own name, he is the
author of *Don't Say a Word*, *Animal Hour*,
Corruption, and, most recently, *True Crime*,
which won the W. H. Smith 'Thumping Good
Read' Award. He lives in London with his wife
and two children and spends summers in
Sharon, Connecticut.

Also by Andrew Klavan in Vista paperback

THE TRAPDOOR

and coming soon

THE RAIN

ROUGH JUSTICE

ANDREW KLAVAN

THERE FELL A SHADOW

VISTA

First published in the USA 1988
by Bantam Books

First published in Great Britain 1990
by Coronet paperbacks

This Vista edition published 1997
Vista is an imprint of the Cassell Group
Wellington House, 125 Strand, London WC2R 0BB

A catalogue record for this book is
available from the British Library.

ISBN 0 575 60229 5

Printed and bound in Great Britain by
Caledonian International Book Manufacturing Ltd,
Glasgow

97 98 99   10 9 8 7 6 5 4 3 2 1

This book is for
Doug and Mary Ousley

"Last night, ah, yesternight, betwixt her lips and mine
There fell thy shadow, Cynara! thy breath was shed
Upon my soul between the kisses and the wine;
And I was desolate and sick of an old passion,
    Yea, I was desolate and bowed my head:
I have been faithful to thee, Cynara! in my fashion."

Edward Dowson

It was the night of the first big snow. I remember that. A slate December sky had threatened the city all that day. The clouds had seemed heavy with the coming storm. The air had seemed brittle with it, like a pane of glass the wind was about to shatter.

Then, around eight that night, the clouds gave way. The air did shatter. The wind blew in. The snow swept out of Jersey and across the Hudson. In Manhattan, at about 8:05 p.m., a single flake drifted gently through the red glow of a Forty-second Street stoplight. It landed daintily in front of Grand Central Terminal and melted to a gray dot on the sidewalk. By 8:07 the air was white and whirling. The gray spot was covered by a white patina. The white patina grew thicker, higher. The red stoplight became a dull rose glow sunk deep in the blizzard's midst.

The last commuters rushing toward the terminal's front doors turned their faces away from the biting wind. They wrestled with their umbrellas or held their newspapers up as shields. The men had to clap their hats tight to their heads. The women had to press the skirts of their coats down against their legs. Bandannas and jackets fluttered everywhere.

Next, as the streetlamps grew halos and dimmed, the horns started. The cars jammed up bumper to bumper on the broad boulevard. The drivers—who by all rights should have missed the evening rush—grew peeved. Their horns wailed and cursed and bleated. The noise rose up and danced in the dancing snow above Forty-second. The line of cars trudged on slowly under the terminal toward the East River Drive.

Manhattan was cold and beautiful. It snowed and snowed. The air around the lighted peak of the Empire State Building seemed almost alive with the whorls and waves of it. The stone lions flanking the steps of the library looked grim and comical under peaked caps of it. And over the bold, arching entrance of Grand Central, the sculpted Mercury spread his arms to it and welcomed it like the god he was.

As for me—as for me and Lansing and McKay—we drank. There was nothing else for us to do. Nothing better, anyway. The Lady and the Tiger story was covered from every angle. The story on the Brooklyn park was solid as I could make it. The bulldog's deadline was past. The late edition was all laid out. The work was done. The snow was heavy. Drinking was just the thing.

We were in the Press Club. Just down Fortieth from the terminal, around the corner from Vanderbilt Avenue and the offices of the *New York Star* from which we'd come. We had beaten the worst of the storm by minutes.

It's a fancy little pub, the P.C. A dark, oaken room. A long bar running through the center. Round oak tables everywhere. Heavy chairs with leather seats and backs held fast by brass studs. The walls are decorated with old newspapers, framed. Not just the splashy headlines like some of the other press bars. Not just Lindbergh and V-E Day and Men Walk On Moon. The good stories, too. The small stories done well. Breslin dancing in a pothole. Clines watching miners go to work in the Pennsylvania dark. Even Lupica giving it to Steinbrenner. Even me, on Frankie and Johnny: the one about the hooker who gunned her pimp down on the Minnesota Strip. The yellow light from yellow lanterns gleams on the fading pages, reflects off the glass in the frames. The rest of the room is dim and pleasant. Not too crowded tonight. Just enough people to keep a buzz of conversation going.

Lansing, McKay, and I sat in a corner by one of the front windows. We watched the snow hit the glass and melt. We watched the glass streak with droplets of water. We squinted through the droplets and watched the snow cover the bags of garbage leaning against each other at the edge of the sidewalk. We drank scotch.

"It's not the tiger banner," Lansing said. "I don't mind that. I don't mind the sidebars. I don't mind any of it." She was leaning back in her chair, her arm resting on the table, her hand wrapped casually around her glass. She smiled and shook her head. Her long blond hair slapped at her face lazily. Her hair gleamed in the lamplight. "It's him I mind," she went on. "It's the way he drools over the blood that gets me. The way his face fell when we told him she'd only lost an arm."

"The man's an idiot," said McKay. His mouth drew down at the corners as he studied the surface of his drink. His baby face almost managed to look severe. "That thing with the parents . . ." He shook his head. He couldn't finish. He was too ticked off.

Lansing reached over and patted his arm. She turned her face to me. "And then when you got confirmation on the borough president, I thought he was going to take your head off. Like you were intruding. Messing up his sleaze with news."

I laughed.

"Come on, Wells," she said. "Don't laugh. You know it bothers you."

She gave me a look. High cheeks. Blue eyes. Rich lips. Rich, rich lips. I stopped laughing. I shrugged instead.

"And don't shrug," she said.

"Can I drink?"

"Yes."

"Thanks," I said. I drank until the ice rattled against my teeth. I set the empty glass down on the table with a thud.

The subject under discussion was Robert Cambridge. He was the managing editor of the *Star*, had been now for a year and a half. They'd hired him off a California paper. His mandate was to revamp the old tabloid. Make it more exciting. More "relatable," he called it. "Think about your audience," he'd tell us in his weekly staff meetings. He'd slouch in his chair at the conference table to show us what a regular guy he was. His voice would uncoil softly, like a snake at suppertime. "Does your audience wake up in the morning wondering what happened in South Africa or Iran? No. Of course not. They think about the things that will affect them, that will impact on you and me. That everyone can relate to. Think like them. Think you-and-me. Think relatability. Don't just go around thinking news, news, news all the time!'' And here he'd make a dreary news-news-news face. ''Think—*infotainment*.''

McKay was right. The man was an idiot.

Last night, up at the Bronx Zoo, some vandals had played a practical joke. This morning a pretty young zookeeper named Suzanne Feldman had become their punch line. And our headline. The vandals had somehow crept into the zoo and cut through the mesh of the tiger's cage. Maybe they'd planned to free the beast. As it turned out, all they managed to do was open one or two of the squares in the mesh. Come morning, as Suzanne was going about her duties, she noticed the damage.

At that point, she should have called her supervisor. Instead she hopped the fence and went over for a closer look. The tiger—her name was Antoinette—was lying down peacefully. She was all the way back against the enclosure's rear wall. Suzanne deemed it safe to poke around at the damaged wire with her hand.

She deemed wrong. Antoinette pounced lazily. Witnesses said it was the movement of a second. A couple of strides and a flying leap. That was all. Suzanne Feldman was yanked tight against the cage. She was screaming as if her arm were being torn off. It was. By the time two janitors rushed to her side, she had fallen away from the cage. She was sitting upright against the fence. She was not screaming anymore. Instead, she was staring wide-eyed into the cage where Antoinette was enjoying a second breakfast.

''Look. She's eating my arm,'' Suzanne Feldman had said quietly to the janitors. Then she fainted.

The press has a lot in common with Antoinette: other people's misfortunes are its meat. I've been a newspaperman since I left my brother and sister to bury our mother and hoboed down to New York out of Maine. I was twenty one. Twenty-five years ago. I know a good story when I hear one. I know how to get it and write it and play it big. The Lady and the Tiger could handle the banner Cambridge would lay on it. But Lansing was right. He didn't have to drool over it.

''Did it kill her?'' he said, when Lansing first gave him the word.

"No," said Lansing. "It just ate her arm."

"Oh. Gee. Well, still. Even so: I love it. Great, great story. Take McKay up there with you, he can do the color. And I'll give you Gershon for the pix." Making these assignments was the city editor's job. But Cambridge couldn't leave a story this big to the city editor. He couldn't leave anything to anybody. In fact, before McKay left for the Bronx, Cambridge pulled him aside and put his arm around him. He can do that to McKay because McKay is young and has a wife and kid and needs the job.

"Once you get up there," he told McKay in a confidential voice, "ask around, find out, you know, did she have a husband or a boyfriend. How's he gonna feel now she's only got one arm? You know? Is he gonna sue the zoo or what? And how about her mother? Call her mother, you know. She'll cry. It's good copy."

McKay's plump cheeks turned beet red. He nodded. He slithered out from under Cambridge's arm. He walked away.

While all this was going on, I was in one of our better Times Square movie emporiums. I was watching the early showing of "The Perils of Francine." It was a sensitive, insightful epic about a young woman who manages to touch the lives of every male creature in the state of California. It was tough for me to follow the story line, though. The guy sitting next to me kept talking. He was a young lawyer who worked for the city parks commissioner. What he was talking about was the construction of a Brooklyn playground. That playground had now been under construction for seven years. Its projected cost was now five times more than the original estimate and still rising. Slouched in Francine's flickering shadows, whispering in nervous bursts half-lost beneath the cries of passion from the screen, the young lawyer outlined the process by which the contract for the playground had been funneled to a construction company owned by a gentleman named Anthony Giotto. Giotto—who was currently awaiting trial on federal racketeering charges—had apparently directed the payment of a large bribe to a top Brooklyn official. The young lawyer could not give me the name of the official. He didn't have to. I'd been working on the story for two weeks. I knew pretty well who it was.

That evening, about three hours before we adjourned to

the Press Club to watch the storm, I got it solid. I'd landed myself a borough president: Glen Robins. I had him dead to rights. I called the man. Gave him a chance to defend himself. He told me to talk to his lawyer. His lawyer refused comment.

I brought the story to the city editor, a decent old guy named Hugh Rafferty. Rafferty sat at the city desk, rapping angrily at his computer. He was going over the day's minor stories. The big story was the tiger. Cambridge had taken charge of that.

"Talk to *him*," said Rafferty grimly.

I sighed. Cambridge does not look upon me entirely with favor. He seems to feel I oppose his mission to relatabilitize the newspaper. He says I have an attitude problem. He says I have a "problem with authority." He has invited me into his office for informal chats on the subject. Somehow the problem only grows worse. I'm told he's now convinced I'm trying to "undermine" him. If it weren't for the fact that revelations of widespread municipal corruption keep appearing in our paper before any of the competing papers, I do believe he'd let me go.

But I had no choice. I took my story to Cambridge. He was in Lansing's cubicle. His jacket was off. His tie was undone. He was bending over her shoulder as she sat at her computer terminal. He was telling her how to write her story.

"You better have a look at this," I said to him. I handed him the pages I'd pounded out on my old Olympia.

He looked at them. He looked at me. "Well, what do you want me to do about it?" he said. Sarcasm dripped from him like Spanish moss from a Georgia live oak. "You want me to stop the presses? Replate page one? Jesus, Johnny, we've got a big story here. I got a fucking zoo can't keep its tigers away from the customers. I got people getting their arms ripped off right and left. I mean, okay, great, he's a borough president, it's a decent story. But I mean, what am I supposed to do about it?"

Lansing turned in her chair. "You got a borough president?"

"Corlies Park," I told her. "I finally found the bribe."

"Oh, man! Great stuff." The way she smiled at me made my teeth hurt.

It was Cambridge's turn to change colors. He selected

chalky white. I don't think he likes it when Lansing makes my teeth hurt.

"Hey," he said to her, with an ingratiating smile that hurt yet another part of my anatomy. "What's the matter? Don't you like having your story on page one?"

The look Lansing gave him—that was the first hint I got that it was going to snow.

"I can't wait," she said to me now as we sat and drank and talked it over in the Press Club. "He'll give you the skyline today. Tomorrow, the *News,* the *Times,* and *Newsday* will lead with it. We'll get beat out on our own story."

"Maybe they'll notice upstairs." McKay was wilting now over his second scotch. Knocking on Mrs. Feldman's door to ask her about her daughter had taken a lot out of him. "Maybe they'll fire him. Maybe they'll bring charges. Send him to court. Execute him."

I jammed my cigarette out in the table's huge glass ashtray. "That's not the way it works. I've seen a lot of Cambridges in my time. That's not the way they go."

The two young folk lent an ear to the ancient mariner.

"He'll be fired all right," I told them. "Another six months, a year, year and a half at most. But it won't be for incompetence. The guy who hired him will make sure of that because if his hire looks bad, then he looks bad. But, one way or another, soon enough, relatability will become the status quo. They'll want something new, something with more pop to it. Just like they wanted when they brought Cambridge in. Then Cambridge'll be gone."

"Then there'll be another Cambridge," said McKay.

"There'll always be a Cambridge," I said. "But Cambridge is one of the worst."

McKay sank disconsolately toward his glass.

"Shouldn't you be getting home?" Lansing said to him. She said it kindly. Then glanced over at me.

I ignored the glance. Lansing is half my age, and not so tough, I'd guess, when no one's looking. I shook another cigarette out of the pack. Jabbed it between my lips. Lifted a match to it. I kept ignoring the glance. But, as the match flame screened me, I raised my eyes a little. As I did, I saw an answering flame flare up in the rear of the bar, in one of its dark corners.

The burst of fire drew my gaze. At first I thought it was a reflection. Then I saw a man sitting alone at a table in the back. He was lighting a cigarette like I was. I saw his face glow red in the match light.

It was a haunted face, drawn and weary. The face of a fairly young man, no more than thirty-five, with hair still thick and black. But his cheeks were craggy, his expression hard, his eyes sunken, brooding under heavy brows. As he held the match to the tobacco, those eyes peered across the room, fixed and fascinated by something at the front of the bar.

The man shook the match out. He sank into shadow. He sat huddled in the smoke from his cigarette as if for warmth.

I turned, following his gaze. The door to the club had opened. Three men had come in.

2

They stood together in the doorway, stomping the snow off their shoes, shaking it off their overcoats. They cursed the blizzard in booming voices. They sounded like men who had drunk and eaten well.

I knew them. I knew two of them, anyway.

One of them was a friend of mine, Solomon Holloway. He was the bureau chief for one of the wire services here. He was a chubby, elfin man. Dignified in his way. Bald on top with a halo of gray. Small, round, friendly features with mischievous eyes. Chocolate-colored skin that gleamed in the light.

On his left was Donald Wexler, the editor in chief of *Globe*, the newsweekly. Short, thin, small boned. Graying yellow hair, well coiffed. A delicate face, sagging a little. Moist eyes and pursed lips. He tried to hire me from the paper once. We were still on decent terms.

I didn't know the third man. A long, lean, wiry fellow. Tan and rugged. Looked like a cowboy.

They peeled off their coats, draped them over the hatcheck counter. I turned to look again at the haunted man on the other side of the room. His shadow had faded away completely. He was gone.

When I turned back, Holloway had spotted me.

"John Wells!"

Wexler looked my way and smiled. "Wells it is!"

I saluted them. They approached our table, the third man trailing.

Holloway gestured at him. "Timothy Colt, I'd like to introduce you to the dean of New York crime reporters."

"He'd like to," I said, standing. "But I'm all he's got."

Colt and I shook hands. I'd heard of him. I'd read his stuff. He was one of those guys who travels around the world, following the sound of gunfire. A foreign correspondent, and one of the best. He had a way of writing about war as if there were nothing in it but sadness. No right, no wrong, just sadness. I was pleased to meet him.

I introduced McKay. Then I introduced Lansing. Colt's eyes narrowed at her. The three grabbed chairs and sat down with us. Colt made sure he got his seat in next to hers.

A waitress came over. A pretty blond in regulation black tights, white skirt. The three newcomers ordered. Again, I glanced toward the table in the rear. Still empty. Cigarette smoke hung over it.

"So who are you busting today, Wells?" Holloway said. "Am I gonna have something for the morning?"

"Don't look at me," I said. "Our banner's the tiger."

"A farewell to arms." Holloway laughed.

"Yeah," said Lansing proudly, "but our skyline's a bribe to Brooklyn's borough prez."

Holloway's lips parted. "Robins?"

"Read about it in the bulldog, Solomon," I said.

The waitress brought the drinks. A beer in front of Colt, a brandy in front of Wexler, a martini in front of Holloway. Holloway sipped the martini, stared at me over the rim of the glass.

He set the glass down. "Corlies Park, you bastard. You finally got Corlies Park."

"It'll cost you thirty-five cents to find out," I said. "But for that, you get the sports and columns, too."

"You bastard," he said.

"Oh, when will you turn away from the vain life of daily headlines," said Donald Wexler, sniffing at his brandy, "and come to the tropic paradise of the weekly magazine?" He drank.

Before I had a chance to avoid answering that, Colt chimed in. His voice had a rich twang to it. Oklahoma, was my guess.

"Wells, John Wells." He pointed a lazy finger at me. "I've seen yer stuff. Corruption in city government, that kind of thing."

"The voter's friend, that's me," I said.

"Yeah. Yeah, it's good stuff. Got a sort of . . . meloncholy to it. Yeah. Real good."

"Thanks. I liked your pieces from Iran."

He studied me a while, nodding thoughtfully. But in another moment, his gaze shifted direction. He had other business. "Now you," he said to Lansing. "I cain't say I've heard of you before."

He put his arm on the back of her chair. He leaned toward her. She sent a rapid glance at me. I wouldn't play. I reached for the ashtray, crushed out a cigarette, hard. Her gaze was drawn back to Colt. Her cheeks colored a little. He was a good-looking guy. His eyes went deep and there was something vital and electric about them. They kept moving—not nervous, but watchful. I had seen them, after he first sat down, as they calmly memorized the lay of the room. They had seemed to catch the movements at the tables, at the bar. And whenever the door opened, whenever someone came in or out, they turned casually to study them, to file them away.

But right now they were fixed on Lansing. They traveled over her where she sat and seemed to pull every detail of her into their depths.

"What is it you do?" he asked.

"Spot news, for the most part," Lansing said hoarsely. She hid behind her drink.

"She won the AP for the Yorktown Building Collapse," Holloway said.

"AP," said Colt with deep appreciation.

Lansing appealed to heaven. Colt laughed. She smiled.

Wexler helped out: "Colt just got back from Afghanistan."

"Oh?" said Lansing.

"Behind rebel lines," said Holloway. He nodded at Colt. Colt shrugged.

"Oh, come on now, don't be modest," Lansing said. Her voice was warm. "What's it like over there these days?"

Colt shrugged again. "It looked mighty like a war to me."

"And Colt should know," said Holloway, with a jolly laugh in his martini. "He's covered most of them."

The lines of Colt's rugged face turned down in a frown. "It's a livin'," he said softly.

"Oh now, come clean, dear boy," said Wexler. I saw a somewhat nasty gleam in those wet eyes. "You know what Voltaire said: 'Once a philosopher, twice a pervert.' You wouldn't keep going to war if you didn't like it."

I sensed Colt tighten. He withdrew his arm from the back of Lansing's chair. "Voltaire said that about goin' to whorehouses."

There was silence for a minute. I saw Lansing take the opportunity to glance up at Colt's profile.

Then Holloway laughed. His thick lips curled in an impish V. "All I know," he said, "is that Sentu was war enough for me."

"Hear, hear," said Wexler.

He lifted his snifter. Colt smiled, shook his head. His hands closed on his beer. He lifted it, too. Holloway followed with his martini. The three looked at each other. Their glasses came together, touched in the air. Lansing, McKay, and I watched quietly.

"To Sentu," said Holloway.

"Sentu," said Wexler.

Colt echoed: "Sentu."

And, as each brought his drink to his lips, Holloway added: "The making of us all."

They drank. I looked at Lansing. She tilted her head to one side. I glanced at McKay. He gestured uncomfortably with his hands. I glanced, finally, at the three men drinking their obscure toast.

That's when I saw the haunted man again.

He had reappeared suddenly. From somewhere in the back. I remembered there was a flight of stairs back there that led down to the rest rooms and a broom closet. Now he was moving swiftly toward the front door. His head was ducked down behind the collar of his heavy overcoat. His shoulders were hunched as if to further shield him from view. He wove through the tables with smooth, quick strides, looking neither to the right nor the left.

In a moment he'd reached the door. He grabbed the handle and pulled. The wind gusted in. It blew back his collar, bared his face. Snow swirled over the floor, rose around his

ankles. He seemed about to plunge forward, to vanish into the
blizzard.

The sound of shattering glass stopped him.

Startled, I followed the sound. I saw Colt: he had turned
to check the movement of the door. He sat frozen in his chair.
His cheeks were the color of ashes. His hand was still curled
as if he were holding his beer mug. He wasn't. It had slipped
through his fingers. It had fallen to the floor, and the thick
glass had exploded into a million pieces. The pile of them
glittered in the pale light.

When the glass broke, the man in the doorway halted,
swiveled. He and Colt locked eyes. The whole bar had gone
silent. There was only the wild, hollow sough of the wind as
it brought in the snow.

Then—in a hoarse gasp that seemed part of that wind—
Colt said: "You!"

The door handle slid from the man's grasp. The door swung
shut slowly. The sound of the wind died. Colt pushed unsteadily to his feet.

"Colt," Holloway said. He reached for Colt's arm. Colt
shook him off. Wexler made no effort to stop him. He sat
transfixed.

"You!" Colt said again. He growled it this time.

The haunted man stood still and waited. Colt stalked him.
Came near him step by step until he was standing with him in
a small pool of melted snow. Their faces were inches apart.

Colt said quietly: "You're dead! You're a dead man!"

The other reared back.

Colt shouted: "You're a dead man, goddamn it! Goddamn
it, you owe me an accounting."

He grabbed the man by his lapels. I heard a chair scrape
as Holloway started to his feet. But the haunted man's hand
shot up swiftly. He knocked Colt's arm away with a single
sweeping motion. Colt staggered back a step.

"Not here," the man hissed. "Not here, for God's sake."

Holloway stood poised to leap forward, to separate them
with his thick little body if they came to blows. But Colt did
not move. He seemed to consider. When he finally spoke, his
voice seemed almost calm.

"The Madison," he said. His intent stare never left the
other's face. "I'm at the Madison."

The man nodded.

Colt pointed a finger at him. "Tomorrow."

The man nodded.

Then, readjusting his collar, he pulled the door open again. He stepped out and, in another moment, he had disappeared in the whirlwind of snow.

The door swung shut behind him.

3

olt stared at the closed door for several seconds. Holloway sank back into his chair with a sigh. Wexler closed his eyes, daubed the sweat from his flaccid face with a napkin. Colt turned, running his hand up through his hair. He took a deep breath. Walked slowly to the table, and lowered himself into his chair.

At first, he kept his eyes trained on the tabletop. We waited, trying not to watch him, watching him. Finally, he looked up.

"Guy owes me money," he said softly. "That's all."

We nodded at him. We mumbled, fidgeted. None of us knew what to say.

The pretty waitress returned to our table—cautiously now. She was hunched over protectively, as if she were afraid of us. She raised one blond eyebrow. "Uh . . ." she said nervously. "Does anyone, like, want another drink? Or anything?"

That turned out to be just the right question. We all wanted another drink, every one of us. She hurried off to get them.

"Well," said Wexler, a little too brightly, "nothing like a bit of excitement to enliven the evening, I always, uh, say, you . . ."

Holloway tried to pick up the slack. "It's funny, I remember this guy I used to play poker with. Owed me money. Once we'd been playing five card stud, and I had three kings and an ace in the hole with no other aces showing. I was broke and this other guy, Bennett, he bet ten bucks . . .''

Wexler, Lansing, and McKay listened eagerly as Holloway told his story. I pretended to listen. I kept glancing over at Colt.

Colt kept staring at the tabletop. He did not look like he was thinking about money. He looked startled, like a man who'd just had a lynchpin plucked out of one of the sockets of his universe. Like the guy who finds his wife in bed with his best friend or gets a tragic phone call in the dead of night. I knew the feeling.

The waitress brought our drinks. We all went for them in a single motion: grabbed and lifted them to our lips in unison. Colt gulped his beer fast and fiercely. He sat in silence while the rest of us made efforts at talk. We talked shop. The talk went on for a while, then died away. We ordered another round. We talked politics. We drank. The waitress swept up the shards of Colt's beer glass. By the time she was done, we were ready to refill.

So the conversation went on in fits and starts. The incident at the doorway stayed there with us. It made it hard to talk. It made it easy to drink. Easier to drink than not to. We ordered another round. The snow fell. Beer, martini, brandy, scotch. We drank.

Around us, the murmur of the bar had started up again. No more than an occasional nervous glance came our way from the dimly lighted recesses of the room. This was the big city, after all. Colt's encounter was nobody's business. It certainly wasn't mine. I shrugged it off, stopped watching him. I sat and smoked quietly, half listening to the others. I blew smoke out in a thin stream. It rose into the darkness near the ceiling. Vanished there.

I glanced out the window. The snow was still falling, though not as thickly as before. By now, it had piled up high on the street and sidewalk. The garbage near the curb was just a white hulk. I imagined the whole city—the whole soar and dip of its skyline—was just a series of white hulks out there beyond the tavern walls.

The talk faltered yet again. There was yet another stretch of awkward silence. Colt set his beer glass down heavily. He wiped the foam from his lips with his hand. He put on a grin.

"What is it we were talkin' about anyway?" he said. "Before we were so rudely interrupted."

"Sentu!" said Lansing quickly. My attention returned to her. She sat up very straight. Took a deep breath of relief. She was wearing a pink blouse and we all watched it rise and fall. "I was wondering about that," she said. "What was all that about Sentu? The making of you, you said. What is Sentu, anyway?"

McKay narrowed his eyes. He was studying his latest drink carefully. "It'sh a coun . . . a coun . . . a country. Ishn't it?" He was not much of a drinker, our McKay.

Holloway peered into his martini.

"It was," he said. "It was a country."

McKay lifted a finger in the air. "Africa. They had a revelation there. A reva . . . a reva . . . you know, a lution. A revolution."

"Ten years ago," said Wexler. He exchanged glances with Holloway and Colt.

Then Colt gave a snort. He shook his head. "Je-sus, you fellahs never quit," he said.

McKay grinned at them. "What?" he said. "What?"

"Yeah, come on," said Lansing.

I sat quiet in the rising warmth of the liquor. I listened.

Holloway tapped a palm on his belly, leaned back in his chair. He held his martini under his nose. Stared across the top of it into space. "We were there, the three of us," he said. "Sentu. We were freelancers there. We used to feed dispatches to anyone who would take them. Looking for a big story. Looking for a big break." He laughed a little. "Although— as for me personally—I was looking for a way to escape from Moses Holloway."

"Moses," said McKay. "Yeah. Moses Holloway. I've heard of him. He your father?"

Holloway nodded. "That he was. My father and, I may say, one of the most distinguished black journalists of his generation." He looked at each of us in turn. "The first black man ever to be awarded the Pen Medal. The first to break the color barrier of the White House press corps. First in ties, first in tails, first in the hearts of his countrymen. My old man." He swirled his liquor meditatively. "Not his fault, of course, but a lot for his son to live with all the same." With a deep breath, he came around again, said more brightly: "At any rate . . . At any rate, Sentu was the perfect little country for me. For the three of us. It wasn't big enough for anyone to send a staffer. But it was just rich enough in precious metals for everyone to take the occasional dispatch. And if it fell . . ." He cocked his head, chuckled his wicked, elfin chuckle.

"If it fell to the rebels . . . That was a story worth covering. And it did. And it was. And we were there."

"So now," Colt said, "every time I wander through town, these two corral me and force me from my warm hotel room out into the cold dark night."

"Yes, it's real hard to do," said Holloway.

"Then they ply me with liquor til I get all sentimental-like and tell them what great war correspondents they were before they got fat and rich and old."

"By God, we *were* great," said Wexler. Colt made a face. Holloway laughed. Wexler went on: "No, now wait a minute, wait a minute. I admit that Holloway and I have . . . how shall I put it? Matured, over the years. Moved on to other things, positions more in keeping with our dignity. We haven't merely . . . continued in the same rut day after day."

"Pitiful," said Colt. "I mean, pitiful."

"But the record here is clear," Wexler announced. "Crack correspondent Solomon Holloway managed a series of interviews with the rebel leaders that brought the story to the front page for the first time. I remember hearing how they waved the clips of it in each other's faces on the Senate floor as they debated what the U.S. should do. And you have to understand: the rebels hated us. I mean, they *hated* the western press with a passion. Solomon scooped us all, the black buzzard."

"Yeah, yeah," Holloway said. Colt snorted into his drink. "But this is the man," Holloway went on, indicating Wexler, "who got a Pulitzer out of it."

"Ah!" said Wexler, dismissing it with a wave of his hand. "But I was just trying to get out of there alive."

"I have to admit: it's kind of amazin' you did," said Colt with a laugh. Then, to me: "Wex was sending stuff out of Mangrela when most of us were runnin' for our precious little lives. That was the capital city, Mangrela. Man, when it fell, the rebels . . . They came in there, there was shittin' and shootin' and shellin' enough for everyone. After the U.S. choppers left . . . Well, none of us stuck around to find out what happened after that.''

"Except Wex," Holloway said.

Lansing and McKay looked him over appreciatively. So did I. He shimmered a little through the haze of scotch that was now floating before my eyes. Still, he did not look like the heroic type. He seemed too elegant, too well kept. Sometimes, though, those are the best ones: the playing fields of Eton type.

I called to the waitress. A round for the playing fields of Eton.

"Well," said Wexler. "I had something to prove, too, I suppose. I'd come to New York from the mainline of Philadelphia. Used a number of connections to land myself a fairly prestigious journalistic post. And then promptly had myself fired." He said it lightly. He drained his glass with a casual flair. The pain of it flickered only dimly at the corners of his mouth.

Colt said, "Hell, that was a long time ago."

"Yes. Yes, it was," said Wexler. "But it was something of a scandal at the time. In its minor way. You see, I'd done an exposé on a cult that had started up just a little north of here. Such things were just beginning to become *à la mode*, if you remember. But I was the first to infiltrate a really big one like that . . ."

My mouth opened on a breath of smoke. I knew this story. I'd forgotten that was Wexler.

Wexler noticed my expression. "You remember, Wells?"

"It was . . . I mean, everyone said the story was a fake," I said.

"Oh God, it was worse than that, dear fellow," Wexler said. "My sources were shown conclusively not to exist. I was said to have made the whole thing up in my hurry to . . . shall we say, achieve a position on the newspaper that was in keeping with my social standing."

I could see it all a little better then. I could imagine Wexler in his youth. Rich, pampered—and exiled in disgrace. Alone in the jungles of Africa and its jungle cities. Sweating through the heat and the bugs. And the revolution. The slaughter. The shellfire. I thought of all that, a little drunkenly, and I looked at Wexler now. His moist eyes gleamed with the bitter memories. I could imagine the desperation that had made a hero of him.

"You were set up, weren't you?" Lansing said.

Wexler smiled ruefully. "Set up by the Temple of Love. That was the name of the cult. It had been coming under some examination from the government on a little matter of back taxes. By getting me to disgrace them, then disgracing me, I suppose they hoped to make themselves out to be victims of persecution."

"Di . . . uh . . . wha wash I gonna say?" said McKay.

"You were gonna ask if it worked," I said.

"Oh yeah. Thash right."

"No," said Wexler, with a sudden, incongruous giggle. "The IRS apparently didn't get the joke."

We laughed. We ordered another round. For the IRS. Outside, I noticed, the storm was letting up. Inside, the club was beginning to empty out. Sodden reporters and editors were turning from their drinks to squint out the window at the slackening snow. Every few moments, one would head for the door, vanish into the night. The comfortable hum of voices was fading into silence. The further reaches of the club were slipping into emptiness and darkness. The barkeep was beginning to give us the eye.

"Last round, folks," the waitress said as she dealt out the drinks.

"Hey," McKay said. He lifted his head for the occasion. He pointed irritably at his watch. "Hey . . . ish only ten after midnigh here."

"That's the little hand, goofball," Lansing told him. "It's two a.m."

Poor McKay's mouth fell open hard. He tried to take his Lord's name in vain but couldn't handle the esses. He tried to stand up. He didn't make it. "I gotta call my wife," he said finally.

"Oh hell, Mac, you can't do that," I said.

"She'll be asleep. Anyway, you'll wake up the kid," Lansing said.

"Thash righ . . . Thash righ . . . Then . . . then . . . I gotta go home. Thash it!"

"Now you're talking," I said. "That's the old steel trap."

Satisfied with himself, McKay tried to rise again. This time, Lansing got up and helped him.

"Come on, old sot," she said. "We'll find you a cab." Steady as a rock, she stepped to the hatcheck counter. She returned to us with McKay's overcoat and her own belted black fur over one arm. "I guess I better head home myself," she said. "I'm sure to have more tiger work in the morning. Probably be assigned to cover the tiger's stomach as it digests Suzanne Feldman's arm."

McKay turned green. His cheeks puffed. Lansing shunted him into his coat. Colt jumped up to help her into hers. I saw him smell her hair as he stood behind her, holding the collar while she closed the front around her.

"Maybe I ought to come with you," he said to her. "Help you home."

Lancer belted the coat, turned. She gave him a long look. "I know the way," she said.

He nodded. Smiled down at her. "Maybe I could call you then," he said softly.

Again she considered. "Let me ask you something."

"Anything."

"When are you leaving town?"

His smile soured a little. "Friday. For Nicaragua. I'm doing a piece for *U.S. News.*"

Lansing nodded once. "Another time, Colt," she said.

He took a breath. "Fair enough."

Lansing waved to us. She hung her purse on one arm and McKay on the other. Colt opened the door. The two went out onto the drifted sidewalk. I watched through the window as they wandered toward Madison, in search of a cab.

Holloway laughed as Colt sat down. His laugh seemed bigger, more wicked than it had before. Less like an elf's, more like a giant's laugh. "Well, he's been through a snowstorm already. But I suspect a wifely shitstorm lies ahead for our friend McKay." He laughed his giant laugh again. Wexler looked heavenward.

"Nah," I said. "I know her. A good kid, definitely. She'll just wag her finger a little in the morning, that's all. Bring him the bromo. Mrs. Mac is okay."

We hoisted our final round. To Mrs. Mac.

"Well," said Holloway.

"Yes, it has been lovely," Wexler said.

"Oh, don't tell me you guys are packing it in already,"
said Colt. "I got a whole bottle of J&B back in my room."

But Holloway and Wexler had had enough. Their movements stiff and a bit unbalanced, they worked their way to the
hatcheck. Colt and I followed.

The four of us stepped out of the Press Club. The chill hit
me hard. It forced me to breathe. The cold breath went to my
head. The tall concrete office buildings around me tilted. The
bunting of snow that hung from their ledges clung weirdly
when it should have fallen. I shook my head. The buildings
righted themselves. I was officially smashed.

We strolled to Madison. We had to kick through the snow
to get there. The street was still piled high with it. Madison
had been shoveled, though, and lightly sanded. Miraculously,
when we reached the corner, we saw a cab wending its cautious
way up the otherwise deserted street. Its toplight was on. It
was empty.

We said good-bye to each other. The booze made us af-
fectionate. But when Wexler and Holloway and Colt clasped
hands, it was genuine enough. They had been through the fall
of a country together. That welded them. It always would.

Holloway, Wexler, and I decided to share the cab. Colt
was near enough to his hotel to walk. I held the door while
Holloway and Wexler slid into the backseat.

"Well . . ." I said to Colt. He looked forlorn, standing
alone on the sidewalk, ankle-deep in snow. I could almost see
the empty hotel room in his eyes. Nothing better was waiting
for me. A one-bedroom up on East Eighty-sixth where the light
from the movie marquee showed up the cracks in the wall.
The old place had brightened some since I'd started going out
with Chandler Burke. She'd hung some pictures. Bought a
couple of chairs. Fought off the cobwebs whenever she came
into town. She hadn't come in for a while, though, and the
apartment showed it. Solitude seemed to be creeping out of
the corners.

"Oh what the hell," I said. I shut the cab door. I saluted
through the dark window. Holloway and Wexler were driven
off.

I joined Colt on the sidewalk. I felt the cold snow cover my shoes.

Colt grinned his slow cowboy grin. The crags in his face lifted. He patted me on the shoulder.

"Well," he said, "I guess it's you and me, pardner."

We started up Madison together.

4

Madison Avenue stretched downtown before us, a canyon of snow. The snow limned the mansard roof of the Polish Consulate hulking above us. It covered the solid Palladian block of the Morgan Library just ahead. It hung from the window ledges of the seedy gray apartments over the Korean grocery. It hung from the edge of the gutter. It hid the dirt and the gritty stone. It frosted them over, made them softer somehow. It muffled the hum and throb of the early morning.

Colt and I walked side by side in silence. We looked at the street around us. The light was like crystal in the thin, cold air.

"Nice town," he said after a minute. "Nice town, Manhattan." He was slurring his words a little.

So was I. "Yeah. In the snow. It's quiet in the snow."

He gave me a glance. "Ah. You're not from these parts, are you?"

"Nah."

"Massachusetts?"

"Maine."

"Maine," said Colt. "I was wonderin'. I knew you weren't city bred anyway."

"Oh yeah? Why's that?" I made an overly expansive gesture. "I got rid of the accent years ago, man."

"I know, I know. And you're a city slicker now but . . . I saw it in you. I did." He shoved his hands in his pockets, breathed plumes of mist into the night. "The way I figure it, a man always has something in him from the country. If it was ever in him at all, it stays that way."

"Aw, it's a long time ago, Colt, long time ago. I haven't even been back."

"Still," he said. He gazed down the street. "When you come from the country to the city, it's always as if you were living a second life somehow. There's always a whole part of your mind set in different places, with different colors, different smells."

I grunted, nodded. "I was just thinking about that. I was just thinking how when I was a kid, when the first snow came, my old man used to take me up into the woods. On this mountain out in front of our house, see. And he'd take me way, way up there and man, sometimes, it's just like you say: sometimes, standing right in the middle of town here, I can still hear the quiet of it. So quiet. And white. And nothing moving. No motion at all except sometimes you'd see a drift tumble out of the highest branches of the pines, and then you'd hear it go whump in the snow." I looked over at Colt. He hoisted his shoulders. Shivered. He was gazing way downtown now where a golden campanile gleamed against the black sky. "He was a forest ranger, my old man," I said. "He'd take me to this stream he knew. All frozen over except for a trickle down the center between the ice. And he'd show me the tracks in the snow where the animals came down to drink. Raccoons, deer, even moose sometimes. He taught me all of them. I could tell them all."

"Yeah," Colt said vaguely. Then more clearly: "Yeah, that's what I mean. City folks never know that stuff. Not really. And we never really know what they know either. Doesn't matter how long we stay."

"What're you?" I asked him. "Oklahoma?"

He laughed. "An Okie from Sutterdale, that's me. A town with a population of seven hundred, and most of them lived out on ranches, somewhere way the hell out in the plains. I'll tell you, I can remember runnin' through the dust of the streets of that town, out to the edge of it. Standin' there on the brink of this plain of grass that I swear to God went on as far as the ocean. I'd run out there to catch sight of the train, the freight train, rollin' out to the northwest." He took one hand from his pocket. He raised it in the night air. Extended it to show me the train rolling away from him. "I'd stand there and watch it, Wells, this long, long line of cars runnin' deeper and deeper into the plains. And I'd stand there at the edge of town and, so help me, if my soul could have left my body, I'd have been on that sucker. I'd've been gone, boy. Gone, gone, gone." He laughed again. "Hallelujah."

One corner of my mouth lifted. I didn't have to answer.

"That's what I mean, I guess, more than anything," he said. "What I mean is: I been everywhere, man. Everywhere. I seen everything, been shot at, captured. . . . You ever cover a war?"

"Nah. I was a local crime boy from the start."

"Yeah, well, it's something. I mean, you just see everything." Colt stopped on the sidewalk. I stopped, turned to him. He shook his head at the long stretch of avenue ahead. "And no matter how much I see, no matter where I go, sometimes I feel like I'm still just standin' there at the edge of town. Like there's still someplace out there I'm tryin' to get to." He faced me. "Like I never got on that train. You know? Just like I never got out of Oklahoma."

We stood silent for another moment. "Oh hell," I said.

He snorted. He slapped my shoulder. We started walking again.

We reached the hotel. Young men dressed in black flanked broad glass doors. We passed into the lobby, the boys attending. Colt collected his key. We passed into the elevator. Silently we were hoisted up to the seventh floor.

I leaned back against the wall.

"Whoosh," I said.

"Yeah," said Colt. He laughed. "All that air."

He let me into his suite. Two rooms, both small. There was a sitting room with two stuffed wing chairs in the middle of it, a sofa against the wall. A coffee table, long, low, and topped with glass. A TV in the corner. A bureau beside it. A window on Madison. A door into the bathroom, another into the bedroom. I glanced through the bedroom doorway, saw the usual pair of beds crushed close to either side of a lampstand, a writing desk under a mirror against the wall. All of it fancier than most, I guess, but a hotel room is a hotel room just the same.

I took my coat off, dumped it on the sofa. Sat down heavily in one of the chairs. Colt carried his coat into the bedroom. There must have been a small refrigerator hidden in there, because he came out with two plastic cups filled with ice. He extracted the scotch bottle from a drawer in the bureau. He poured with a liberal hand. He took his place in the chair across from me.

"She's something," he said. He'd been following some thoughts of his own. When I raised my eyebrow at him, he said: "Lansing. She's something all right."

"Yeah," I said. "She's something."

"She sure can hold her liquor."

"Oh, man. Can she ever. You ought to see her some-times."

"Damn! She any good?"

"What's that?"

"As a reporter, I mean."

"Oh. Yeah. Yeah, she's good. She goes for it, anyway. She once drove me up Fifth Avenue at maybe sixty miles an hour to beat the cops to a murder scene." I paused for effect, sipped my scotch. "Fifth Avenue goes downtown."

I saw something flicker in Colt's hard brown eyes. The crags around them bunched together. "I reckon that was just to impress you," he said.

"Oh hell. What's that supposed to mean?"

"What's that mean? It means she's mad about you, buddy."

I waved him off.

"She is. The way she looks at you."

"She's twelve years old, Colt."

He laughed once. He drawled: "She ain't twelve. And you ain't eighty. She's . . . what? Twenty-five?"

"Close enough."

"And you're fifty?"

"Forty-six, thanks. Just worn by hard living."

"You married or something?"

"Something. Divorced."

"Kids."

"I had a daughter once," I said. "She killed herself when she was fifteen."

"Christ," said Colt. "That is hard livin'."

He drank. He did not drink lightly. He did not drink like

a man already drunk, trying to make it last. He took a long draft, like he wasn't there yet, wherever he wanted to get to. Wherever the pain ended.

He came gasping out of it. "So are you really as good as they say?"

"Hell, no. Are you?"

"Nah. But I'm good."

"Yeah. Yeah, you are."

"You, too, my friend."

I shrugged. "They make it easy for me. The pols in this town. This town . . ." I waved a hand around. "Politically, this town is about as healthy as a cancer on a leper's ass."

He tilted his head, eyed me shrewdly. "And what're you? The good doctor?"

I heard myself make a harsh, guttural noise of dismissal. "I'm just taking notes in the cesspool, pal. I don't fix it, I just write about it."

Colt made a quick movement with his tongue, like a man spitting the Oklahoma dust from his mouth. "So how come you're too all-fired pure to make it with a pretty young thing who's dyin' for you?"

The question took me off guard. I shifted uncomfortably between the wings of my chair. I was beginning to feel like I was being interviewed. I didn't like it. If I'd wanted to be held accountable for myself, I'd have gone into another business.

"I got a woman," I said tightly.

"She doesn't seem to be waitin' up for you," Colt shot back.

"She works upstate. Runs a suicide hot line up there."

"Ever see her?"

"When I can. Right now things are kind of busy."

Colt sat relaxed, one leg crossed over the other at the knee. But his eyes stayed sharp. His hand gripped his glass tightly. "When's the last time you saw her, Wells?"

"What?"

"You don't see her. I'd bet cash money on it. You never see her."

"What is this, Colt?"

"Ah," he said drunkenly. "You don't give a shit. I know your type."

"You're drunk."

"I know your type. You don't give a shit about anything."

"You're drunk. What is this garbage?"

He pointed a finger at me. "You're workin' all the time. Right? You bury yourself in your work. You don't *want* to give a shit, that's what. That's why you keep away from Lansing."

"Oh yeah?"

"You think I don't know you."

"That's what all this is, huh. That's what it is."

"I know you, Wells. I know you. I was just like you once. I was just like you."

I'd had it. "Cut the shit, Colt. Just because Lancer kissed you off, I don't have to take this shit."

That seemed to stop him finally. The fire in his eyes dimmed. He looked down at the standard, hotel-issue shag rug.

We sat in silence for a few seconds. My head was spinning. My mind was dull. Vaguely I found myself wondering about the incident in the bar. The confrontation between Colt and the haunted man. We'd all politely let it go unmentioned, but it had cast a pall over the night. It had sparked the serious drinking. Now it seemed to me that this discussion was related to it in some strange way. Some way I couldn't make out. It was all too complicated for my pickled brain.

Colt started talking again. To add to my confusion, he seemed to have gotten off on a whole new topic.

"We were in Jacobo when the rebels broke through." He was still staring at the rug. He spoke quickly, in a low, feverish murmur. "Me and Wexler. We knew the capital, Mangrela, we knew it was going to fall. You have to understand. There'd been weeks, months of . . . of boredom. Of nothin' but the heat and the mosquitoes. Then there'd be some sudden rush of vengeance out of all them jungles around the cities. The rebels would come whompin' down on some little town, kill the men, rape the women. Then the government'd hit back and a bunch of rebel sympathizers'd up and disappear. And then . . . and then it would all calm down. All sink back into the heat and the boredom. It didn't seem to us like anything would ever really . . . happen."

He took a long breath. It shuddered as it came out. He wiped his mouth with one hand. "And now it was comin'. Finally. All of it. The bloodshed . . . not just bloodshed . . .

the . . . the torture, the mutilations. The long, long killings in the hot, hot sun. Mangrela was goin' to fall, man. Me and Wexler, we knew we had to get back.'' He lifted his eyes to me. Eyes as haunted now as those of the man in the bar. ''Not just to get the story, Wells. Not just to get the story. We had to get out. That's where the yank choppers were. The capital. And once the capital belonged to the rebels, we were finished. All of us.''

His whole body shook once in the chair as he let out the memories of a decade ago. He blinked—hard. He was fighting the liquor, but soon it would win. He wanted to get it all out first.

''We didn't even know if we could make it back,'' he said softly. ''I left that morning, as soon as we got the news. Wexler thought he'd have a better chance in the dark.'' Colt's eyes filled. I could barely hear him. ''It gets awful dark in Sentu at night. The stars . . . I was afraid to travel in the dark.'' He started to bring his drink to his lips, then lowered it. Another shot would probably have finished him. ''Even in the day, it was a nightmare. The shellfire never stopped. The jungle was exploding everywhere. The roads . . . the dirt roads. They were filled with refugees . . . children, women, bleeding, desperate, dead. And soldiers—you couldn't tell what side they were on anymore. They'd stop you, check your ID. You didn't know if they were goin' to blow your head off or let you pass. They didn't know. It depended on . . . God knows . . . luck, their mood. It was chaos. It was a jungle where all the animals were humans, and all the humans left were either murderers or dead. . . . They stared at you out of the undergrowth. And the shells kept falling. . . . Wells, I've never been so afraid.''

I stared at that weathered face of his. It was not the face of a coward. Not at all. It was the sort of face you wanted beside you when the shooting started. Calm, hard, unwavering.

''You see what I'm sayin'?'' he said to me quietly. ''You see what I'm tryin' to say?''

I opened my mouth to answer. I didn't answer. I didn't see. I didn't understand why he was telling me this. I was drunk and I couldn't make sense of it.

Colt ran his hand up through his dense brown hair. With the other arm, he pushed to his feet. As he did, his drink fell from his loose grip. The glass tumbled onto the rug, spat its liquor into the shag. I saw the shag darken with scotch. I heard, in my mind, the beer glass shattering when he dropped it in the tavern. I couldn't shake the idea that everything was connected.

Colt towered over me where I sat. He swayed. He put his hand to his forehead.

"I didn't just go back there for the story," he said. "Not just to get the story. Not just to get out." Stumbling, he headed for the bedroom door.

"Colt," I said. It came out slurred.

He reached the doorway. He faltered, leaning against the jamb. I heard him say something. His voice cracked as he said it. I couldn't make out the words.

He straightened, swayed. This time, I heard it.

"Eleanora," he muttered. "Eleanora, Eleanora, my love, my love."

He staggered out of sight into the bedroom.

I waited. There were no other sounds.

It took me a moment to fight my way to my feet. I set my drink down on the coffee table. I walked to the bedroom door as if I were balancing on a tightrope. I peered in. Colt lay sprawled facedown across the nearest bed. I saw his back lift and fall with his breathing. I heard him start to snore.

I turned unsteadily. I don't know why. I dared the tightrope back to the sofa to get my coat. I picked up the coat but decided it would be best to put it on sitting down. I sat down heavily, with the coat on my lap. The sofa seemed very deep, very soft. I blinked. I blinked again. I blinked several times over. Maybe it would be better, I thought, to put the coat on lying down. I lay down. I pulled the coat up over me. I closed my eyes.

I opened my eyes quickly when I felt the whole world start to spin. My stomach flipped as I lay on the sofa. I stared at the lamp in the ceiling to bring the room to a halt. I had to fight to bring all the split images together. For many long minutes, I hung in that precarious place where it is impossible to keep your eyes open and sickening to close them.

Then, mercifully, I passed into oblivion.

An insistent knock—and a taste like sand—brought me round. The room was bright with morning. It was a piercing brightness: the optical equivalent of a dentist's drill. I groaned when it hit me. I tried to go to sleep again. The knock kept on. My head ached with it. I blinked. I ran my tongue through the sand in my mouth. I sat up. I groaned.

The knocking kept on. I figured it out. Someone was knocking on the door. The door, I noticed now, was not where it usually was. The window was not where it usually was. I, as it turned out, was not where I usually was. The knocking continued to hammer at my head from the outside. A dull throbbing began to answer it from within. I called up the memory of the night before. I remembered Timothy Colt. His hotel room. I looked down at the coat on my lap.

The knocking kept on.

"All right!" I shouted. The sound of my own voice ricocheted off my internal organs like a pinball. "All right," I said more quietly.

I tried to push myself off the sofa. It seemed a long way. I tried again, my stomach heaving.

I stood. The room rocked this way and that. The knocking—which had paused when I shouted—started up again. I cursed. I turned slowly to find the door.

"I'll get it!"

The voice startled me. It was Colt. He had come, not from

the bedroom to my left, but from the bathroom to my right. He came striding out vigorously. He was dressed and pressed and ready to meet the day. His wiry frame was wrapped in a natty tan suit with a western cut. There was a string tie in a neat bow around his neck. His chin was clean-shaven. His hair was wet and slapped back on his skull as if he'd just come out of the shower.

I groaned at the sight of him. He grinned at me as he passed to the door.

"You look awful there, friend," he said. "Go on back to sleep for a while."

I made the only response I could think of without the use of a pistol. Colt laughed. He grabbed hold of the doorknob and pulled the door in. I stumbled into the bathroom.

I heard Colt say: "Well, hey!" He sounded surprised and pleased.

I heard a low, breathy voice answer, "Compliments of the house, Mr. Colt."

Colt laughed. "Fine by me."

I relieved myself, then stumbled to the sink. I splashed water on my aching face. I looked up in the mirror. It was not a pleasant sight. The usual crags and lines of a thin, fierce face had sagged in the light until I looked like a basset hound. Above the high hairline, my gray hair lay damp and tangled.

Behind this travesty, I saw the reflection of the sitting room. A bellboy had entered carrying a tray. He took it to the coffee table in the center of the room.

As he bent forward to put the tray on the table, I saw Colt come up beside him. The reporter reached into his pocket, brought out his money clip. He thumbed through it for a tip. I turned away from the mirror. Walked to the bathroom doorway.

I was looking out the door when the bellboy straightened, turned around. He and Colt faced each other in profile before me, Colt to my right, the bellboy to my left. The bellboy, I saw through bleary eyes, was dressed all in black, like the doormen. His face was dark brown with deep-set, intense eyes. He wore his hair cut close, almost in a crew cut. He couldn't have been more than twenty, if that, but dark lines creased his brow and pinched the corners of his mouth.

Colt fumbled with his money clip. He found a couple of bills and held them out to the kid. The bellboy killed him.

I saw it this way. Suddenly the kid had a knife in his left hand. He must have slid it out of his shirtsleeve. It was a wicked-looking dagger. Its blade was short and curved like a scimitar's. It flashed once as he brought it up under Colt's ribs. It went into the reporter with no more noise than a whisper of tearing cloth and flesh. Colt gave a soft little "oof." He bent forward with the blow. As he did, his killer twisted the knife expertly. Colt's face went blank. He hadn't even had time to be surprised.

With a smooth flick of the wrist, the bellboy pulled the dagger free. As he did, Colt keeled over. He hit the coffee table. The tray rattled with the blow. Colt rolled onto the floor, landing on his back. At last he lay still, his eyes staring up at the ceiling, his arms splayed inelegantly. Blood was bubbling up through the hole in him.

That's when I realized he was dead. That's when I cried out: "Colt!"

That's when the bellboy turned and saw me.

That's when he knew he had a witness.

Only the slightest hesitation raced across the young-old
face of the assassin. His eyes shifted toward the door.
He was wondering if he should break for it. I was still staring
dumbfounded, my eyes flashing back and forth from the killer
to the body of Timothy Colt. Not five seconds had passed since
the kid had pulled the knife.

The fountain of blood burbling out of Colt's midsection
grew weaker. His white shirt was now soaked scarlet. As I
fought to grasp the fact of the reporter's death, the bellboy
made up his mind. He came for me.

It was an expert approach. He moved in, crouched low,
the knife gripped lightly, held close to his side. He kept his
intense eyes trained on my chest, like a basketball player watching for the fake.

I tried to rouse myself. I was dull with hangover and shock.
I glanced at the door to gauge the possibility of escape. The
killer thought with me. He circled around me as he came on
until he had blocked the path to the exit.

I had two ways to go and a second to choose. I could either
retreat into the bathroom and fight cornered, or move out into
the room and keep away from him as best I could. I saw that
unswerving stare, that curling blade, no more than two steps
away. I moved out into the room, my back to the wall. I
crouched low with my open hands held up before me.

He sprang. I thought—crazily—of Antoinette, the tiger.

He sprang like that. A single, flowing motion, swift as death. But in the moment before he leapt, I saw him reverse the position of the knife in his hand. He held it ready to deliver a quick forehanded slash at my cheek. That would turn my head to one side and leave me open for the returning backhand that would plunge the blade into my throat. It was a good move. If I'd never seen it before, I'd have never seen it again.

But I had. A drug ring enforcer from Washington Heights had shown it to me to impress me with his abilities. I was impressed. Impressed enough to remember.

The assassin reversed the blade in his hand. I had a fraction of a second to prepare. He sprang and slashed in one motion. I leaned way back, as if dodging a right cross. The blade flashed by my eyes. For an instant, Colt's killer was exposed, his arm extended. In that instant, I drove the stiffened fingers of my hand deep into his armpit.

He cried out, fell back a step. He should have been hurt bad. He wasn't. He recovered and jumped at me. He swept the knife up toward my gut.

I dodged to the left. I felt the blade pass by my shirt. I slammed into something—a lampstand. It toppled over and so did I. I hit the floor on my back. The wind was knocked out of me. This was definitely one of the worst hangovers I'd ever had.

The killer had stumbled a step away from me, carried by the force of his own missed jab. He steadied himself and turned. He leapt on top of me, pinning my arms with his knees. He raised the knife for the kill.

I lifted my right side off the floor. The movement took all my strength, but it pitched him over. I rolled in the opposite direction. Scrambled to my feet. Spun around just as he rushed me again.

I caught his knife hand by the wrist. His fingers gripped my right hand as I went for his eyes. We locked like that, inches apart, my eyes burning into his, his into mine, our teeth bared, our hot stale breath whistling into the small space between us. I tried to knee him in the groin. He blocked it with his legs. He tried to cut his way free. I shoved him. We both went down.

We rolled over and over on the floor. The blade of the knife kept flashing on every side of me. I kept fighting for a grip on his wrist, losing it, finding it again just before he plunged the dagger into me. I was bigger than he was, but he was tough like jerky, sinewy. I was fighting for my life, but he was doing a job he knew well.

I was weakening. The booze of the night before seemed to have eaten away at me. The cigarettes of a lifetime were making me wheeze as we rocketed back and forth across the stale shag carpet.

We went over again, the two of us, locked together. His brown face was twisted with effort and rage.

We slammed into the coffee table. I was hit hard. I landed, dazed, with my head on Colt's leg. The killer pulled his left arm free and belted me in the mouth. I felt my lip split. He jerked his knife hand clear.

Again the blade went up as he sat atop me. I threw my left arm in front of my face. I felt the metal pierce the flesh just below my elbow. I screamed as he yanked the knife out again. I reached down and grabbed his balls and made a fist. He screamed and rolled off me. He curled up on his side, moaning softly. I curled up on my side, coughing dark phlegm. I could feel the old cigarettes welling in my lungs. I could not catch my breath.

My head was swimming. My forearm burned. I fumbled for purchase on the coffee table. I slipped, hacking, and splashed into Colt's bloody shirtfront. I felt the give of the breath-empty flesh beneath. I slipped off him to the floor again. His blood was smeared all over my cheek, and the carpet shag stuck to it. I got up on my hands and knees. I could not stop coughing.

Vaguely, I saw the assassin uncurl. He climbed to his knees, too, bent over, heaving, cradling his crotch with his hand. He swept the floor with his eyes. I realized he was looking for his knife. He'd dropped it. I looked around frantically.

We saw it at the same time. It had been flung over near the sofa. We both started crawling to it. I got there first. I wrapped my fingers around the handle—a golden handle with rubies inlaid. But before I could use it, the assassin climbed onto my back. He grabbed my head under the chin and tried to rip it off my neck. He dug a thumb in my eye for good measure.

With a yell, I let the knife go and thrashed around wildly,

trying to shake him. He slammed into the sofa and fell off me.
I crawled toward the knife again.

The room blurred as my left eye streamed. I lost my sense
of perspective. I was groping for the handle. I was stretched
out, reaching out, when he jumped back on top of me. He
tried to bite my cheek. I raised my arm, and his teeth sank
into my shoulder through my shirt.

"Agh!" I said. I rolled onto my back. With my free fist,
I hammered and hammered at his face. His mouth slackened.
He dropped away. Wheezing, I went for the knife a third time.
He grabbed hold of my ankles. The gold handle swam into my
sight, but I could not get it. I stretched as far as I could and
took a swat at it. The dagger spun away over the rug, out of
reach.

The assassin let go of me. He got to his feet and went for
the knife. I swung my legs around and tripped him. He toppled
forward with a grunt. He smashed face first into the coffee
table. His nose exploded in a pink blast. He bounced onto the
floor.

Sobbing, I began to crawl slowly toward the open door. It
heaved and yawed in front of me. Blood poured down my
forearm. Tears poured from my damaged eye. Snot poured out
of my nose. The door and the hall and escape got closer bit
by bit.

Behind me, I heard the killer moving, groaning, sobbing
like me. I wondered if he'd try for the knife. If he went for
the knife, I might have a chance, time to get out.

I pitched forward about a foot from the door. My face fell
into the soft carpet. It felt very comfortable, very warm. I
considered resting there a while. Not long. A minute, maybe
two was all I needed. Just enough for a little shut-eye. Instead
I reached up, grabbed hold of the edge of the door. Pulled
myself onto my knees again. Crawled a few more inches.

I got out. I got my head out the door. My head was stretching into the hall. Then he got me.

He must have left the knife behind. He must have chased
after me, crawling, too. He collapsed on top of my legs. He
wrapped his arms around them. I was flattened by the impact
of it.

Cursing in a language I'd never heard, he began to drag

me back into the room. I had no more strength to fight him. I raised my head a little.

"Help," I said.

No one answered.

When he had me inside, he dropped me. He pushed the door shut. I rolled onto my back. Wearily, he fell onto me. He wrapped his hands around my throat and squeezed.

Everything seemed strangely silent then. Almost peaceful in a way. I saw his face contorting close to me. I saw the insanity in his eyes. I saw the dark circle of blood where his nose and mouth had been. I felt my lungs heaving for air. But there was no sound. Everything drifted before me in slow motion. It was as if I were underwater: the world was floating dreamily into darkness.

Dreamily I lifted my hand and dug my thumb into the gory hole where his nose had been.

I surfaced immediately as the silence was shattered by his squeal of pain. He flew off me like a man who'd accidentally sat on a hot stove, his arms wide, his mouth open. He sat down hard on the floor, not far from me, cradling his face in his hands. I propped myself onto my elbow, turned over, and vomited violently onto the rug.

And, as there had at the beginning of this lovely winter's morning, there now came a knock at the door. There came a shout: "Is everything all right? Is everything all right in there?"

The knocking became a pounding. Someone was hitting the door with his fist.

I tried to call out. I could only make a high, whistling sound deep in my throat. The knocking continued. I wondered if maybe I'd been struggling to wake up all this time, struggling to answer the door, to make the knocking stop. Maybe all this had only been the nightmare of a moment.

There was a shout. "Open up in there. Now!" It was the voice of authority. Hotel security maybe. Or the manager.

I began to think about getting to the door again. Maybe I could slide on my belly, dragging myself along the rug. As I was considering this, my old pal was on the move. He took hold of one of the chair arms and pulled himself to his knees. From his knees, he grabbed the high back of the chair and pulled himself upright. He was breathless, crying.

Outside, there were more voices now. The knocking had stopped. I thought I heard the jangle of keys.

The assassin staggered to the window. He lurched toward it like a zombie in an old horror film.

A key scraped in the lock. I heard the latch turning.

The assassin reached the window. It was tall and pivot-hung. He grabbed hold of it and swung it in. He hoisted himself to the edge of it so that from the waist down he was inside. From the waist up, he was hanging seven stories above the earth.

The door opened. People began rushing in.

The assassin hurled himself out into the open air.

7

"Eesh," said Fred Gottlieb. "What a mess."

He was talking about my face. It lay—this face of mine—pointed up at the ceiling of a hospital room. It felt lumpy, like a potato. Like a potato that hurt. All of me hurt. My eye watered. My throat was sore from being choked. My arm stung from being stabbed. The rest of me throbbed in a sort of generalized agony.

Fred Gottlieb stood in the doorway, shaking his head. "Eesh," he said again.

The homicide detective was about my age. A burly man, built thick and low to the ground. His tan corduroy jacket was stretched tight across his shoulders. His purple paisley shirt was stretched tight across his chest. The shirt was unbuttoned at the top. Generous tufts of hair spilled out of it. It was barely buttoned at the bottom; his round belly pushed against it, trying to break free. His face was circular and rocky. His curly black hair receded on top from a wide brow. He was clean-shaven, but the stubble on his cheeks was thick and black, adding to his look of gruffness. Only his eyes gave him away. They were small and brown and deep, like little pools of water in the ground.

He shuffled into the room. It was a regulation hospital box. Four green walls. Two stark beds. Bars over a window with a river view.

There was a metal chair next to my bed. Gottlieb pulled it close, sat down.

"They tell me they're going to let you out as soon as they get your X rays back."

I nodded. The sore throat made it hard to talk.

"You think that's such a good idea? I don't know." He narrowed his eyes at me. "You don't look so good."

"Thanks," I whispered.

"I read an article in *Newsweek*, they said because of hospital overcrowding they sometimes release patients too soon. A couple of days later, they find them dead in the bathtub. It's a terrible situation."

I nodded.

"On the other hand," he went on, "you could stay here, they put someone in the bed next to you with an infectious disease, you have to share the bathroom. You're here for a couple of cuts and bruises, the next thing you know: hepatitis. You didn't get a blood transfusion, did you?"

I tried to smile with the unsplit corner of my lips. I shook my head.

Fred breathed a sigh of relief at the same time as he hunched his huge shoulders in concern. Beneath his open jacket, his holster showed a moment. The black butt of his detective special blended nicely with his shirt's lavender swirls.

"Hospitals," he proclaimed softly, "are very unhealthy places. It's a terrible situation."

I nodded.

He widened his eyes wearily. "So," he said. "So what's the story?" I opened my mouth. Gottlieb said: "Wait: maybe you shouldn't talk. Here, I'll give you a pad, you can write it down."

I stretched my neck to ease the pain as a laugh escaped me.

"Right, that's stupid, too complicated," Gottlieb said. He waved the idea away with his hand. "I'll tell you what. . . . Fill in what we don't have already, all right?"

I nodded.

"Okay." He nodded back. "What we have so far: we have Timothy Colt, the big-time famous journalist, and he's dead. He's murdered." He shook his head. "Such a waste, too. A successful man like that."

My eyes shifted away from the detective's stern face. I thought of Colt. His tough cowboy features. The humor and the sadness in them. I didn't get to know him very well, but I got to like him. And I knew his work. He was one of the good ones.

His round, worried face hovering there above me, Gottlieb continued. "The hotel manager and the two bellhops who rescued you, they saw the man, the killer, go out the window. After that, Miss Kelsey, downstairs . . . he half scared her out of her wits. Such a pretty girl, too, it's a shame. A singer with some kind of a rock band."

My sudden breath squeaked like a new sneaker on a basketball court. "He got away? How . . . ? How could he?"

"Uy!" Gottlieb shook his head. "Don't ask. He could have killed himself. He could have killed everybody. People on the street. I don't even want to think about it. What does he do? He goes out the window. He swings down onto the ledge below. This little tiny ledge, he's gotta be like an acrobat. There's another window there. He breaks the glass—with his knee, says Miss Kelsey—and goes falling in. As for Miss Kelsey: I left her, she was still crying." He waved his hand again. "I'm telling you: it's been an awful morning. They woke me up at seven o'clock with this. I heard it was you, I didn't know: were you dead, were you alive, what? I read in *Science Times* last week, they said not getting enough sleep cuts down on your resistance to infection. Maybe I shouldn't stay around here too long." He closed one eye, presented his face to me. "Do I look okay?"

I nodded.

"I don't look pale or flushed or anything?"

I shook my head.

"Good. Because you look just terrible. Are you sure you want to leave?"

I nodded.

"Okay. I mean, if you want to stay, they have to keep you." I nodded again. He sighed again. He went on: "Anyway, we got a description from the Kelsey girl. But, you know how it is, she was half asleep, she'd been to a party. . . . She's a show business person, who knows what she's doing at seven o'clock in the morning? That's last night to her. You see what I'm saying: I could use a description."

I gathered up my strength. "Okay," I whispered.

He leaned back in his chair, held up a hand. "You don't have to give it to me now. Rest, relax. Get better."

"S'alright. I'm just a little hoarse."

Gottlieb shrugged, but he went into his jacket pocket and brought out a notepad. He went into his shirt pocket and brought out a pen.

I took a deep breath. Coughed a little. Said: "He was five-seven. Wiry. Bullet head. Thin, oval face. Black—dark brown." I forced each word out with an effort. I felt like I'd accidentally swallowed a Brillo pad. "Big eyes, very mean. Thin lips, very mean. Sunken cheeks. Very mean. Not much nose anymore. Lots of bruises. Probably looks about as bad as me."

He glanced over his notes once quickly. Flipped the book shut. "Thank you very much. Much better than Miss Kelsey, who said, and I quote, 'He was like a happening bizarro thing, man, with short hair.' I should issue an APB."

I inhaled again. It sounded like wind passing through a church organ. "You get the weapon . . . the knife?"

"Yeah." He raised his eyes heavenward. "And I mean, what is that, a Swiss Army scimitar?"

I laughed. "Oh," I said. "Don't make me laugh."

"Sorry, but I mean it looked like some kind of ceremonial whatchem with the tribal drums. You kill a pig and it rains." He chuckled, then stopped chuckling at once. "I don't know. It's a terrible situation." He shook his head, worried. "Anyway, so when you feel better, it doesn't have to be today, you could come down and look at some mug shots. It couldn't hurt. I'd appreciate it."

I gave him yet another nod. I prepared myself to speak at length again. It wasn't getting easier. The pain in my throat was growing worse with every word.

"The knife. Colt traveled to all kinds of exotic places. Just back from Afghanistan. Headed for Nicaragua."

Gottlieb nodded his coarse, curly head. "I know all this. I talked to his friends. I talked to your friends, Lansing and McKay. Lovely woman, Lansing. Make a nice wife for someone. She should have children. She shouldn't be running around writing about dead people." He studied his pointy black shoes.

"They tell you about the bar?" I wheezed. "The argument Colt had with the guy in the bar?"

"Yes, they told me, they told me. It doesn't help me, but they told me. Mr. Holloway and Mr. Wexler said they recognized the man as someone named Lester Paul. He used to hang out in a country named Sentu. I'm supposed to have heard of this."

"Yeah. Yeah," I said slowly. "The three of them covered a revolution there. Ten years ago. That's how they got started." As I fought to speak, my battered mind clouded again with that feeling of connection: the sense that every fact was linked to every other. It was hard to make sense of it, and hard to shake.

"Right. Terrific," said Gottlieb. "Anyhow, what they can tell me about this Lester Paul—who has an argument with Colt a few hours before he's mysteriously murdered—what they can tell me is not a lot." He opened the notebook again, flipped back through its pages. "Mr. Holloway and Mr. Wexler, they tell me he hangs around Mangrela, the capital city. I say: 'He hangs around doing what?' They say: 'We don't know.' I say: 'He has a job, this mystery man?' They say: 'We don't know.' I say: 'So what's his beef with the late Mr. Colt?' They say: 'We don't know.' A very informative interview. The public pays for this." He flipped the notebook shut with the same decisiveness as before.

"Colt . . ." I said. I had to catch my breath, start again. "Colt said, 'You're dead!' Or 'You're a dead man!' Something like that."

"Right. Very good. You remembered that. So did Lansing. She really is a lovely girl."

I laughed some more. It hurt some more. "You're killing me, Gottlieb. Would you ask your questions?"

"All right, all right. I'm just mentioning," the detective said. "So—what were we saying? Oh yes. 'You're a dead man.' I asked Holloway and Wexler, they said they'd heard Paul, this shadowy person who suddenly shows up in a bar arguing with Colt just before he, Colt, gets knifed to death . . . They shrug their shoulders, these two distinguished journalists, and they tell me Lester Paul was supposed to have been killed by the rebel armies when they took over this country of Sentu everyone's heard of but me.'' Now, he actually slipped the notepad back into his pocket. He leaned forward, his hands resting on his knees. ''So—I put out a bulletin for the man. We'll find him, we'll ask him questions, we'll arrest him, he'll get life for murder. Anything else I should know?''

I stared at the cracks that crisscrossed on the white ceiling. I tried to think. The throbbing pain made it tough. The hangover was still there, too. In my stomach. In my brain. Nothing seemed straight. Nothing seemed clear. Finally my voice trailed out of me on a labored breath. It sounded like the voice of the wind in a ghost story.

''Eleanora,'' I said.

Gottlieb cocked an ear at me. ''Pardon?''

''Colt. He mentioned a woman. Eleanora. In Sentu. I think. I don't know.''

''A woman?''

I nodded.

''Just a woman. That's it.''

I closed my eyes against the haze floating through my mind. I opened my eyes. The haze was still there. ''I don't know,'' I said. ''It was on his mind . . .''

The detective rocked his head back and forth, uncertain. Pushing off his knees, he stood.

''Well, if you can think of anything else about her, let me know. If you can think of anything else about anything.''

I sighed, giving up the effort. I nodded.

''And you'll come look at mug shots?''

I nodded.

He laid a thick hand on my shoulder. ''And don't let them chase you out of the hospital.''

I nodded.

''And don't get hepatitis,'' Gottlieb said. With a wave, he plodded to the door.

It was two in the afternoon before my doctor finally showed up: a Puerto Rican kid in his twenties. He wore thick black spectacles on his little-boy face. They slid down over his pug nose as he read the chart tied to the foot of my bed.

"You're forty-six, is that right, Mr. Wells?"

"Yeah," I croaked. I could still feel that bastard's fingers on my throat.

"Well, happy birthday," said the doctor. He let the chart drop and looked at me. "Most of your internal organs just turned sixty."

I cast my eyes heavenward. "Can I go home now?"

"How much do you smoke a day?" the whippersnapper asked.

"A pack," I lied.

"How much do you drink?"

"A glass of brandy for medicinal purposes."

He studied me closely over the spectacles. He probably wore them just to look doctorly. "We took a blood test, Mr. Wells," he said. "It's been passed on to Scotland for bottling. What's your excuse, man?"

"A life haunted by tragedy. Can I go home or not?"

Dr. Doom sighed, nodded. "Sure. A man ought to spend his last days in familiar surroundings."

I started to work my way out of bed. "Nobody lives forever," I said.

"Thank you, Mr. Kierkegaard. You're a philosopher." He tapped his white-shirted chest with a pen. "I'm a doctor. Take better care of the machinery, pal. Or you're a dead man."

With which he let me go.

I got dressed and hobbled outside onto First Avenue. The day was chill and bright, the way it often is after a blizzard. The cold bit into me, frosted my breath. The sky was cobalt. The sun was white. I could imagine the daylight glinting off the undisturbed snow of the Maine forests. I could imagine the way it would dazzle you. It was not dazzling here.

The pristine beauty of the night before was gone. The city had crushed it under its heels and wheels. The dirt of urban life had turned the unbroken white to soggy gray. The Sanitation Department shovels had crowded it up against the curbs. The buses had churned it into slush. Now the sun was cutting through the chill to melt the slush into icy puddles. The puddles collected at the corners. Pedestrians had to leap across them. Cabbies raced through them to slash fantails of water over the pedestrians' clothes. There were cries and curses everywhere. New York City is a winter wonderland.

I went limping and leaping through this mess until I found a newsstand. I picked up a copy of the *Star*. Then I hesitated. I thought about what the doctor had said. Then I bought a pack of cigarettes. I don't like doctors, anyway.

I stood on the wet sidewalk. I slapped a cig between my lips and lit it. The smoke rasped against my hurt throat. I endured it, took another drag, and scanned the paper.

A surprise. A pleasant surprise. Cambridge had bannered the borough president. "Robins Bribe Probed." He used the bottom half of the front page for a picture of the tiger with an inset of the lady. He then played the tiger on page three, and the bribe on page seven. That was as good a way as any to do it. Either Cambridge had caved in to city room pressure or he'd been force-fed mind-altering drugs. Either way, it had turned out all right.

With renewed faith in my chosen profession, I hailed a cab. I rode through the puddles to Vanderbilt Avenue and the concrete tower that houses the *Star*.

I tumbled out of the elevator on the twelfth floor and stood before a wall of glass doors. I could see myself reflected in them. My tie was gone. My jacket was torn. My face was purple. My arm was wrapped in gauze. I pushed the reflection away and walked into the city room.

The place was a maze of white cubicles under white fluorescent lights. It greeted me with a kind of white silence. That steady non-noise was the whisper of fingers on computer terminals, the hum of printers encased in glass along the wall, and the muffled rattle of newfangled phones. At the long, central city desk, editors and reporters conferred quietly. They leaned over monitors and pointed at sentences. They gripped phones to their ears or bowed their heads together. They spoke only when they needed to. They spoke in hushed tones. There was no reason for them to be so quiet, but they were.

When I had first come into the business, I had come into a life of pounding wire machines and typewriters, of shouted orders and jokes, of phones that really rang and rang often. But then there was the war, and Watergate. The glamor of presidential scandal. Newsmen making news. It got to be a different business after a while. A bigger business. More distinguished. Quieter. Nowadays, sometimes, when I came into the *Star*, I thought the place would start to rattle with my footsteps, like a fancy house full of knickknacks when the big clumsy plumber comes to call.

The white noise stopped. You could hear it die with a sort of hydraulic hiss. Lansing, leaning on a divider in earnest conversation with McKay, was the first to speak.

"Wells!" she said.

Heads turned at the city desk. Faces popped up over the cubicle partitions. Someone else called out my name and someone else. Someone waved at me. A crowd gathered around me. I nodded at them as I pushed past.

"How you feeling?" they said again and again.

Again and again, I told them, "Fine." My voice was already beginning to recover.

They peppered me with questions. For a while I entertained them with tales of the battle. For a while longer, I griped about the hospital. They shook their heads in wonder at my bravery, resilience, toughness, integrity, decency, Americanism, and good breeding. Then they returned to work. Even McKay had to answer a phone call. In the end only Lansing remained.

I was leaning against my desk. She was standing right before me. I could smell her. She smelled good. She was wearing pale pink slacks and a striped pullover shirt. She looked good. She looked bright and new. But her eyes filled as I studied her. She put one hand up to her mouth. I saw the fingers trembling.

"Stop that," I said.

"You look dead," said Lansing.

"I'm okay. I need a shower and a change of clothes, that's all."

"You should be home. You should be resting."

"Yeah. The doctor says I should give up cigarettes and liquor, too."

She bit her lip, took a breath. "Silly doctors. What'll they come up with next?"

"Crazy, isn't it?" I looked around me at the huge expanse of a room. "Anything going on?"

"Oh God, Wells," Lansing said. "The place is a madhouse."

"What else is new?"

"I mean it. Go home and get some rest."

"He's playing this big, huh?"

I faced her again. Caught her swiping at the corner of one eye with a finger. She nodded. "Half the room's working on Colt, the other half's doing the snow."

"Blizzard Hits As *Star* Newshound Routs Assassin?"

She nodded. "He wants you to write your part of the story, too. Exclusive: How I Fought A Killer And Found God. He's been calling your apartment to see if you're back yet. He keeps telling everybody that Wellsey won't let him down."

I cringed. "He's calling me Wellsey again?"

"Head for the hills." She tried to smile, but it stuck as she looked into my battered face.

I pushed on quickly. "What happened to the tiger banner?"

"Sandler." Sandler was one of The People Upstairs. The big-boss types we rarely got to see. "Rafferty got fed up," Lansing said. "He sort of quietly let it drop to Sandler what was happening down here. About a half hour later, Sandler came down and casually asked to see your Borough Prez banner. Cambridge turned beet red. You should have seen him. He . . ."

It was a game try, but she couldn't finish. Her lips started to tremble. She turned away, her face to her shoulder.

"Come on, Lancer, knock it off," I said.

"You look dead," she whispered. "You look just dead."

I reached for her shoulder, thought better of it. My hand fell to my side. I stood there stupidly.

Robert Cambridge called to me from across the room. The sound of his voice made every aching part of me ache even more.

"Wellsey! Wells, Wells, Wells."

Lansing stiffened. With a quick toss of her hair, she walked away from me. She didn't look back. She didn't speak another word.

"Wellsey, I knew you'd come in! I knew those old doctors at that old hospital couldn't hold an old bird dogger like you."

I gritted my teeth. I prepared the semblance of a smile. I turned to greet him. He looked tall and trim in a dark blue suit. His round face was damned near cherubic with its welcoming grin. His dark hair dangled rakishly on his brow. His face was tan, of course. That winter tan of his never ceased to amaze me.

He swung his hand around in a broad arc to clasp my shoulder. He squeezed it, sending radiants of pain up the back of my neck. His expression turned serious. He considered me.

"So—you look good," he pronounced. One guy to another. Cambridge is nothing if not one of the guys.

"Thanks, Bob," I said manfully. "I feel just grand."

He tapped my shoulder. I fought back a shriek. "You know, the other papers, the radio and TV people, they've been calling here for hours. They all want to interview you. They even asked to talk to Lansing and McKay."

"Oh yeah?"

"You know what I said? I said: Fuck 'em. Fuck 'em. Let 'em quote a police spokesman. I mean, do you work here or what?"

He laughed. I made a noise.

"So, uh, Johnny," he went on. "You gonna write me an exclusive on your little brush with death?" He smiled deprecatingly as he said this: just another brush with death, old sport.

"You betcha, Bobby," I said.

"Good, good." He slipped his arm full around my shoulders now. He smelled better than Lansing. "Now, I'm going to have Wally Wilkinson write the lede . . .'' I cleared my throat. Wilkinson was a reporter Cambridge had just hired out of California. He was, as Cambridge himself might have said, 'with the program.' Relatability was his life. When the Chinese pandas came to the Bronx, for instance, he volunteered to cover it. On the other hand, he wouldn't have recognized a hard news story if it sat on his eyelids. Cambridge continued: ''What I want from you is a fast, tight sidebar on the actual events as you experienced them. Do you see what I'm getting at?''

''Gee,'' I said, ''I think so.'' After a quarter century in the business, I really felt I was beginning to catch on.

Encouraged by my quick intelligence, the managing editor gave me a little more to handle. ''Don't be afraid to express your feelings. Your shock at seeing Colt killed. Your fear at being stalked by an assassin. Your sense of—of—triumph when you realized you had survived. Am I giving you a sort of idea of what I'm looking for here?''

''It's beginning to take shape for me, Bob,'' I said hoarsely. I coughed. My throat was tightening again.

''Good!'' Cambridge said. He slid his hand off my shoulder, slapping my back as he went. This time, I could not suppress a groan of pain. ''Think you can have that on my desk by five? Give me a chance to look it over before I pass it on to Rafferty.''

I hesitated. This was a little tricky. Cambridge had edited my copy before. Made it more relatable. In one instance, he had made it so relatable that I was nearly sued by an entire county. In the wake of this experience, he and I had come to certain understandings. He was allowed to tell me how to write my stories beforehand. I was allowed to ignore him. He was allowed to make suggestions on the finished copy. I was allowed to stick two fingers up his nose and yank hard if he changed any of it. Normally, all went well. He worked on making the newspaper relatable. I worked on making the newspaper a newspaper. Lately, however, it seemed to me that this arrangement was beginning to weigh on his sense of authority. Added to that, he couldn't be too happy about Sandler forcing him to banner my Borough Prez story. I feared for the life of my sidebar if Cambridge got his hands on it before the city editor did.

''Well,'' I said finally, with a manly chuckle. ''I'll sure

try, Bob. I'm still feeling a little low, truth be told, but I'll do the best I can." I whipped out a cigarette, lit it, took a drag. I blasted the smoke out in a great haze that spread over us both. Cambridge paled. He does not like cigarettes. He worries about my health, he says. I took another drag.

Undaunted, he pressed the point. "You know, it's only quarter to three now. . . . I just want a sense of how to coordinate the whole layout that we're doing, so if you don't mind I'd appreciate it: on my desk by five." He paused. Grinned through another smoky blast. "Okay, guy?"

"Uh . . ." I said.

"Yo, Pop, you got a visitor!"

The call came from the copyboy, Alex. He calls me Pop. Charming kid. I left Cambridge eagerly. I returned to the glass doors. Alex was there. He pointed me out to a woman who'd just come in. She was small and slender, almost lost in her big cloth overcoat. I guessed she was thirty-five or so. Every year of it was written on her pale face in lines that were carved deep into the corners of her mouth and eyes. Still, it was not an unattractive face. It was pert and sharp, with birdlike features under red hair cut short and bobbed. Her green eyes were bright and clear and intelligent. They followed Alex's gesture quickly. They measured me with a single glance.

She extended her hand. I took it. The skin of her palm was dry and cold. Up close, I saw she had too much lipstick on. She wore too much blush, and her cheeks seemed feverishly bright.

"Mr. Wells?" she said. She spoke crisply. She seemed to be forcing her smile.

"I'm Wells."

She took another deep breath. "My name is Valerie Colt," she told me. "I'm Tim's wife."

"They made me come in to identify the body," she said. She pushed out a sad laugh. "I hadn't seen him in over a year, I didn't know if I'd recognize him."

We were in my cubicle now. I'd pulled an extra chair in there for her. I was seated against one wall, leaning forward, my elbows on my knees. She was seated across from me, leaning back, her head resting against the divider. Between us, my Olympia—the last typewriter in the place, I think— was almost buried under a mass of pink notes headed "While You Were Out." A metal ashtray was balanced precariously on top of these.

Mrs. Colt closed her eyes wearily. "Poor Tim," she said. "He didn't have anyone else."

I took out my cigarettes. I jerked one between my teeth. I slid another one out for her.

"You were divorced?" I said.

She nodded, waving off the cigarette. "Five years now," she said. As I went to put the pack away, she reconsidered, reached for them. I shook one out for her. "I shouldn't really," she told me. "The kids don't have anyone else."

"How many kids?" I held my lighter up for her. She leaned into it. The flame light ran red through the lines beneath her makeup.

She leaned back again, her head to the divider. She blew

smoke at the fluorescent lights. "Two," she said. "A boy and a girl. Six and seven."

"That's a lot to handle alone," I said.

"Yes," she answered quietly. "It's a lot to handle. Alone."

I watched her. I waited. I wondered why she'd come.

Her next words seemed to answer the question. "I wanted to tell you how sorry I am that you got hurt." She smiled. It was a tired smile. "Someone always has to—had to—do that with Tim. Apologize, I mean. People got hurt when they were around him. Someone had to . . . do the niceties, you know? Offer the apologies. Pick up the pieces."

"Someone like you," I said.

She took a long drag of smoke, thinking. She let the smoke out with the single word: "Yes."

"Even now."

She nodded. "Even now. I mean, he just kept on, didn't he? All that charm. All that intensity. He was like . . . a magnet."

I didn't answer. I didn't know what to say. I didn't know what she wanted.

"I mean," she continued, "he just kept on charming people and running off on his dangerous adventures and . . . and people followed him. Cameramen always wanted to work with him. Officials always wanted to talk to him. Women always wanted to . . . to be with him. They followed him. And somehow . . . somehow, they always got hurt. They got shot or . . . or arrested or . . ." She lowered her gaze to me. ". . . or abandoned," she said. "And he just kept on, unhurt, untouched, as if he were under some kind of invisible protection. Until now." Her eyes blurred as the tears welled suddenly.

"You must have loved him very much," I said. It sounded lame even to me.

"Oh!" With a short, quick, stabbing motion, she killed her cigarette in the ashtray between us. "Oh, I know what you're thinking," she said. "Poor woman. Poor woman carrying a torch for a man who ditched her five years ago. A man who was never really there to begin with, always . . . always off somewhere, some other country, never . . . Damn." She had laid her purse down next to the chair. She reached for it quickly now, unsnapped it, brought out a tissue. She dabbed at her cheeks with an expert gesture, caught the tears before they carried her mascara away in black streams.

"I wasn't thinking that at all," I lied.

She snuffled once. "Do you know where I live, Mr. Wells?" she said. "Do you know where I live with my two children? I live in one-half of a brick house in Astoria. One bedroom. One bathroom. A yard no bigger than a square of carpeting. I'm a teller for a bank out there. I can just barely afford what I've got. Between the rent and the day-care . . . he never . . ."

I crushed out my cigarette carefully, slowly, watching my hand, giving her time to recover.

"And now that he's gone, I'm sure there's nothing left for me. I'm sure he spent it all on . . . the fine hotels and the fine food and the fine liquor that the . . . the sources and the women liked." A lock of red hair fell forward on her brow. She brushed it back impatiently. The motion brought her face up again. She looked at me blankly, as if something had just dawned on her. "You won't write this, will you? I didn't mean . . ."

"You want to go off the record," I said.

"That's right. I want to go off the record. Can I do that? Is it too late to do that?" An edge of panic crept into her voice.

I shook my head. "It's not too late."

"I didn't . . . I heard you had to say it first. I thought maybe . . ."

"Politicians have to say it first," I said. "You can say it now."

She smiled a little, nodded. "I say it now."

"Fine." I lit another cigarette. She didn't take one this time. I leaned against my desk, rested an elbow on it. I glanced down at the messages strewn atop the typewriter. I saw the name Chandler Burke written on one of the pink sheets. I looked up at Valerie Colt. "Mrs. Colt," I said without thinking, "why did you come here? Why did you come here to talk to me?"

She was sitting, just then, very erect. Like a little girl. Her knees were pressed tightly together. Her hands lay clasped in her lap. She was smiling slightly, ruefully, as if she were almost amused at the bitterness of her situation. Her green eyes were still glassy with a sheen of tears, but behind that there seemed to me to be a kind of nakedness. I knew, looking at her, that whatever she was about to say would leave her exposed and vulnerable, completely stripped of pride. I wanted to lay my hand upon her mouth and hush her. But whatever she wanted from me, it had driven her this far. She could not go back. She could not help herself.

"I came here . . ." she said, stiffly, primly, as if reciting. "I came here to find out what he said. At the end. If he . . . mentioned me, at all. At the end? Just . . . something, you know? Anything he might have . . . said, I . . ." We could hardly bear to look at each other. "Now," she said, her chest rising with a breath. "Now do you understand why I've come? Why the poor, deluded woman has come?"

I grappled with it for what seemed a long time. People went by the cubicle's opening. The business of the city room seemed to press in on the little space. The seconds went by.

"Mrs. Colt," I said finally. "It was so fast. He—I mean, he died so fast, there was no time . . ."

"But before that." She no longer bothered to hide the sound of panic. "You were with him before that, the police told me, you were drinking with him, he must have talked to you, you must have talked about . . . about . . . things . . ."

"Well . . . I . . ." I moved my hand about helplessly. The cigarette held between my fingers left a spiraling trail of smoke. "Yes," I said. I forced my mouth into a slight, self-effacing smile. "You have to understand, I was a little the worse for the liquor, I . . ."

"Yes," she said eagerly. "You didn't remember . . . everything . . . of course, I . . ."

"That's right, I . . . forgot, we . . . We talked of you at great length, in fact . . . quite a lot, he, uh, Tim, he spoke very, very fondly of you, in fact, I . . ."

"What did he say? Please. What did he say?"

"Well, he spoke about how fond he was of you. What a wonderful wife you were. He said, I remember now, he said . . ."

"Oh God!" It was a soft cry, but on the instant it escaped her, she pitched forward. She doubled over in her chair, her hands coming up to cover her face. Her whole body shook as she sobbed and sobbed. "Oh God," she said again. "Oh God, oh God. Eleanora! Eleanora!"

I sat and smoked and watched her cry. I did not touch or

speak to her. I did not think it would help. She sobbed for about a minute. The sobbing steadily slowed. She fought for breath painfully, swiping at her cheeks with one hand, unsnapping her purse with the other.

She laughed through the tears. "And now I'm a mess on top of everything, right?" she said gamely.

I smiled.

Her red forelock dangled limply. Her eyes were becoming swollen. Her cheeks were already shadowy with smeared mascara. She dabbed at the shadows with her tissues. She took out a circular compact and opened the top. Peering into the mirror, she smoothed the shadows away. She was still sniffling, but the tears had stopped.

She returned the compact to her purse, snapped the purse closed. "I'm sorry," she said. She did not look at me.

I shook my head. "Forget it."

"It was foolish of me to come here, to look for . . . for something you couldn't give me, no one could give me. No one but Tim. I was an idiot."

"We'll all be in jail when they make that a crime," I said.

She forced a smile. "Well!" she said decisively. She stood up. She still hadn't raised her eyes to me.

"Who was she?" I said. I watched her closely. "Eleanora. Just out of curiosity. Who was she?"

She gazed at her shoes. Cheap flats, I noticed. Tan, well worn. The shoes of a woman who was on her feet all day. Finally she lifted her face. Her voice was squeezed back in her throat, back where she was holding the unfallen tears. "She was the woman he loved," she told me. She made a little noise filled with humor and despair. "Oh, she was a lot more than that, I guess, by the time he finished with her. By the time he finished building her up in his mind, romanticizing her, she was . . . everything. Everything Tim loved." She laughed. Not a happy sound. "In Tim's mind, Eleanora was adventure and work and I don't know what all. His youth. She was more than any *living* woman could have been to him. More than I could be anyway."

"You mean she's dead?"

Valerie Colt nodded. "So I gather. I didn't know that much about her, of course. Only that he called for her at night. Only that he sometimes . . . called her name when he was with me.'' Her face contorted. She raised a crumpled tissue to her eyes for a moment. This time, the tears did not come. She lowered her hand. "Other than that, he didn't tell me very much really. I mean, she was my rival, after all. And it isn't easy competing with a dead woman, let me tell you. It isn't easy." She laughed and sniffled. Her words came quickly in her high, hard voice. She seemed relieved to be talking about it.

"I guess not," I said. "But who was she? Did he tell you anything?"

"Oh . . . yes, sure. I mean, there was a time, after he came back from Sentu, when he spent most of his time writing letters, contacting ambassadors, trying to find her. He had to tell me something then."

"Is that where he met her? Sentu?"

She nodded. "That's part of what she was to him: the memory of that first success, that first adventure. She was some sort of a nurse there, I gather. Something like that . . . I don't really know." She sounded surprised when she said this. She'd probably lived with the woman's image so long, she was startled to find out how little she really did know. "He met her in Sentu and I guess they . . . fell in love . . . and she died when the rebels came into the capital. I guess . . . I guess that's all I know for sure. I don't think even Tim was sure what actually happened to her. Just that she couldn't get through the rebel lines. And that he couldn't find her." Now the tears were gone completely. Now she looked at me undaunted. "I lived with Timothy Colt for a year before he went to Sentu. I lived with him and Eleanora for five years afterward. I don't really care who she was, Mr. Wells. I'm sure she was . . . beautiful and . . . and brave and . . . and whatever else." She slung her purse over her shoulder. She raised her chin proudly. "But I was real," she said. "And I was there. I was always there." She moved to the entrance of the cubicle. "I'm sorry if I made a fool out of myself."

"No . . ." I said.

She ignored me. "But do you know what it's like? Do you know what it's like to lose the one person you love most in the world?"

She turned on her heels and was gone. I heard her flat shoes slapping wearily against the floor tiles as she vanished.

For a few minutes I sat alone in my cubicle. I sat alone with my cigarette and her question.

Then I put out the cigarette. Then I answered the question.

''Yes,'' I said to the emptiness.

A long time ago, it must be almost ten years now, back when I first came to the *Star,* I covered a sniper attack on Fifth Avenue. It was Christmastime, December twenty-second. The Avenue, between Thirty-fourth and Fifty-ninth, was one long steady river of humanity. It was a colorful river. Red hats and green scarves, blue and yellow and brown coats all blended together into what seemed a single mass. That mass flowed steadily from where the mechanical dwarves hammered out presents in the window workshops of F.A.O. Schwarz's toy store, past the high towers covered with tinsel, electric lights, and starbursts, past the enormous color-dotted tree outside Rockefeller Center, to the bottom of the Empire State Building, which presided solemnly over the whole great human continuum.

The sniper's name, it turned out later, was Wilfred Campbell. He was from the Bronx, a black man with a jowly face and mournful eyes. He was a window washer. Worked in Manhattan mostly.

About three months before, he'd hit the numbers. It was not an enormous jackpot, but there were a few grand at least. He went out to celebrate at one of the neighborhood spots. It was in an old wooden box of a building, green paint chipping from the boards. There was a sign above the window with the words ''Girls! Girls! Girls!'' painted on it and a picture of a cocktail glass tilting to one side. Campbell had never been in the place before. He was a churchgoing man, married, couple of kids. He usually stayed away from places like this.

But he went in this night. He watched girls in G-strings dance on top of the bar. He took to one of them, a skinny little teenager who called herself Yvette. He paid her to dance on top of his table. He bought her a couple of overpriced drinks. He told her about the jackpot he'd won. After she got off work, she let him come home with her. She lived only a few blocks away from Wilfred's place.

Wilfred stayed with Yvette for two months. That's how long his money lasted. During that time, he lost his job for not showing up. His wife left him, moved back in with her mother. His kids stopped talking to him. Wilfred didn't seem to care. He bought Yvette dresses with spangles on them. He bought her shoes. He rented limos to take her to dinner in. All of this, Yvette later told me, she took with no strings attached. She continued to dance at the bar. She even turned tricks sometimes. Wilfred never complained. Sometimes, she said, she couldn't even stand the sight of him, couldn't bear his touch. He didn't seem to care about that either. She let him live with her. That's all he seemed to want.

When his money ran out, she told him, "Sorry, honey, but now you got to go." He nodded. He seemed to understand, she said. He left without a fuss.

Now Wilfred owned two guns, a .38 caliber pistol and a small caliber rifle. A .22, I recall. He went home and got them both. He put the pistol in the pocket of his army jacket. He put the rifle in a duffel bag. He took the subway into midtown Manhattan.

He carried the duffel bag into a building on the corner of Fifth and Fifty-fifth. It was about six in the evening then. The shopping crowd was thickening with the rush hour crush.

Wilfred walked right past the security desk. He carried his duffel bag onto the elevator. He rode up to the fourth floor. There was a movie company up there. It took up the entire floor. Wilfred had frequently been the guy to wash their windows. He knew just the one he wanted.

The secretary at the front desk was gone but the door to the story department was open. Wilfred walked through, carrying his duffel bag. He came into an empty hallway. There were doors to offices on either side of it. He walked to the first door on his right and went in.

A young woman was sitting at the desk in there. Behind her was a broad window looking out on the brownstone steeple of the Presbyterian church.

The woman looked up at Wilfred. She smiled brightly. She asked him what she could do for him. Wilfred wrestled the big .38 from his pocket. He pointed it at her and fired. Her smile vanished in a burst of red. Her body rocketed off her chair. It thumped onto the floor.

Wilfred kicked the door shut and locked it. He carried the duffel bag to the window, set it down next to the woman's twitching body. He unzipped the bag and brought out the rifle.

Wilfred shoved the barrel of the rifle out through the pane of glass. The glass shattered. Gleaming triangular shards of it spun down through the air toward the people below. Three adults and four children were injured when they were struck by the falling glass. Wilfred took aim and opened fire.

With that big a crowd, with all the music and the lights, it took a long time before the people knew they were being slaughtered. The victims fell silently. The people behind them shoved to get by. On the steps of the church, a young salesman visiting from Houston, Texas, collapsed backward into his wife's arms. She saw his eyes staring upward. She saw the round, raw, red hole between them. She screamed as he slipped from her grasp to the pavement. Her scream became a gurgle. Wilfred had shot her in the throat.

The people passing beneath the church saw that. They'd looked up when they heard the scream. They'd seen the blood bubble suddenly out of the woman's neck. They panicked. The panic spread. The mob on the Avenue surged and shrieked and fell away again and again like the waves of a stormy ocean. Cars stopped short as people tumbled wildly off the sidewalk. The scream of horns joined the screams of the people.

Wilfred kept firing calmly, expertly. He saw a little girl lost and crying in a bookstore doorway. He shot her in the chest. He saw a man scrabbling up the church stairs over the fallen body of an old woman. He put a hole in the back of his skull.

By the time I got there, following the cops, seven people

had been shot dead. More than twenty-five had been wounded. That was the end of it for the most part. Wilfred ran out of ammunition and quietly gave himself up.

When they led him out of the building, I pressed in close to the protective cordon of police. The other reporters shoved up against me. Between one blue-uniformed arm and another, I saw Wilfred pass. His head was bowed. His hands were cuffed behind him. Two cops had him by the elbow, escorting him through the storm of shouted questions and flashing bulbs. He passed within two feet of me. So I shouted at him. That was my job. I shouted the only question I could think of.

"Hey, pal, why'd you do it?"

Wilfred lifted his sagging face as he was urged on. He stared at me with his big, yellow, melancholy eyes.

"Because, mister," he said quietly, "I loved her that much."

He hanged himself in his cell the next day.

I thought about old Wilfred when I got home that night. I thought about his answer. I thought about Timothy Colt and how he died. I thought about a lot of things.

Before that, I hadn't had time to think. I'd been busy serving the greater good of journalism. After Valerie Colt left, I dashed off my sidebar on my fight with Colt's killer. Standard stuff. Took about half an hour to write. When it was done, I pretended I was working on it a while so I could keep from handing it to Cambridge before deadline. As it turned out, my relatable friend was fairly pleased with it. He didn't give me too much trouble.

A little after six o'clock, I took myself home. I felt sick and sore. My throat was raw from too much smoke and talking. My belly stung from too much aspirin, too little food. The rest of me hadn't stopped aching since that morning. By the time I trudged into the crumbling old brick apartment building on Eighty-sixth Street, I wasn't thinking of anything but a shower and a drink and bed.

My apartment on the fourth floor was dark when I came in. Dark but for the glow from the triplex movie theater across the street. That glow gave a hard, glinting quality to the night pressed against the window. It touched the shadows of furniture with gaudy tones of gold and red.

I pounded my fist against the wall a couple of times to chase the roaches away. Then I turned on the light. I threw my copy of the paper down on the couch and headed for the kitchen.

My bottle of J&B was on the counter. I grabbed it with one hand, pinched a glass with another. I carried them out to the living room. I set them down at the desk by the window. I set myself down in the desk's swivel chair. I poured a drink.

The first sip of the liquor made me feel better all over. The hangover I'd had all day disappeared. The pain in my stomach eased. The soreness in my limbs faded. I stared out the window at the movie marquee. I thought about Wilfred Campbell.

I thought about Wilfred, and I thought about the doctor who'd talked to me that afternoon.

Take better care of the machinery or you're a dead man.

I sipped the scotch. It tasted bitter. What did he know, anyway?

I thought about Wilfred, and I thought about Valerie Colt. I thought about her sadness, about her crumbled pride.

Do you know what it's like to lose the one person you love most?

Yeah, I knew. I knew, all right. I'd loved my wife once. Constance. And my daughter, Olivia: I'd loved her more than anything. But one day my wife decided she didn't want to be my wife anymore. And another day, years later, my daughter decided she didn't want to be alive. She was fifteen then. She lived in Europe with her mother. She was working as a counselor in a summer camp. She wrote me a letter from there. She told me she was learning to find beauty in the real world with all its sadness. Then she walked into the woods and hanged herself from a tree. I thought about her now. I thought about Valerie Colt. I thought about Wilfred Campbell.

I thought about Wilfred and I thought about Valerie's husband, Tim. Timothy Colt, one of the best in the business.

When's the last time you saw your woman, Wells? When's the last time you saw her?

I thought about him saying that to me.

You don't see her. You don't give a shit.

I thought about him lying dead in the morgue with no one to identify his body but the wife he'd deserted. The wife he'd deserted for a dead woman. For an obsession. I thought of his words that night, that drunken declaration of his loneliness and his anguish.

Eleanora. Eleanora, my love, my love.

And then he died. Without warning. Without even a chance to cry out, to bitch about the unfairness of it. His arteries slit by an expert twist of a curved knife. That's what I call not taking care of the machinery.

You don't give a shit about anything.

I thought about Chandler Burke.

When's the last time you saw her, Wells?

She lived over fifty miles away, up in Grant County. That hadn't seemed to matter at first. At first she'd come down to the city a lot. I'd take an occasional trip up there. Mostly, when we could, we'd spend our weekends together in the big bed in the next room. She liked to make omelets in the morning. I'd wake up to the smell of them. Over the weeks, she covered the cracks in my walls with posters and photos and drawings. We shopped for them in the little stores downtown. There were pictures of the Flatiron Building, Madison Square Garden, Central Park, and so on. Scenes of little old New York seemed to be the theme of it. I hung them up while she gave directions. She was grim and fussy about it in her old-maid schoolmarm way. It made me smile. I even smiled when she bugged me about how much I smoked and how much I worked. I liked to shut her up by kissing her. She was not fussy or grim when we were making love.

When's the last time, Wells?

I guess we just liked to play house in the beginning of it. We'd both of us lived alone too long. Chandler even seemed willing to put up with the life I led. The phone call dragging me to a crime scene in the middle of the night. The unexpected source opening at the last minute. The weariness that comes of getting home at three a.m. The cynicism that comes of dealing with criminals and pols. She seemed willing to put up with all of it. And it was good in the beginning. I don't even know how it faded away.

I guess I'd gotten busy lately. The scandal in city government was heating up. I was digging my way closer to the mayor's office, maybe toward the governor. I was working weekends, round the clock.

You bury yourself in your work. You don't want to give a shit.

About a month and a half ago, I'd been doing a story on a small-time triggerman namd Vitorelli. Vitorelli had killed a rookie traffic agent, a twenty-five-year-old named Russ Clinton. Clinton had had the temerity to reprimand Vitorelli in front of his friends for double-parking on a street in Greenwich Village. Clinton was also black. Vitorelli didn't like being embarrassed in front of his friends by a black guy. Clinton vanished two days later. He was found about a week later distributed among three garbage bags in the Bowery.

I could tell from the start that the cops weren't on it. They made a lot of serious faces at the TV cameras. They talked vaguely about following leads. But I had it on good authority that the fix was in. The constabulary was just killing time until the murder was knocked from the top spot on the six o'clock report. Soon, they knew, the clean, happy faces of the local anchormen would begin jabbering about something else, about the latest fire or sexually transmitted disease. The camera has a short memory.

But the pen remembers forever. I went after him—Vitorelli. My cop sources put me on to him and I went after him hard. In three days, I had him nailed. I had eyewitnesses to his argument with Clinton. I had his movements, his weapon, the holes in his alibis. I had enough circumstantial stuff to put him away. More than that. I had enough to force the cops to bust him.

Vitorelli, though, he had his sources, too. The night I filed the story, he and one of his goons caught up with me as I was hunting for a cab. They bundled me into the back of a car at gunpoint. They regaled me with humorous stories about what they were going to do with me if the story actually appeared in print. Their descriptions were graphic and unpleasant.

They were good enough to leave me off in front of my office so I could run right upstairs and tell the editors to kill the story. I neglected to do this, however. I hailed a cab and went home to bed instead.

Vitorelli was arrested. Then he was set free on a quarter million bail. I spent the day he got out at the movies with Chandler. I spent the night in bed with her. I had a nightmare there. I dreamed Vitorelli was chasing me. I dreamed he was chasing me and my daughter, who was already dead. Vitorelli was threatening to kill her again if he caught her. He said I'd have to watch her die.

I woke with a shout, sweating. Chandler sat up beside me, touched my arm. I shrugged her off. I went into the living room and lit a cigarette. I stood at the window in my underwear, smoking. Chandler wrapped my bathrobe around her and followed me in.

"What?" she said softly. "What is it?"

"A dream," I said.

"About Olivia?"

I turned around, surprised. She watched me carefully. Her eyes were kind. "Yeah," I said. "Yeah, and Vitorelli. That guy, that killer I just . . ."

"Yes, I know." She waited, studying me. I felt the sweat begin to gather on my brow again. "Tell me."

"Forget it. It's just a dream."

"Tell me anyway.".

I hesitated. The sweat ran down the side of my face, into the stubble on my jaw. My heart beat harder. I couldn't tell if it was the dream that was spooking me or the idea of telling it. I told it anyway. Chandler was silent. She listened.

"So?" I said when I was done. "You're the counselor. What's it all mean?"

She smiled a little. "You're supposed to tell me that."

"I told you what I think. I think it's just a dream and we should go back to bed."

She nodded slowly. "All right," she said. She turned away.

"I'm afraid," I said to her. I was angry suddenly. "Vitorelli is tough. He's tough and he's mean and I'm afraid, all right?"

She faced me again. Her eyes were soft. The robe fell open around her. "That's not so bad," she said. "I spend most of my time afraid."

We stood there together, half-naked and too damned old to look good at it. We stood there, looking into each other's eyes, and seeing the fear inside. For a few seconds I felt we were approaching some kind of common border. Someplace where each of us ended and began at once. Someplace where, if we took just one more step, we'd be together in a different way than before. A more complete way.

We didn't take that step. I dropped my eyes. Chandler moved suddenly, nervously toward the kitchen.

"I'll make us drinks," she said.

She almost never drinks.

When was the last time you saw her?

Vitorelli vanished the next day. Hasn't been seen since. The wisdom on the streets is that some of his friends were afraid he would talk rather than do time. They also didn't like him messing with reporters. It causes trouble for everyone.

So it was then, the night I had that dream: that was the last time I'd seen Chandler Burke. I kept calling her at first. Kept making excuses for not arranging a time to get together. But somehow, it just didn't happen. I'd be busy or she would. There was always something. Then about two weeks ago I stopped calling.

You think I don't know you? I know you, Wells. I was just like you once.

I sat at my desk with the hard, cheap light of the triplex marquee blinking at the night window. I sat and I drank my scotch and I found myself thinking, for no reason at all it seemed, about Wilfred Campbell. Wilfred Campbell in his urban aerie with his rifle and the waves and waves of panicked people below him rising and falling at the pull of his trigger finger.

Because I loved her that much.

I could remember what the place looked like before Chandler hung the pictures. I could remember Chandler casting her eyes over it and saying: "It looks like you're just passing through, John. It looks like no one lives here."

The phone was on the table before me. I came forward in my chair, setting down my glass, pushing the scotch bottle aside as I reached for the receiver. I dialed Chandler at home.

"Hello," she said.

"This is John."

There was a short silence. "I called. I called earlier," she said. She had a deep, warm voice. But it was a hesitant voice, too. Her words proceeded as if they were shuffling forward in the dark. They were careful, wary of pitfalls.

"I—I heard about you on the radio. I was worried. Are you all right?"

"I'll do. The doctor says I'm going to die if I don't stop smoking and drinking so much."

"Yes. Yes, the doctor is right."

There was a pause. "I got beat up bad, Chandler," I said.

"Yes." She nearly hid the quaver on the word. "Yes, that's what I heard."

"I'm gonna be okay, but I got beat up pretty bad."

She said nothing. I did not know if she was crying. I did not know if she was angry.

I said: "I'm sorry I haven't called you."

"It's all right," she answered softly. "I've seen the paper. It's a busy time."

I nodded without speaking. The silence drew out over the seconds. I could picture her sitting there alone in her apartment. Sitting erect in her chair, the phone held to her ear. Staring directly before her, while the cat wound around her ankles. Her expression pensive, her mouth tight. All of her motionless in the silence as it dragged on. I could picture her round, serious face, white cheeked and sad eyed, her hair dull brown. I could picture her pale lips. They were soft lips when you kissed them. Her body was lush and soft to the touch.

"Come down," I heard myself say finally. "Come down this weekend. Friday. Can you?"

The line crackled.

"What?" I said.

"Yes. Okay."

"Okay," I said.

She waited for me to go on. I couldn't think of anything to say.

"I miss you, John," said Chandler Burke finally.

My lips parted. I said nothing. My lips closed.

"See you Friday," she said.

She hung up. I laid the receiver down in the cradle. I stared at it. It was silent. *He knows who I am, Chandler*, I thought. *He knows I can identify him. He's sure to come back for me. He's sure to.*

I reached for my glass. I raised it. I watched the theater's red and gold lights expand in a line around the outside of it, encircling the amber scotch. With my other hand, I pulled a cigarette from the pack in my pocket. I put it between my lips and lit it.

I sat in my chair and I stared out the window.

I loved her that much, Wilfred Campbell had said.

I thought about Chandler Burke. I thought about Timothy Colt.

I thought about Wilfred Campbell.

"**W**hy did you want to see me, Wells?"

"I want to know more about Timothy Colt."

Donald Wexler sat in a wing chair of red leather. I sat in another, facing him. We were in the library of Wexler's town house. There were bookshelves on two of the walls. They were filled with ribbed, leather-bound volumes. And there was a huge leather reading chair with an ottoman before it and a standing lamp behind. To my left was a window partly covered with red velvet drapes. The window looked onto the swank brownstones of East Ninetieth Street.

It was quite a place. A place fit for a man with an elegant background and an elegant job and an elegant Pulitzer Prize. When I'd walked in the front door, I'd entered an expansive hall. The floor was tiled with squares of black and white marble. The light of a crystal chandelier glinted off them. A winding staircase led up to the second story past a wall lined with portraits.

A maid in a black uniform had led me across the hall and through a draped doorway. We went through a living room. There were marble statues there. Greek youths and maidens rose from behind sofas and chairs. Their sleek lines were reflected in gilt-framed mirrors. We passed on into the library.

Wexler was waiting for us. He rose to meet me, extending his hand. He was dressed smartly in a gray suit, a maroon tie.

He was getting ready to head off to work, I guess. It was 9:30 in the morning. I had phoned an hour earlier to ask if I might drop by.

We sat down in the wing chairs. He called for coffee. We drank it. We talked. Wexler asked after my health. I told him it would do. I told him about the assassin, about how Colt had died. He listened silently, gazing out the window. His face sagged; he looked weary, depressed. His damp eyes seemed to be looking at something very far away.

And that's when he turned and asked me: "Why did you want to see me, Wells?"

"I want to know more about Timothy Colt."

"Oh? I wouldn't think they'd let you cover this one."

"I'm not. Not the investigation. Lansing's on that."

"I see. You're doing the side angles?"

"I guess. I don't know. A man gets killed in front of you, it kind of makes you curious, that's all."

He gave me a wintry smile. He considered it for a long moment. "The funeral is tomorrow, you know," he said softly. "Up in Valhalla. Will you be there?"

"I'm not sure. It's kind of strange to first meet a man on the night he dies."

"Yes," Wexler said. "Yes, I suppose it is. It's too bad, really. He would have liked you, too. You're his sort. Oh, go ahead, there's an ashtray somewhere."

I had taken out a cigarette. He rose and went to an antique rolltop desk against the wall behind him. He took a tiny china ashtray from one of its compartments. Set it next to the silver coffeepot on the small round table that stood between us. I practically filled it with the first tip of ash. Wexler took his chair again.

"Who was Eleanora?" I asked him. I watched his face carefully when I said it. The name registered there. The pouches of flesh above his cheeks gathered as his eyes narrowed. His thin lips tightened till they nearly disappeared. He didn't try to hide his reaction. He looked down at the table, still smiling that cold, sad smile.

"He must have been very drunk," he said.

I nodded. "He was. We both were."

"He never mentioned her unless he was. Not to me, anyway. But then, he and I, you know, we met by sheer accident. We became close . . . well, merely due to our circumstances. You, as I say, were more his type. Still, he was fascinating."

"Was he?"

"Yes. At least, I thought so. He was . . . big. Bigger than life, I guess you'd say. He had a way of making you feel your own life was insufficient. Drab. Everything about him seemed a little more—exciting than the rest of us. He had a quality of—vitality? Some kind of yearning in him. I don't know. Something, though. Something most of us forget eventually, or learn to do without."

I knew what he meant. I thought of Colt on the edge of the Oklahoma plains, watching that freight train roll and roll into the endless grass. "All right," I said. "Then why? Why was he like that? What did he have that the rest of us don't?"

Wexler studied me. He seemed to come to a decision. He laughed once and said, "Eleanora, for one thing."

I nodded slowly. "So who was she, Wexler? I came to you because he told me he was with you the day the capital of Sentu fell. He said you went back to cover the story, and he went back for her. Who was she?"

As he answered me, his attention drifted. Into his memories of Africa and revolution. They couldn't be far from the surface of his mind just now.

"Eleanora?" he said. "She was a missionary. English, I think. An Anglican missionary." He shook his head. "No, I don't suppose that's entirely fair. She was something of a legend even then. Even before Colt made a legend of her in his mind. We heard about her now and then, the reporters. We spent most of our time, of course, in the Hotel Victoria, in the bar there. We traded stories. You know how it is. There were several about her."

I listened. I imagined the reporters gathered at the bar's round table. I imagined their voices murmuring.

"It was said, you see, that she ran an underground railroad. A sort of rescue operation for those caught up in the fighting, those—targeted, I suppose you'd say, for execution. What made it all so remarkable is that she took no side in the fighting. She had no political point of view." His slim, well-manicured fingers reached for the silver coffeepot. He refilled our cups. "If you were wanted by the government—which meant you were subject to sudden arrest . . . I mean, Wells, you have to understand: it meant that you and your wife and your children could disappear silently in the night, that you could be dragged from your home and taken to the cellar of a place they called Imperial House. And in Imperial House, my friend, you could scream your lungs out while they killed you inch by inch. While your neighbors huddled together in fear pretending you'd moved away or never existed. . . .'' He paused. He sipped his coffee delicately. "So, as I say, if you were wanted by the government, there was a rumor that Eleanora could hide you, that she had a network of safe houses and guides who could get you out of the country, up the coast possibly to Morocco or down to South Africa. Maybe it was just something people told each other. A hope they conjured up when there was no hope left. At any rate, the same applied—so the story went— if you were being hunted by the rebels. And what a charming bunch they were.'' Wexler raised his eyebrows as if he were talking about a group of boorish party crashers. "Oh, they, in the name of liberation and justice, they would come battering down your door with the butts of their machine guns and . . . I had a friend, a conservative editor named Briley, Joseph Briley. He was vacationing in the countryside when the glorious rebels burst into his house one night. They shoved a gun barrel up one of his nostrils and made him and his two children watch while they raped and murdered his wife. Then they cut one of the children, a little boy, to pieces with a machete while the other child, a girl of three, looked on. I won't tell you how they killed her.''

"How do you know all this?'' I said. My voice was hoarse.

"I was coming over to his house that evening. I arrived ten minutes after the rebels left. Briley was still alive. He was bleeding to death, but he was still alive. He told me what had happened while we waited for the police. Frankly, Wells, I thanked providence when he died in my arms.''

My imagination kept going. I saw the scene. I didn't like what I saw. I tried to focus on the well-coiffed, well-dressed, well-situated man sitting before me. It seemed impossible he'd ever knelt in the blood and sweat of a massacre to cradle a dying friend.

One corner of Wexler's mouth lifted, as if he knew what I was thinking. But he only said: "So . . . if the rebels were looking for you, you could also go to Eleanora. She made no distinction. She would risk her safety, her operation, her life for anyone in need. That's what they said about her at the Hotel Victoria in Mangrela. That was the story."

"If it was true, why didn't anyone stop her?" I asked.

"Ah, my friend, that's just the point. When I say she was a legendary figure, I mean just that. No one had actually seen her in years. No one who returned to tell about it at any rate. The government couldn't find her to arrest her. The rebels couldn't find her to assassinate her. She came—like a good fairy, rather—when you needed her, and not a moment before. In fact, I think that was the aspect of it that tantalized Colt the most."

"Finding her."

"Yes. When no one else could."

I crushed a cigarette. I lit another. I nodded. I understood.

"Once the fever of the thing got into him," Wexler said, "he couldn't let it go. At first, whenever the subject of Eleanora would come up, he would wave his hand at us and say it was all nonsense, that if she were real, someone would have found her. All the same, he wouldn't let the conversation die. He wanted to hear all the stories. He listened to them all." I heard a clock strike ten in some other room. As Wexler put his cup down, he glanced at the gold watch on his wrist. "I have a meeting in half an hour," he murmured. "I really should go."

"Did he find her?"

Wexler glanced up, surprised at the hint of urgency in my voice. The story gripped me. I could see it all.

Wexler inclined his head. A stream of cigarette smoke poured from my mouth as I relaxed. He went on.

"What happened is this. We were drinking one night in the hotel bar. Just as usual, only later than usual and more than usual. I had the feeling Colt was doing it on purpose, building himself up to something. Not that he needed an excuse to drink, God knows, but there was something feverish about it that night. I'm not just saying that now, either. I thought so at the time. He drank and he drank, scotch after scotch. Even the usual gossip and complaining died after a while and it became so quiet we could hear the small-arms fire on the other side of the city." Wexler looked at me, but he wasn't seeing me. He was gone again, back to that bar, back where they told the stories of

Eleanora while the flash of small arms lit the night like fireflies. I was there with him. "And he said—Colt, I mean, he said: 'I'm going to find her, Don. I swear it. I have to find her.' Those were his words. He staggered to his feet. I was too drunk to stop him. I just sat there, watching, openmouthed. I can see him to this day, his khaki pants all rumpled, the back of his white shirt gray with sweat, his jacket gripped in his hand. And while I sat there and watched, he stumbled through the folding doors, out into the lobby, out into the night."

I did not ask again, but the question hung there between us: Did he find her?

"He was gone for two weeks," Wexler said. "He was gone so long, I put an official inquiry in motion to see if he'd gotten himself arrested or killed. Somehow, I must admit, I didn't think so. Not Colt. That wasn't . . ." He coughed. Then he finished it: "That wasn't the way he was destined to die. No, he turned up again. One morning. I came down with a few of the others—Charlie Oberkfell was there, Jack Mars— do you know them?"

I shook my head. "No."

"I came downstairs," Wexler said. "They served breakfast in the bar in the morning and we all went in for our coffee and cruller. And there was Colt. He was at the table we'd been drinking at when he left. He was drinking scotch as he had been. He was drunk—just as drunk as he was before. So help me, Wells, it seemed like the intervening weeks had never occurred. We sat down with him, ordered our coffees. Colt, I remember, was studying the depths of his scotch. And he looked up. He looked up directly at me. And he said, 'She's real, Donny.' The look on his face . . ." Wexler turned away. He peered out at Ninetieth Street as if something fascinating were out there. I followed his glance. All I saw were a few fur-coated matrons passing along the sidewalk, down through a lane carved between drifts of dirty snow. But Wexler kept staring. " 'She's real, Donny.' And he said—he said she was beautiful. Beautiful in the English way, he said, with the swan's neck and the pale blue eyes. The golden hair piled high on top. He talked about the way strands of her hair fell on her cheeks when it was hot. When it was hot and she moved among her people, her refugees, touching them, whispering to them, giving them, Colt said, a portion of her courage."

Wexler blinked, turned from the window. "It was then, of course—when he told me how the gold strands of her hair fell onto her cheeks in the heat and all that—that's when I first realized he was in love with her."

I waited, thinking he would go on. He continued to gaze at me in that bland, open way. The heat from my cigarette brought me around. It had burned down to my fingers. I put it out.

"Was that it? Did he see her again?"

Wexler made a vague motion with his hand. "I imagine so. I believe he did at the very end. You have to realize this was only a month or so before Mangrela fell. Much of that month I spent in the city of Jacobo to the north."

"But what about Lester Paul? Did he have anything to do with it? With her? What the hell was that all about in the restaurant last night?"

"That I can't tell you. Whatever was between Colt and Lester Paul, there was only one other person who knew about it. That was Robert Collins, the British journalist. And I believe he was killed when the rebels entered the city." Wexler straightened the front of his jacket. "And now, Wells, I'm sorry . . . you must excuse me. I'll be late."

At the same moment he stood, a woman appeared at the library door. Wexler smiled fondly at her.

"Darling," she said, "don't you have a board meeting this morning?"

"Yes, my dear," Wexler said gently. And to me: "John Wells, this is my wife Anne."

I shook hands with her. She was a woman in her early forties. A fine, sculpted creature who'd been well cared for her whole life. She had short, carefully crafted auburn hair. A thin precise face softened by bright, kindly blue eyes. I'd seen that face before. In the society columns. Vaguely, I even remembered the pictures that appeared there seven or eight years ago. Society queen weds prizewinning journalist from mainline Philadelphia.

"It's a pleasure to meet you," she said as I released her hand. "I've heard so much about you."

I mumbled something.

"I do hate to steal Donald away from you like this, but he really does have to go scrap with the board."

"It's all right, darling," said Wexler. "We were just finishing up."

She nodded at him, her red lips slightly curved. She flowed gracefully out of the room. He watched her go, the fond smile lingering on his lips. When she was gone, he looked at me sheepishly, slightly embarrassed by his affection.

"Well . . ." he said.

"Who killed him?" I asked. "Who do you think killed him?" I thought of that expert assassin and added: "Or had him killed?"

"Good Lord," said Wexler, surprised. "Good Lord, I don't know. It could have been anyone. It could have been Communists who don't want him to write about Afghanistan or Capitalists who don't want him to write about Nicaragua. It could have been anyone who didn't want him to write about anything. It could have been a jealous husband, for all I know. Let me give you a piece of advice, Wells." He laid a hand on my shoulder—carefully. His manicure probably cost more than my suit. "If it's a story you're after, get your story. Write your story. But if it's personal, if it's just because you happened to be there, let it drop. Let the police handle it. It's what they're there for. Don't become too—hooked, as it were, on Timothy Colt. He was a fascinating man, as I said. Almost like a drug in a way. And like a drug, he really wasn't very good for people."

As we stood together in the rich morning sunlight that fell through the rich curtains into the rich library, I studied Wexler's face. Was he warning me? Warning me off? I looked to his damp brown eyes for a clue, but saw nothing.

But when I was outside and alone again, I remembered Valerie Colt. *People got hurt a lot around Tim.* That's what she'd said. *Someone always had to pick up the pieces.*

I walked along Ninetieth with my hands shoved in my overcoat pockets. I watched the pale light of the near-winter morning glare up at me from the puddles of melted snow in the gutter. Maybe Wexler was right, I thought. Maybe I was just fascinated by Timothy Colt. Maybe it was an unhealthy fascination. Maybe it was deadly.

12

I took a subway back to the *Star*. I sat in my cubicle, my feet up on the desk. I opened my mail. I stared at each piece dutifully before I tossed it into the wastebasket.

McKay came by to greet me. He leaned against the cubicle partition, his hands behind him.

"How you feel?"

"Creaky, but better. How do I look?"

"Like shit, but better. Thank God, too. That battered-up face of yours really did a number on Lansing."

"Yeah, well, she's funny that way."

"I asked her if she wanted a cup of coffee yesterday. I was going downstairs to the diner. She said, 'Stop bothering people, McKay.' "

"Kid can't control her emotions." I lit a cigarette. I went through a few more letters. Tossed the rest out all at once to save time.

"Nice piece on your fight to the death," McKay said.

"That what they called it? I haven't seen the paper."

"Yeah, in the subhead. The exclusive story of his fight to the death with an assassin."

"Kind of overlooks the fact that neither of us died, doesn't it?"

"Don't be picky, Wells. It's a good spread, and I couldn't have written it better myself."

"Yeah," I said, taking a long drag of smoke. "Yeah, you could have."

"Well, yeah, I could have," said McKay, "but he'd have *killed* me."

"Life's unfair. What can I say?"

Alex, the copyboy, passed. I told him to get me a cup of coffee or I'd break his legs.

"Sure, Pops," he said.

"I may break his legs anyway," I told McKay.

"He's nicer than Lansing."

I laughed. "So what's up today? Where's Captain Relatable?"

"He's coming in late. He worked till almost six last night."

"Now, now."

"He called to check in."

"To make sure the assignment editor didn't make the assignments?"

"You got it." McKay had a wicked half grin on that baby face of his. "Lansing's got the follow-up on Colt. She's hot for it, too. I think she wants to track down Lester Paul herself. Vengeance is mine, sayeth the Lance."

"He the suspect? Paul?"

"According to Lansing. She's got it pretty much figured out. Paul hired the assassin to settle his old score with Colt."

"What old score?"

"The one they argued about in the tavern."

"Oh yeah. That old score. What do the cops say?"

"Well, you know Gottlieb."

"Yeah, in fact I talked to him," I said. "He'll find Paul, they'll sit, they'll chat."

"Right. He hasn't said much more than that, far as I know."

"Hard to believe he's the meanest tec in the south, isn't it?"

"Is it true he once shot a matchstick out of Fats Thompkins's mouth?"

"Who knows? The way I heard it he lit the match with the bullet."

Alex brought me coffee. I let the snotty little bastard live. I ditched the nicotine and went after the caffeine.

"So anyway," I said, "Lansing's doing the follow on Colt. What about you?"

"Something of my own. Homeless children. With the snow and winter coming on and all."

"Sure." I waited. McKay said nothing. I finally had to ask him. "What about Wellsey? The old bird dog? The man who duels to the death?"

McKay lifted his eyes to the fluorescents, bounced his butt against the hands folded behind him. "Well . . ."

"Don't tell me: The Day After I Fought An Assassin and Found God."

"Worse. You see the *News* this morning?"

"No. I haven't seen anything."

"They led with Colt, same as us. But they dumped the second-day snow stories and page-three'd a copyrighted piece on the Corlies Park bribe."

"They page-three'd my two-day-old story? Did they have anything new?"

"Details. An interview out of the U.S. attorney's office. Not Ciccelli. Basically the same stuff."

"So they're saying we got the story first but now they're gonna run with it."

"Right," said McKay, still watching the fluorescents. "So—sort of casually this morning, while he was telling the assignment editor his job, General Cambridge says, 'I'd use Wells on Colt but, of course, he'll be bird-dogging the scandal. I mean, obviously that's our big story.' "

I was taking a long sip of coffee when he spoke. I nearly scalded my sinuses. I put the Styrofoam cup down, wiping my mouth with my hand. "That son of a bitch," I said. "Suddenly it's a big story."

"So unless you were planning something else . . ."

I thought it over. "No," I said. "I want to do something on Colt, but not yet. Maybe a profile after the funeral tomorrow . . . No, this is what I was going to do anyway, I guess. I just hate to make it look like he thought of it."

"Life's unfair. What can I say?" said McKay. He pushed off the partition. "Anyway, I'm glad you look like shit but better. I gotta get to work."

"Okay," I said. "Thanks, Mac. If you see Alex, kick him in the face, then tell him if he doesn't bring me a copy of the *News*, you'll do it again. The *Times*, too."

"Sure thing."

Off he went.

I got on the phone. I checked in with my friend at the parks department. I left a message with borough president Robins. I wrangled with Ciccelli's secretary. She's a divorcée with orange hair who feels that answering the phone in the U.S. attorney's office is pretty much the same as running interference for a quarterback with shaky knees. I got nowhere with her.

Alex brought me the papers. I looked them over. The *News* was pretty much as McKay had said. They'd filled in a few blank spots and called it an exclusive. The story still belonged to me. I started hunting through the *Times*. As I did, I got the sensation I was being watched. I glanced up. I was being watched.

"Yo ho, there, Lansing," I said.

"Don't go around yo ho–ing me," she said grimly. "How do you feel?"

"Super. Great," I said.

"You look a little better."

"I'm telling you. I haven't felt this wonderful in years. I should be nearly killed more often."

"I'll say."

"How's the Colt case?"

"Have you had breakfast?" she asked me.

"Uh . . . yes."

"Liar."

"Okay—no."

"Idiot."

"What's the right answer here?"

She thumped a paper bag down on my desk. "Here's a bagel," she said. "Eat it."

I dug into the bag. The bagel was a toasted garlic with cream cheese. My favorite. There was orange juice, too.

"Gee," I said.

"Just shut up and eat it."

"Mmmpf," I said around a mouthful of bagel. "Sho howsh the Colt cashe?"

Lansing shook her head at me, sighed. She crossed her arms under her breasts. She leaned her shoulder against the partition. "Fine, fine," she said. "Gottlieb's after Paul. He gave out some stuff this morning. Says it looks like Paul's some kind of international smuggler type. Nothing fancy. Stones, metals. Fencing for pickpockets. Some guns, too. Some drugs. Whatever's happening.''

"How does Gottlieb get this?"

"He's been busted—Paul, I mean. In Morocco and again in France. He's even wanted for questioning in a pornography case out of Boston.''

"Charming guy.''

"Kind of elusive, as I understand it,'' Lansing said. "Escape artist–type. In Morocco, they actually had him in prison. One of those little stone boxes where people draw pictures of windows on the walls for twenty years and then die. Eat the bagel, Wells.''

I ate the bagel. "Urph?'' I said.

"So one day they walk in, he's gone. No tunnel. No hole in the wall. Just gone. Three guards lost their jobs over it. He beat the gendarmes, too. In France. That's where they keep the gendarmes. And the cops in Boston still can't figure out how he got away. Even Interpol's had him cornered a number of times. He's pretty impressive.''

"He's never met Gottlieb.''

"That seems to be Gottlieb's attitude. Speaking of which, he says you're supposed to come in and look at some mug shots. He says the guy who beat you up is probably some kind of international hired-gun type. Hard to ID, but it's worth a shot.''

"We beat each other up.''

Lansing let that pass. "Gottlieb says Holloway and Wexler are being helpful not at all so anything you can do would be appreciated.''

"Yeah, I talked to Wexler this morning. He wouldn't give me anything either.''

"You talked to Wexler? What for?''

I shrugged as casually as I could. "Background,'' I said. "I might do a piece on Colt after the funeral.''

Lansing straightened. Her high white cheeks turned red. "Back off it, Wells,'' she said. "It's mine.''

I was taken aback. "Boy, McKay was right about your mood.''

"McKay's an idiot. Just stay off my story.''

Now I began to be a tad peeved. "Your story? The guy got killed right in front of me.''

"That's right," she snapped, "and the killer saw you."

"So what?"

"So just keep a goddamned low profile, okay?"

"What's that supposed to mean?"

"If you get killed on this, Wells, so help me, I'll be really, really mad."

We glared at each other for a second. "Get out of here," I mumbled, turning from her to the paper on my desk. "I'm busy with Corlies Park. Trying to find out what the *Times* did with it, for crying out loud. They're burying this stuff, I swear it. I think they're sleeping with these people over there."

I continued to mutter to myself until I heard Lansing shift behind me. "Just eat your goddamned bagel, Wells," she said. When I sneaked a look, she was gone.

I went back to work. It was slow going. There were no big breaks to be had. It would take me all day just to leapfrog over the *News* with a few new details of my own. I took a new tack, running down a few old rumors about Giotto, the mobster who'd gotten the contract for the playground. I was on the phone so long I felt my ear was welded to the receiver.

Around three that afternoon, McKay returned. He thumped a paper bag on my desk.

"What am I, an underprivileged nation? What is this?" I said.

"A BLT," said McKay. "Lansing says eat it or she'll kill your cat."

"I don't have a cat."

"She says she'll buy you a cat and then kill it. She'll name it Scruffy."

"Man," I said, "she's tough."

I exhumed the sandwich, bit into it. Leaned my head back and stared at the ceiling, chewing.

McKay sat on top of the papers on top of my desk. "You look beat," he said.

"I thought I looked like shit."

"You look like beat shit."

I chewed a while. "You ever think about birdcages?" I said.

"What, you mean, like, the lining thereof?"

"Yeah."

"Sure. You bust your ass, you get it, you write it, you

print it. Next day, they use it to line birdcages. Or wrap fish. Who doesn't think about that?''

"Doesn't bother you? Good writer like you? You could write books.''

"I'll write books.''

I nodded. "Sure you will," I said. I took another bite of the sandwich, closed my eyes. I hardly had the energy to chew. I was beat, like the man said. I opened my eyes. The fluorescents made them ache. "I'll bet Colt would've written books," I said. "Good books.''

"Hell," said McKay, "you'll write books, too.''

I laughed. "I don't even read books.''

He pushed off my desk. "Nowadays, that's not a problem.''

When he was gone, I finished the sandwich. I smoked a cigarette. I smoked another. Finally I turned to the papers scattered on the desk before me. With a sigh I gathered my notes on Corlies Park. I began to assemble them into a story. There wasn't much to work with. I'd gotten a guy in Ciccelli's office to give me a little on their investigations into Giotto's construction company. If I led with it, it would look like we'd gotten something new the *News* had missed. I could do to them, in other words, exactly what they'd done to me.

I started writing it. My typewriter clacked loudly in the room filled with quiet keyboards. It was routine stuff. The background was copied straight out of my original story. My mind drifted as I copied it. It drifted to Colt. I thought about him writing books. He would've done it, too. He would've written the books that I would never write. The stuff I wrote would just keep lining birdcages.

My mind drifted on. It drifted to Eleanora. I thought about her moving among her refugees, whispering to them. What was her voice like, I wondered. English, Wexler had said. Did she have one of those sweet, melodic British voices you hear in the movies? Deborah Kerr, that sort of thing. When you saw her—when Colt saw her—walking among the sick and suffering, did he suddenly feel there was something more to life? Something better than lining birdcages?

I finished the story around five o'clock. Around 5:01, all hell broke loose.

It started with a shout from the city desk.

"Lansing!"

I had just gotten up to bring my story to the editor. I was in the aisle when Lansing came tearing out of her cubicle across the room. She had her purse strapped over one shoulder, a camera strapped over the other. She was wearing a tight wool dress, dark green, with a skirt that flared. It lifted from her legs as she stepped briskly toward the desk. Reporters, editors, and copyboys stopped in the aisles to watch.

She was halfway to the desk when she called out to Rafferty: "Got him?"

Rafferty's old, bald, bullet-shaped head nodded in imperturbable calm. "Maybe," he said—quietly, but so it carried to her. "Just heard a call over the scanner. There's a raid on at Thirtieth and Madison, the Hotel Lincoln. Thought I heard Paul's name. We're calling on it."

Lansing changed directions. She headed toward the glass doors. The reporters, editors, and copyboys watched her green skirt. "I don't want to wait," she called over her shoulder. "I wanna be there. Get me on the two-way if you get it confirmed."

I walked up to our medical reporter, a guy named Vaughn. I stuffed my story into his hands.

"Stop drooling and give that to Rafferty," I said. I left him there staring and ran after Lansing. I caught up with her as she threw the big glass door open. I held it for her, followed her out to the elevators.

We stood next to each other, waiting for the doors to open. Lansing did not turn. She pressed her lips together. She tapped her foot angrily.

The elevator bell rang. The door slid back. The box was empty. We got on, pressed the button. We watched the arrow above the door sweep toward one.

"Why are you doing this?" she said.

"Because I was there, Lansing. And hell, if he wants to find me, I'm in the book."

She bit her lip. The elevator touched down. "Okay," she said.

Even before the door fully opened, we were hurrying through the lobby to the street.

Lansing's car was parked in the press section just out front on Vanderbilt. She drove a Honda Accord, a semisnazzy hatchback, all red. She had her keys out of her purse as she came around the driver's side. She let herself in and leaned over to snap open the passenger door for me.

It was rush hour. It was dark. Up in front of us, we could see the glaring lights of the traffic packed tight on Forty-second Street around Grand Central. We could hear the horns as motionless cars fought for space amidst motionless city buses. The cold purple of the evening air seemed to shimmer with the rising exhaust.

On one side of Vanderbilt, the stream of cars flowed slowly but steadily toward the logjam up ahead. On the other side, sparser traffic zipped toward Forty-fifth. Lansing turned the key in the ignition, flicked on the headlights. She hit the gas and made the engine roar. With one fluid motion, she looked over her shoulder, put the car in gear, turned the wheel, and shot out into the street.

The horns went up behind us like flares from a sinking ship.

"Jesus!" I said. I reached for my shoulder harness.

Before I could get it on, I was thrown sharply against the door. The strap flew from my hands. My left elbow hit the edge of the dashboard.

"Yah!" I remarked.

Lansing was making a U-turn.

The disparate flares of car horns united into a single screaming flame. Brakes screeched on the wet pavement. Headlights swiveled this way and that. Lansing's Accord wove and swayed through spaces that were barely there as she shot into the uptown stream. Cursing, I grabbed the shoulder strap again.

The strap flew from my hands as my shoulder slammed into the door. Someone screamed curses in a deep, guttural voice. The tires of the Accord answered with an agonizing squeal as Lansing swung the wheel around to point the front fender down Forty-fifth Street.

The cars around us bucked and stopped and started again. But Lansing kept her heel pressed to the pedal. The Accord wove forward like a fish through the weeds.

"It's shorter this way," Lansing shouted over the noise.

"Life?" I shouted back. I reached for the shoulder strap.

We made it to the corner of Fifth Avenue. We stopped at the light. To our right, the white headlights stormed at us, heading downtown. To our left, the red taillights swept away from us in a single body toward the Bowery. Above the other sounds of horns, I was dimly aware of the rising howl of a police siren. I yanked the belt across my chest, felt around for the latch.

"Here they come," said Lansing.

I glanced up as I struggled with the belt. The sea of headlights was parting, shifting to one side of the Avenue and the other. Down the middle came the revolving red and white flashers of an onrushing cop car.

The siren rose to a screaming peak, Dopplered down suddenly as the cruiser went past. The shoulder harness flew out of my hands as Lansing hit the gas. She ran through the red light, spun onto Fifth. The car's rear tires slid to the side on the melted snow, then straightened. Lansing bore down on the gas, edged her front fender up behind the cruiser's tail. The whirling glare of the flashers filled our windshield. Together the cop car and the Accord raced down Fifth Avenue as the traffic around us ducked and dodged for cover.

I reached for the shoulder harness. The cops ahead zigzagged through sudden spaces in the traffic. Lansing's car clung to the cruiser's rear fender. Christmas decorations rushed by me on every side. The fairies in the window of Altman's gamboled and cavorted a moment and then vanished in a blur.

The Empire State Building—lit red and green—towered over us to the right and then was behind us. The flashers swallowed everything as they passed.

The seat belt flew from my hands. This time I was tossed into the corner between the door and the dash. The cop car had made a sharp left turn. Lansing had gone after it. I immediately grabbed the belt again, wrestled it over me, down toward the latch. Ahead of us, the gloaming sparkled with red and white. Police cars were jammed together, flashers spinning, in the center of the street. One cop stood in the middle of Madison Avenue, battling the traffic with his bare hands. Alone, he made way for the oncoming cops, waving the cruisers in to join their brothers.

The cruiser before us dashed across Madison. Lansing dashed after, past the traffic cop, into the wild dance of flasher light. I grunted as the seat belt fastened with a loud snap. The harness held me in place as Lansing pulled roughly to the curb. She braked to a stop.

She was out of the car while I was still unfastening the belt. I tumbled out the passenger door a moment later. Police men and women were rushing by, crouched, their pistols drawn. Some of them carried rifles. All of them were raked by the spinning lights, brought into relief and plunged back into silhouette as the glare caught and released them.

The cops closed in on the building right before me. It was six stories of chipped brick two slots from the corner. The Hotel Lincoln sagged like the shoulders of a man in mourning. The light revolving on the front of it dashed over broken windowpanes covered with cardboard and canvas curtains with blackness showing through the holes. A lighted sign with the hotel's name in brown ringed a skewed metal awning over the crumbling stoop. Under that sign, police officers were coming out of the building into the night. With them were the poor, broken, dispossessed inhabitants of the place. Scrawny black women, old white men, children with long-suffering faces. The police ushered them out one by one into the chaos, evacuating the hotel in case shooting started.

I shivered. I was chilly. I had forgotten to put on my overcoat. I stuffed a cigarette in my mouth. I stuffed my hands in my pockets. I followed Lansing into the confusion of flashers and dusk.

I found her in the middle of the street. She was hovering over a shorter, stockier figure. A man in a camel hair coat. I heard her voice as I approached.

"Is it him? Is it Paul? Just tell me: is it Lester Paul?"

And the answer: "Sheesh, Lansing, would you stop already? Do I call out half the department to catch a litterbug? Move back to the sidewalk so you won't be ashamed I'll have you carried away."

"Is he armed?" Lansing asked.

I moved up beside her. I nodded a greeting to Gottlieb. The burly cop gestured at my colleague. "Is it me, Wells, or is she giving me a hard time? I got a maybe killer up there, he shot through the door at a cop who tried to question him, almost blew his foot off." He shook his head, worried. "There could be shooting, there could be killing. It's a terrible situation. Who knows what'll happen? Move back to the sidewalk, Lansing."

I took her by the arm. "He's right."

She shook me off. "Okay," she said. "Just—which room is he in?"

Gottlieb sighed, wiped the sweat from his high round forehead with one heavy palm. "Right there, fourth floor, corner window, see it? Soon as I finish the evacuation, we'll move in, we'll arrest him, we'll see what's what."

I took Lansing by the elbow. I drew her back.

"Are there cops stationed in the hall up there?" she called out.

"No, an escort to the bus station it should be easy he escapes," said Gottlieb. "Wells, marry her she won't be out on the street where they shoot people."

Raising his hands, he turned away from us. He faced the building as a few more cops brought a few more lost-looking souls out into the night.

Other cops ran and crouched and raised their guns around us. I kept tugging on Lansing's elbow, bringing her back from the front of it. Finally I got her up onto the sidewalk. A low wall of cruisers, flashers, and armed police stood between us and the hotel. No one was coming out under the awning anymore.

Lansing and I stood side by side. She unstrapped the camera from her shoulder, brought it to her eyes, and started firing. I

watched the corner window on the fourth floor. I could see a
light on in there behind the canvas curtain. It seemed a harsh
light, like a bare bulb burning. For a moment, as I stood and
watched, the street seemed to fall silent. There was only the
crackle of police radios and the buzz of Lansing's camera.

It was just then that I heard a sound behind me.

I glanced over my shoulder. There, in the doorway of the
building at my back, I saw the small shadow of a man. I almost
turned away again before I recognized him.

"Holloway?" I said. "Solomon?"

He stepped forward. White light flashed on his bald, chocolate-colored dome. He let out a rough laugh.

"I didn't notice you," he said.

He came up beside me. The three of us faced the building.
I saw Gottlieb talking to a uniformed officer. They were getting
ready to go in. Lansing took pictures.

"Since when does the wire send its bureau chiefs out to
cover busts?" I asked.

Holloway chuckled. "I heard it on my car scanner as I was
heading home," he said. "I'm curious."

But as we waited, as the seconds went by, I took a sidelong
glance at his face. It was tight, intense. His eyes were focused
grimly on the building.

We heard a shout from inside.

"Come on out, Paul! Come on out now!"

I felt Holloway tense beside me. Another second passed.
Lansing's camera clicked and whirred. Then Holloway started.
We heard a crash from inside. The light behind the fourth-
floor window swung crazily. Shadows and silhouettes swarmed
over the curtain. Someone shouted: "Paul!" I heard Holloway
stop breathing.

The curtain on the fourth floor was pulled back. We saw
a lean, red-haired cop wrestle the window up. He stuck his
head out into the chilly December night.

"Lieutenant?"

Gottlieb trundled forward until he stood in plain sight.
"Right here," he called.

The cop shook his head slowly. "He's gone, Lieutenant."

Lansing's camera stopped. She lowered it. She stared.

Gottlieb lifted his two hands. The flashers played on his

camel hair coat. "How is he gone? You're standing outside the door. I'm standing outside the window. Where is he?"

The cop tucked his head inside. He conferred with the others around him. He returned.

"He's just . . . gone," he said.

Beside me, Holloway started to breathe again. He began with a long sigh of relief.

14

We had to rush to make the bulldog. I wrote the lead under both our bylines while Lansing worked up what she had on Paul. It went well together: an escape artist works his art on New York's finest. It was good stuff. By the late editions, we had it polished to a reasonable facsimile of perfection.

It was nearly ten-thirty when I bought Lansing a drink over at Flanagan's. It's a good solid sports bar next to the terminal. Pictures of ballplayers on the wall. Semicircular bar around a couple of TVs. Baskets of popcorn on the tables. We sat in the back and hoisted a couple of scotches.

We were tired. We stared into our booze a lot. After a while, Lansing smiled. Brushed the long blond hair back over her shoulder.

"What?" I said.

She waved me off. Then she answered. "I was just thinking: we haven't worked together on a story like that for a while."

"The drug den fire, wasn't it?"

She nodded fondly. "Yeah. I didn't think you'd ever pair with me again after I ran in the doorway for that picture."

I laughed. "It wasn't that. It was the drive to the scene."

Her mouth opened in surprise. "Oh, come on!" she said. "I'm a *great* driver."

I plugged in a cigarette. It kept my mouth shut. Somehow I'd known she would say that.

I lit a match. Behind the flame, Lansing's expression grew serious.

"Listen," she said. "I got this job because of you."

"You got this job because you're good."

"And you backed off a story once to let me prove it."

I shrugged, blew smoke at her.

Lansing looked at me hard with her blue eyes. There's something about those eyes. They can flash at you like polished steel. But behind that, just behind it, there's something else. Something fearful, maybe. I'm not sure. Something it would be very easy to hurt.

She said: "If you want this one—Colt, Paul, the whole thing—if you want it, it's yours."

"I don't want it."

"I'm just saying . . ."

"It's your story, Lansing. There's just some angles I want to cover. Maybe I'll do some sidebars on it. . . ." My voice trailed off.

She lowered her face, stared into her drink. I looked at the part in the center of her hair. The thin show of white scalp. I thought of her sitting in front of a mirror in the morning, making that part with a brush.

She looked up. "It got to you, didn't it?" she said. "Colt? He got to you."

I jabbed out my cigarette quickly. "Come on, Lansing," I told her. "Let's get out of here."

She drove me home, up Park Avenue. Mostly the cabbies owned it now. They whizzed by quickly, fighting each other for inches and dimes. Lansing made her way uptown slowly, clinging to the right lane. When she wasn't on her way to cover a story, she drove like an eighty-year-old dowager trying to outlive her kids.

We didn't talk much on the way. When we got to Eighty-sixth Street, we didn't talk much some more. She parked outside my building, and we sat together silently in the dark of the car. All around us, Yorkville was bright with movie marquees and streetlamps. Lansing gazed through the windshield for a long moment.

"What was it?" she said. "About Colt, I mean."

"Forget it, Lancer. Thanks for the lift."

"Come on, Wells, I can be curious, too. Think of it as a favor."

"Forget it," I said.

"I mean, you've seen people die before."

I sighed. "I guess. But Colt seemed . . . I don't know."

"Too much alive to die," said Lansing sadly.

"Yeah. Like he had something he lived for, anyway. Something he gave a damn about. Maybe it just seems a waste, somehow." I reached for the door handle. "Or maybe I'm just getting old."

"You're not so old," Lansing said. She turned toward me. Her face caught the streetlight's glow. There was no trace of steel in her blue eyes now. "And I'm not so young, either."

I had my hand wrapped around the handle when she spoke. I was about to pop the door. I stopped. I tried to look out the windshield, not at her. I saw the neighborhood's young lawyers and stockbrokers in their long overcoats hurrying home with tomorrow's *Times*. They scurried past the drug dealers. The drug dealers jerked up and down on their toes at the corners, their hands clasping their stashes in the pockets of their army jackets. Overweight women were out strolling their sleeping kids around. Overweight husbands in Giants sweatshirts followed, headed toward the newsstand for the *News* or the *Star*. The bulldog was out already. Tomorrow's birdcage lining today.

Lansing kept looking at me with her easy-to-hurt eyes. She was beautiful. She even smelled beautiful. She was twenty years younger than I was. I felt like an idiot.

"Chandler's coming down tomorrow evening," I said to the windshield. "Coming down for the weekend."

"Is she?" Lansing turned to the windshield, too. "That's nice. I'd like to meet Chandler sometime."

I nodded. "Yeah, that'd be great."

I popped the door open.

"Nice working with you tonight," said Lansing. She sounded a little hoarse.

"Yeah," I said. "See you tomorrow."

I didn't watch her drive away. I headed straight for my front door. I heard her engine rev behind me. When I glanced up, I saw the Accord swiveling under the green traffic light onto Lexington. I went inside.

I heard the phone ringing as I came down the hall to my apartment. I hurried to get the key in the door. I pushed into the darkness, hit the light switch. I moved straight through to the desk by the window.

I grabbed the phone, looking down at the triplex marquee. There was no line outside the theater. *That big Christmas sci-fi picture must have bombed,* I thought. Then I heard the deep, measured voice on the other end of the wire say:

"John Wells. This is Lester Paul."

He waited for me to answer. "You've got my attention," I said. I pulled open the desk drawer fast. I rooted through the mess for a notepad, flipped it onto the desk, flipped it open. I pulled a pen from my pocket.

"I want to tell someone my side of the story," the voice went on. He had a trace of an accent. I couldn't place it. "I want to tell you."

"On the record?" I said.

"Yes, you can print it all."

"Okay, when?"

"Tomorrow evening. Ten o'clock. Are you familiar with the American Museum of Natural History?"

"Yeah, sure."

"Walk by it on the park side. Across the street, you understand?"

"Yeah. Ten o'clock." I scribbled it on the page in front of me.

"I'll drive by and pick you up in a blue Chevrolet."

"You got it."

"And Wells . . ."

"Yeah."

"If there are any police, I'll drive by and blow your brains out."

I went and watched them bury Colt. I was one of many. They turned out in number to see him lowered into the snow-covered earth. There were reporters and editors I knew, some foreign correspondents I'd only heard of, others I didn't even recognize. It was hard to tell who was covering the affair and who was attending it.

Solomon Holloway was there, and Donald Wexler. Lansing was there, on the outskirts of the small crowd, taking pictures, taking notes. Valerie Colt stood close to the graveside. A little boy stood on one side of her, a little girl on the other. The boy sucked his thumb as he looked down into the hole at the box with his father in it. The girl stared at nothing. Mrs. Colt began to weep into a lace handkerchief. Her red hair bowed to the frosty air. The workers covered the coffin with earth. I looked around and saw other women weeping, too.

The crowd began to disperse. The snow crunched under us as we moved to the street. Lansing hung back, getting quotes from some of the famous journalists there. I walked alone. Holloway and Wexler were just in front of me. They leaned their heads together and spoke quietly. They kept their hands clasped behind their backs.

The two moved apart as they reached the street. Wexler went toward a maroon Mercedes. I expected a chauffeur to jump out and open the door for him, but he got in and drove it off himself. Holloway had a long brown Lincoln. I moved up beside him as he opened the door.

"Can I get a lift home?" I said.

He turned. His eyes, normally wide and merry, narrowed at me a moment. I saw his tongue move between his lips.

"I'd ask Lansing," I said, "but she's working the crowd."

He still hesitated—then said: "Sure. Get in."

He tooled the big car out into the street. We rolled past the glittering water of the Kensico Reservoir, the flat-faced wall of its dam. We got on the highway and sped by the city of White Plains. The only thing that glittered there were the silvered windows of its faceless office parks.

Holloway kept his eyes on the road. I smoked a cigarette, toyed with it.

"Nice service," I said.

"Yeah. Weird, though," Holloway said. I looked at him, waited. He went on in his low, rolling voice. "Couple of days ago, Tim's sitting at the table with us. Laughing, telling stories. Making passes at your pal Lansing. Man, he had the heat on for her, you could tell." He wound the car onto the Bronx River Parkway. Plenty of trucks, traffic into the city. It kept moving. Holloway paid close attention to the road. "What I mean is: he was *alive*. Thinking things, saying things, wanting things. A couple days later they put him in a box, put the box in the ground, and that's the end of it."

I sneered at my cigarette. "Anyone ever tell you it'd be different?"

"No, I know, I know. It's just weird, that's all. That's all I'm saying."

I nodded. "Yeah," I said. "It is."

Outside the windows, the gray winter woods of Westchester were giving way slowly to the gray towers of the Bronx. Holloway let out a heavy sigh.

"So," he said, "can the bullshit, John, let's have it."

I smiled. He was right. He was a friend, and I couldn't con him. I'd met him five years ago, when he first came to New York to take over the bureau there. Before that, he'd been in Lebanon and London. Before that, there had been Sentu. As long as I'd known him, he'd been as he was now: tough, wicked but restrained, with a quiet sense of mockery.

But you heard stories about Solomon Holloway, about the way he was before he'd proved himself in Africa. Then, with the shadow of his famous father hanging over him, it was said he could be pretty wild. Hard drinking, quick with his fists. They said he'd been fired off a paper in Chicago for it. There'd been an editor there, the story went, who lopped off the last two graphs of one of his stories. For space. It happens all the time. My friend Holloway apparently approached said editor at the city desk and uppercut him so hard the guy's head hit the floor before his butt did. In those days, I'd been told, Holloway had a red-hot rage buried in him that could erupt at any moment. There was, as far as I could tell, no sign of that now.

Holloway could still surprise you, though. He surprised me the day I met him. That was at a press convention at the Harlington Center, one of the glitzy Sixth Avenue hotels. The theme of the conference was supposed to be "Responsibility in Media." The actual subject was: "How Can We Avoid It?" At that time, the news business was rapidly shedding the grim-watchdog guise of the post-Watergate era and revealing the party animal underneath. News executives were catching a lot of flack for ditching depth in favor of sensationalism. Basically, a bunch of managing types had decided to hold this conference to convince everyone that dull stuff like facts, balance, and restraint didn't have to get in the way of fun stuff like ratings, circulation, and profits. Perelman had ordered me to attend.

In the dark days before Cambridge was hired to make the *Star* relatable, Perelman had been hired to give it zing. He did not think I was zingy enough. He thought three days of zingy seminars would help. I was on my second day when I met Holloway. I was not feeling zingy.

As the new bureau chief for the wire, Holloway had shown up at the conference out of curiosity more than anything. He sat at my table during a dinner lecture entitled "It's Still a Business." He drank martinis throughout this lecture with an intensity and perseverence that would have awed an Irish poet. When the speaker—a TV executive—asked for comments, Holloway stood up.

He introduced himself. Then, in his deep baritone, he said: "My comment is this: Journalism is indeed a business. Like running a factory. People who churn out pablum to the voters of a democracy for high ratings are the same as manufacturers who produce shoddy and dangerous goods for quick profits. In a system of private enterprise, we are each all the more responsible for what we produce." He paused, then added dramatically: "You asshole." He cleared his throat. "And now I'd like to sing a little song." With which, he regaled us with several verses of "Red River Valley," some of which I suspect he made up on the spot.

He sat down.

"Can I buy you a drink?" I said.

"Please," said Holloway.

From that moment on, the conference was a free-for-all. And Holloway and I were pals.

Now, as he drove his long Lincoln past the red-brick projects of the Bronx, I smiled at him from the passenger seat.

"Look," I said, "I'm not a cop. I just want to know."

Holloway chuckled deeply. "Sometimes the things you just want to know end up on the front page. Is this off the record, John?"

I thought it over. Shook my head. "No."

"I didn't think so." He hesitated another moment. "Okay," he said then. "Shoot."

"Why were you there, buddy? At the raid last night. When Paul escaped, you looked like a man whose medical tests just came back negative."

I turned from him, looking toward the window. Beyond the projects near the road, the ashen desert of the northern borough spread away before me.

"I didn't tell the police anything about Lester Paul."

"So Gottlieb says."

"But I knew him. I knew him in Sentu."

I nodded, at the window.

"Look, I mean, I don't want to make any excuses. But most of what I could have told Gottlieb . . . it was in the papers this morning. That Paul was a . . . a criminal. A fence. A smuggler. A wheeler-dealer type. The rebels bought guns from him, the government bought drugs from him, electronics. He had ins everywhere."

I put a fresh butt in my mouth, lit it.

"I mean, hell, man, I would have told Gottlieb," Holloway said. "I would have. But I knew it was all right there in his record. I didn't have much to add."

"Okay," I said.

I heard Holloway take a deep breath. I looked at him. His forehead was furrowed now. The crow's-feet showed at the corners of his eyes. His lips worked over what he was going to say for a long time before he said it. "The thing is," he finally let out, "when I was in Sentu, I got . . . involved . . . with the rebels."

"Involved?"

"You have to understand," he said quickly to the windshield. "No one from the Western press had gotten to them. No one had gotten so much as an interview, and now, I don't know, maybe because I was black, here they were offering me a chance for an exclusive. A chance to make my name." There was a pause. He added quietly: "My own name."

The smoke hissed out between my teeth. It ran out my open window. "What did they want?"

"I had to prove myself to them. I had to let them know I was trustworthy."

"What did they want?" I said.

"Paul had brought in a small shipment of weapons . . . grenade launchers, I think, I'm not even sure. They needed someone—someone clean—to contact him. To talk to him about . . . times and places where the weapons could be exchanged for cash."

"Okay," I said quietly.

I saw the corner of his mouth curl as he drove. "Come on, man. Don't get all ethical."

I snorted. "Who, me?"

"I was ambitious, and there was a price for what I wanted."

"Did you pay it?"

Now he laughed outright. "I'm afraid we'll never know. I was walking the streets, trying to decide, when a jeep drove up beside me, government soldiers jumped out, dragged me into the car, and drove away."

"What?"

"They took me to Imperial House."

The smoke rolled out of my open mouth. I remembered what Wexler had told me about Imperial House. You could scream your lungs out as you died inch by inch in its cellar, he'd said, and no one would know. I glanced at Holloway as he drove. A portly gentleman in a three-piece suit. A witty smile at the corner of his mouth. Intelligence and education in his deep brown eyes. I tried to imagine him in the cellar of Imperial House.

He said: "They had a chair there, Wells. In Imperial House. In the cellar, they had a chair. A chair with straps on it. And all around the chair, there were little stands with trays on them, like you have at a dentist's office. And in the little trays on the little stands, there were instruments. Gleaming, metal instruments I can't begin to describe to you. The minute you saw them, your imagination started working. What were they for? What exactly?" Holloway took a deep breath. He swallowed hard. His expression remained wry as he looked through the windshield. "The soldiers tear your clothes off and then they strap you in that chair. They leave you there: alone, naked. And you wait, alone and naked, staring at those instruments, and you wonder what those instruments are for. And then two men come in. They wear white coats like doctors. And they look at you, you sitting naked there, they look at you the way doctors do, with that look that's somehow both concerned and evil at the same time. With that look that tells you you have completely lost control of your own life. And they say to you—just like doctors—'We understand we have a problem here.' And you want with all your heart to believe in the benevolent sound of their voices, you want to open up to them, tell them everything. But they don't even ask. You hear me, man? You beg them to let you tell them everything and they just start looking through their instruments. Picking them out."

It was cool in the car. The chill air blew back and forth from his open window to mine. But Solomon Holloway's bald head was glistening now with sweat. And sweat ran down from my temples, as well.

"Lester Paul bought me out."

I hadn't realized I was holding my breath till I released it. "Jesus," I said.

"Robert Collins—he was a Brit journalist over there, friend of mine. He came by my room to see me that evening and found it ransacked. He started asking questions of his government sources. Got most of the story. He contacted Lester Paul. Paul pulled a few strings and I was released. Just like that."

"Why?" I asked him.

He shook his head. The skyline of Manhattan rose before

us. Its scarps and pinnacles were gray against the hazy blue sky.

Holloway shrugged. "I don't know. Maybe he felt bad that he was part of the reason for my arrest. Doesn't sound like a smuggler's motive to me, but . . . No one really knew all that much about Paul. Why he did what he did. All I know is that he got me out of Imperial House, man. And that's why I didn't tell the cops anything about him. And that's why I was relieved when he got away."

I wiped the sweat off my forehead with my palm. I took a last tug at my cigarette and tossed it out onto the highway. "What if he killed Colt?" I asked.

Holloway gave me his deep, rolling chuckle. "What if?" he said. "What if? Hell, he probably did. You saw them in the Press Club together."

"And?"

For the first time since the trip from the cemetery had begun, Holloway looked over at me. "The rules were different there, John," he said. "They were different in Sentu. What was between Colt and Paul was just between them."

I thought Gottlieb might disagree. I didn't say it, though. I said: "What was between them? Do you know?"

He frowned. "Nah. Not really. Part of it, I guess. Colt was in love. With a missionary he'd met. A sort of local legend, woman named Eleanora."

For a moment the image of a woman in white rose before me. A woman with golden hair passing among the sick and the frightened.

"Yeah," I said. "I've heard."

"Well, as I understand it, this Eleanora ran something of an underground operation. And at the end, when the rebels were headed for Mangrela, her network collapsed, she had to get out. Colt wanted to help her."

The city loomed larger. Its million windows glinted in the sun. The traffic began to congeal around us. I heard myself say: "Were they—when you say in love, I mean . . . were they lovers?"

"Oh yes, oh yes. That they were."

I felt myself dip inside a little. The way you do when an elevator drops too fast. Startled, I realized I was a little jealous.

Holloway went on: "I mean, Colt was my friend, my close

friend. We'd talk about these things. You know how it is. Man, he would go on and on about her forever. Not like any of his other women. They were lovers all right. He was crazy about her. I remember he used to talk about how white her skin was, like marble. And then he'd say that she'd flush all over when he made love to her, so that she looked like a statue coming to life.'' He gave an evil little chuckle. ''Colt had to be the only man alive who could make sex sound even better than it is.''

I tried to answer with a laugh. It didn't come out that way. I said: ''Yeah,'' again, but this time it was barely audible. I was thinking about what a statue would look like if it came to life.

''Anyway, at the end, with the rebels coming down on us, Colt was desperate to save her. He came to me and asked me to help him find Paul. I guess he thought Paul might have some influence, be able to pull some strings. I directed him to Robert Collins. Collins took him to Paul. And together, the three of them went off to rescue Eleanora.'' The cars gathered thick around us. Holloway guided the Lincoln onto the FDR Drive. The East River sparkled to our left. To our right, the uptown projects towered over us. ''By then,'' Holloway went on, ''by then, man, shellfire was hammering at the outskirts of the city. The exodus toward the sea was never-ending. Men, women, and children with everything they owned on their backs moved in one continuous snaking motion through the streets and off to . . . somewhere. I don't know. Nowhere, maybe. Away. Away from the shells and the rebels. Running for their lives.'' He took a breath. He was trying to tell it calmly.

''The rest of us,'' he said, ''the Westerners—the press— we left according to our ambitions and our fears. I filed stories until the electrical lines went down. Then I grabbed a camera and took pictures of the chaos in the streets. Finally the shells began to score on the city. I knew I had to go.''

The FDR wound south. Manhattan welled up beside us like a stone sunrise. Holloway kept the Lincoln in the right lane, moving slowly. For the first time, I noticed how tightly he was gripping the wheel.

''There was an airlift on,'' he said. ''American choppers had flown in to take embassy workers and the rest of us. I got back to the hotel, packed what I could. I went downstairs, out

past the bar. And as I passed the entranceway, I saw a solitary
figure sitting in the empty room. Sitting at a table, smoking a
cigarette, staring into space.''

''Colt.''

''Yes. He'd come back.''

''Alone.''

''Yes. Without Lester Paul. Without Collins.''

''Without Eleanora.''

''Yes. Collins, I gather, had stayed behind, trying to file
dispatches somehow. We later found out he was killed by
shellfire. Paul—until the other night, we assumed he'd died,
too.''

''And Eleanora?''

''Colt spent months, almost a year, trying to find her. The
word was she'd been captured by the rebels. Died at their
hands. Colt would never tell me what had happened. Why he'd
come back like that, alone. He just sat there in the bar with
the cigarette, as if he were waiting for the place to sink into
the earth, taking him with it. I screamed at him. I said, 'Colt,
we've got to go! Now, man, now!' He just waved at me
vaguely. I grabbed him by the arm. He didn't resist. He didn't
do anything. I dragged him out into the street.''

Holloway stared out the windshield. His stare was hard.
His mouth was tight. I saw his throat working under his tie.
''The sky—it was night, Wells—and the sky was red with
fire. I fought through the crowd toward the embassy compound
where the choppers were. The streets were jammed solid with
people. All I could feel was that soft-hardness of flesh pressed
against me. All I could smell was the sweat and the terror.
Sometimes my feet didn't even touch the ground as the crowd
carried me. Sometimes I could fight for a yard and then another.
Sometimes . . . sometimes I only saw the sky—the red sky
—floating over as the crowd closed in.''

He nodded curtly. ''I just held Colt's arm. I held it and
held it. He was like a rag doll. I held on to him and pushed
toward the embassy. Eventually—like when you get close to
the shore of the ocean—eventually, the tide carried us. The
people—in their panic—were trying to get onto the American
airlift. Trying to get out of the country any way they could.
They carried us to the embassy compound. There was a fence
around it. Marines stood behind it, their rifles raised. The

marines . . ." He snorted. "Teenage boys. Under their hel-
mets, they looked like they wanted to bury their heads in their
mothers' laps and cry for mercy. They stood behind the fence,
fighting off this . . . this tidal wave of humanity. It kept crash-
ing against them and they kept pushing it back. Only when
they saw a white face would they open the gate and let it pass."

I saw sadness in his eyes. I saw bitterness in his smile. "I
dragged Colt to the gate," he said. "They opened it and pulled
him in. Then one of the marines hit me in the chest with the
butt of his rifle, shoved me back. The gate slammed in my
face."

"Oh man," I said.

"The crowd, then, the crowd started to pull at me, to pull
me away from the fence. Clawing at me, trying to get around
me, trying to get close themselves, to talk, to beg, to bribe
the marines standing guard. And I just started to scream." His
voice melted away on the word. He spoke in a near whisper.
"I started to scream, 'Reggie Jackson! Reggie Jackson! Reggie
Jackson!' It was the only ballplayer's name I could think of.
I just kept screaming. I just kept fighting off the hands that
were pulling me away from the gate. And finally . . . oh God,
finally . . . the gate cracked open, and a hand reached out.
And I screamed and screamed, 'Reggie Jackson! Reggie Jackson!' And that reaching hand grabbed me—grabbed me right
by the front of my shirt and pulled me through the gate. And,
Wells, I was looking into the whitest, roundest midwestern
face of a marine you ever saw in your life. And the tears were
streaming down those pink, pink cheeks of his, and he said to
me, 'Pete Fucking Rose, man. Pete Fucking Rose.' "

We pulled off the drive. The city surrounded us. We drove
beneath vaulting walls of concrete. Holloway's hands had relaxed on the wheel now. His stare had softened. His mouth
relaxed, too. He lifted his eyes to look at the buildings looming
above us.

Softly, he said to me: "All these people, Wells. They just
don't know."

"So what was it?" I asked him.

"Hm?"

"Between Colt and Paul? What was between the two of
them?"

For a moment Holloway didn't answer. He seemed lost in

his own reflections. Finally, though, he blinked. He glanced at me.

"I can't say for sure," he said. "But if I had to guess?"

"Yeah?"

"I'd say it was Eleanora."

16

She is a woman who lives in the shadows, who lives with fear. In this small country where the fabric of daily life is often torn to pieces by the sudden cruelties of war, she is a source of hope to some and the target of others' hatred. In a nation where there seems no middle ground between oppressive government and savage revolution, Eleanora Richardson is that middle ground—gone underground.

I sat in the reading room of the public library. A vast room that soared over towering mullioned windows up to ornate ceilings far distant overhead. At the bottom of that cavernous space, I sat hunkered before a microfilm viewer. I squinted through its glare at the newspaper page projected onto the surface below. It was a copy of the *Boston Globe*, over a decade old. The *Globe* had picked up a series Colt had sold to the wires. His series on the underground in Sentu. This was the lead piece on Eleanora.

I went back to the story.

Virtually single-handed, Miss Richardson oversees a secret network of safe houses through which pass revolutionaries targeted for arrest and torture, petty government officials targeted for assassination, and, most frequently, some of the vast number of homeless refugees left orphaned, widowed, and injured by war. With Miss Richardson and her people, they find medical attention, solace, and, sometimes, a chance to resettle elsewhere.

An Englishwoman, Miss Richardson came to Africa seven years ago, a twenty-two-year-old missionary for the Anglican Church. She found herself on a continent volcanic with revolution. In Rhodesia first, and later Zambia and Angola, she made attempts to operate openly under the auspices of the church, helping to run schools, infirmaries, and food centers. Soon, however, various victims of national violence began coming to her for help, attracted by her nonpartisan sense of charity. They came one by one, and then by the dozens. She found herself operating subterranean sanctuaries while maintaining a public show of aboveboard missionary work.

In the last four years, however, this has become impossible. Hounded from nation to nation, Miss Richardson has been forced to sever all ties with the church, and to relinquish much of her contact with the everyday life of men and women.

The cellar of her quiet suburban home has been turned into an infirmary of fifteen beds. Some of the people there on one recent day were suffering from gunshot wounds. Some of them were children. Miss Richardson assured them that a "safe" doctor would be with them before the day was done.

Sitting upstairs in a living room darkened by drawn curtains, with her hair disheveled, her forehead grimy, and her white apron stained with blood, she consented to an interview. She was reluctant to speak in detail about her life, fearing she would inadvertently reveal information that might make her or her operation more vulnerable. She did, however, discuss her past and present situation in general terms, saying that the greatest difficulty of the life she has chosen is her separation from her home, her parents, two brothers, and a sister.

"The worst of it, believe it or not, is not being able to keep in touch with your loved ones," she said. "Letters get through now and then, but you can go as long as six months, more, without a word. It gets terribly lonely sometimes, and that's when the fear gets to you. You find yourself thinking, 'All right, I'll pack it in.' But, of course, you don't, do you?"

I sat back in my hard wood chair. I looked around me. There were rows and rows of viewers on the desk. There were rows and rows of desks. There were people passing among the shelves. There was steady movement, steady murmuring.

For a second I felt as if I had come up from underwater, or out of a movie in the afternoon: I was surprised to see the light. I'd been involved in the piece. I'd imagined Eleanora sitting in the darkened living room. I'd heard her voice. I'd heard it very clearly, in fact. It was a calm, gentle voice. It had no fear in it.

I blinked the feeling away. I leaned forward.

Nothing in her background prepared her for this life. The daughter of an Essex County minister and his wife, she grew up in the rectory of a rural church. She speaks fondly of playing with the sons and daughters of farmers.

"I was a bit the P.K., you know," she said, smiling. "The preacher's kid. The other children accepted me well enough, but I was always the one they turned to to settle their arguments or make the rules of the game. It gives one a tremendous sense of gravity and responsibility very young. Not easy to get rid of it, I suppose."

Strongly influenced by a father she describes as "witty, unpretentious, and kind," she became intensely religious in her youth. She left the country shortly after graduating from Girton with the idea of spreading the gospel among the disadvantaged.

"I'm afraid I was not very enlightened," she says now. "I had this idea that there were all these unhappy Africans, you know, and they were just waiting for me. I suppose I felt that all they really wanted was for someone to come along with the love of Christ in her satchel and sort of spread it around here and there."

She says she is still religious, but that she does not preach much or teach the Bible anymore. "I can't tell a five-year-old who hasn't eaten for a week about the love of Christ. I can't tell a woman who's just seen her daughter bayoneted that He works in mysterious ways. I just can't. One simply reaches a point, you know, where one feels that if Christ is anywhere, He's in one's hands. One's actions. If He wanted His name mentioned all the time, He would have gone into films."

I laughed softly. Then I stopped laughing, the smile pasted to my face. I thought about her talking like that, with her golden hair disheveled and her forehead begrimed. I thought

about her white skin and how it blushed red when she made
love.

I shifted uncomfortably on the chair. I took a breath, focused my attention, and leaned into the glare of the machine
again.

In Sentu, Miss Richardson's organization is thought to be
particularly pervasive. She is spoken of in almost legendary
terms among natives and Westerners alike. She shrugged off
such celebrity and declined to discuss the extent of her network.
She did admit that she did not "start from scratch here," and
used experience and the remnants of previous networks to es-
tablish herself quickly.

In Sentu, she said she has found a situation that is far from
unique in Africa, or in the world: a mixture of real injustices
and ambiguous politics boiling over into violence. Again and
again, she has refused to take sides, and she said she has even
rejected appeals by several governments to allow them to use
her network as a base for undercover operations.

"Each side always seems to feel that this or that adjustment
to the local machinery will make things all right," she said.
"Even when they recognize the complexities, they still see no
alternative but to operate within that machinery, to tinker with
it this way or that. That's what justifies the violence in their
minds: the seeming nearness of the goal. But, of course, the
machinery of injustice, of hatred, of cruelty—these aren't local
at all, are they. They're worldwide. They're not built in Sentu
or Rhodesia or Zambia. We build them here—in the heart. My
heart. All of ours."

She paused, reflected, then let out a surprisingly girlish
giggle, bringing one hand to her mouth with the modesty of a
preacher's daughter.

"Listen to me go on," she said, laughing. "I suppose I'm
still a missionary, after all. Only it turns out I didn't come here
to save Africa, did I? I came here to save myself."

I shook my head. My hand went out to touch the last words
of the article. The shadow cast by my fingers wiped the words
away. I gazed at that shadow. I was not thinking of Eleanora
now. I was thinking of Colt. I was thinking of him again as
he stumbled to the door of his bedroom on the last night of

his life. Staggering under the weight of alcohol, and under the burden of his loss.

Eleanora. Eleanora, my love, my love.

Poor bastard, I thought. Meeting someone like her. Losing someone like her. He must have loved her pretty damned desperately.

What else could he have done?

17

That night, I met with Lester Paul.

He'd said ten o'clock. I left the office around nine-fifteen. I wanted to be there first, to scout the place. I grabbed a cab on Vanderbilt. We headed to Madison, then started uptown.

The air was crisp and cold. The night sky was clear. There was no moon that I could see. Rush hour was over, but the sidewalks were still crowded with Christmas shoppers. Some of them carried stacks of packages in their arms or gripped shopping bags in their hands. They looked warm in their overcoats and scarves.

There were lights everywhere. There were colored lights in the store windows. There were white lights on some of the trees. There were golden lights around the gates of the Helmsley Palace Hotel. Spotlights blanketed the stone spires of St. Patrick's Cathedral. Red taillights sped along in front of us. Green traffic lights hung overhead.

There were lights everywhere. But somehow, two stood out. Two headlights. They'd been following me since I left the *Star*.

I don't know why I noticed them. Maybe I'd been watching for it, expecting it without thinking. I'd witnessed a murder, after all. I knew I was a target. Maybe I was just naturally on my guard.

One way or another, when my cab pulled away from the

Star, I glanced over my shoulder. Through the rear window, I saw the two headlights pull into traffic, too. As we moved toward Madison, so did they. As we headed uptown, they did, too. I didn't think much of it at first. I just noticed.

We passed under the AT&T building, a rose marble tower turned to shadow in the night. Two trees in its open courtyard glittered with lights behind its heavy columns. I glanced back at the headlights. They were still there.

The cab had pulled into the left lane. So had the headlights following. The cab signaled to turn left on Fifty-seventh Street. The headlights edged even further to the left, as if to turn also.

"Go up and through the park," I said.

"Eh?" said the hack.

"Don't turn."

He clicked off his signal. He pulled into the center lane. The headlights behind us did not make the turn either. They followed us.

"Listen," I said to the back of the driver's head. "There's a guy tailing us. Can you lose him?"

"Tailing?" the cabbie said in a thick Levantine accent.

"Yeah, it's worth a dime."

"You no want de Natwal Histry."

"No," I said. "Just lose this guy."

"Lewis Guy?" asked the cabbie. "I no know this place."

"Pull over," I said.

We went by the rear exit of F.A.O. Schwarz in the General Motors Building. Stuffed bears and giraffes peered down at me from the second-story window. The cab pulled to the curb.

I shoved some money over the seat in front of me.

"Uh, Lewis Guy?" said the driver.

"Keep the change," I said.

I got out of the cab. As I closed the door behind me, the headlights went past. I saw a low, sleek, dark-colored car cruise up Madison. I watched its taillights. They turned left one block up, on Fifty-ninth Street.

I glanced at my watch. It was 9:25. Whoever was after me, I had to ditch him fast. If Paul thought I'd brought anyone with me, he might keep his promise to blow my brains out. I needed my brains in case I ever decided to go into another line of work.

I shoved my hands in my overcoat pockets, started walking quickly toward Fifth.

I got to the corner. It was bright and noisy there. The street opened up into Grand Army Plaza. The glass lance of the G.M. Building shot into the sky beside me. The bronze nude of the plaza fountain was surrounded by lighted trees across the way. There were sidewalk Santas ringing bells. The Salvation Army was blowing brass. Shoppers were following the wisps of their breath through the night. All the stores around were open late.

The low, sleek, dark-colored car turned the corner. It rolled onto the Avenue just ahead of me.

I froze. I watched. The passenger door cracked open. Timing the traffic, a slim man slipped into the street. He sidled around the car to the sidewalk. I saw him craning his neck, looking for me. I looked away. I pretended to study the front entrance of the toy store. Shoppers were streaming into the revolving doors and the two other doors that flanked it. A man dressed up as a toy soldier opened the right door and saluted the people going in. A woman dressed up as a clown opened the left door and made faces at the people coming out.

Out of the corner of my eye, I saw the dark car join the traffic. It eased down Fifth Avenue and was gone. The man who had gotten out moved to the railing of the G.M. Building's sunken courtyard. He leaned over it, pretending to look at the make-believe ice pond and the mannequin skaters set up below.

He was not the man who had killed Timothy Colt. But he looked enough like him to make my gut feel like a cold draft had blown through it. He was small and wiry. He had dark skin. His hair was close-cropped. His eyes were fierce and deep. He seemed even younger than the assassin I had battled in Colt's hotel. He was a kid, maybe seventeen or so. All the same, the aches and pains that had sunk into the back of my mind these past hours now rose to the forefront again. I was in no shape for another fight.

He looked over the railing. Christmas music drifted up from below. "God Rest Ye Merry Gentlemen." The kid was waiting. He was waiting for me to move.

I moved. I headed toward F.A.O. Schwarz.

The toy soldier opened the door for me. He was a young guy. He wore a bright red uniform and a black busby. He had pink spots painted on his cheeks. He saluted.

"I love a man in uniform," I said.

"Hey, it's a job, all right?" he muttered.

I went inside.

I came into a large bright room. At its center was an enormous mechanical clock. Its big peach-colored face had eyes and a mouth. It spun and moved and sang. The big clock was covered with mechanical toys. They spun and moved and sang, too. Jack-in-the-boxes popped. Ballerinas twirled. Cars raced. A hot-air balloon rose and sank down. All the while, this tune kept playing. This happy little tune about boys and girls and toys.

Around the clock, the shoppers moved to and fro with their brightly wrapped boxes. Stuffed animals—red mice, yellow giraffes, black bears, orange tigers, and dinosaurs of every color—lay on shelves, hung over ledges, sat beneath windows. They watched the shoppers go.

I moved toward the clock. I glanced over my shoulder. The toy soldier outside saluted again. He opened the door and admitted the punk who was following me.

The punk had made a mistake. He'd panicked when I went inside. He'd come after me too quickly. Now we saw each other over the shoppers passing back and forth. We gazed at each other for a long moment.

He was afraid. I saw it. It was in his eyes. His mouth was open. His tongue kept darting forward to wet his lips. He was not as cool as his assassin buddy.

He had to decide what to do quickly. He decided. He came at me.

I turned away. A doting grandmother carrying an elephant tottered toward the cashier. An eager father rushed the other way toward the dinosaurs. I slipped between them and headed around the clock. The clock sang its little song.

I thought I'd find the rear exit now. It wasn't there. The way out seemed to have vanished. There was nothing against the back wall but a glass elevator. To the left was an escalator heading up to the second floor. At the base of it, a mechanical teddy bear said, "Oh, I do love robots! They're on the second floor! Merry Christmas."

I went for the elevator. I didn't look back. The floor felt slippery under my shoes as I dodged a young man with a tiger under each arm.

The doors to the elevator were on the other side, facing the rear wall. I was lucky. They opened just as I came around to them. I jumped inside and pressed the button marked two.

The elevator rose swiftly. I looked out through the glass wall. The wide, bright floor full of animals dropped away beneath me. As it did, I saw the punk come around the singing clock. He searched for me desperately. He looked up and spotted me as I rose into the air. He dashed toward the talking teddy bear. He began to shove and weave his way through the crowd on the escalator.

Second floor. The door slid open. I shot out into the glassy stares of a thousand golden-haired dolls. Some of them chattered at me in singsong voices. I slid past the knot of people waiting for the lift. I cut left, passing the top of the escalator. I looked down there as I went by. The crowd was rippling with the punk's progress through it. He was about halfway to the top.

I didn't stop to meet him. I walked on as fast as I could. I had to dump this charmer. Had to find the rear door. Get out, make my date. Meet with Paul alone.

Now I was barreling down a wild hallway. Lights blinked. Plastic figures larger than life turned this way and that to either side of me. A cowboy, an Eskimo, an astronaut flashed by me as I humped along.

I reached the hallway's end. The punk topped the escalator. A woman cried out as he shoved her aside. He started swiftly down the hall.

I swung around. Before me was a vast array of electric trains. Big ones trudged from signal light to signal light. Tiny silver streaks zipped through miniature villages in the Alps. There was an old freight rattling round an oval. I almost stopped to ogle them. I didn't. I skittered past the train tables. Turned, kept walking.

There were ray guns to the left of me. Robots to the right. Somewhere, an alien on a television screen was growling. I headed straight on. There, up ahead, was an entire city in miniature: a little skyline of multicolored snap-together blocks. Skyscrapers, brownstones, stadiums, the works. All of it in stunning combinations of yellow, blue, red, and white.

As I headed into the midst of it, a youth who seemed to be made of flesh and blood stepped forward and called to the

shoppers around him. He was a tall, strapping fellow with lots
of yellow hair. His voice was sharp and loud.

"Hi, everyone, I'm the Lego man, and this is Lego Land,
come on in, you know you can, and try your hand in Lego
Land . . ."

And so on. He kept up the patter. He was pointing at a
round table. Children and adults were sitting there, making
their own creations out of the little blocks.

"Try your hand, it's Lego Land, come and see the Lego
man!"

I hustled past him. Finally I saw what I wanted. It was
right there ahead of me. There was the entrance to another
hallway like the one I'd come down. Just beyond that entrance
was another escalator. It had to lead down to the rear entrance.
I was practically running for it.

I was at the edge of the hallway when the punk came out
of it.

He'd gone around the other side, cut me off. He'd come
tearing down the hall. I guess he'd slipped on the slick floor.
He slammed right into me.

I let out a cry of fright as we collided. I thought maybe he
had a knife. One of those curved jobs, like his buddy had used
on Colt. Maybe he'd already slipped it into me and I hadn't
felt it yet.

I reacted without thinking. I grabbed hold of him, caught
him by the front of his coat. I hurled him to one side.

"Wo-o-oh!" he commented.

He skated across the floor, backpedaling on his heels. The
edge of the little round table caught him right behind the knees.
He went down on top of it. The crash sent a spray of yellow,
red, white, and blue into the air.

The table turned over. The punk went with it, thudding
onto a bed of scattered plastic.

"Gentlemen!" cried the strapping blond. "Gentlemen, stop
it! This is Lego Land!"

I didn't wait to argue. I pivoted and headed for the escalator.

"Wells!"

The scream stopped me. It was high-pitched, broken. I
turned. The punk had clambered to his knees. He pointed at
me.

"Stay out of it, Wells!" he screamed. "Stay out of it or you're a dead man! He'll kill you, I swear, you saw him and he'll kill you, and we don't want anyone else to die, but you saw him and he'll kill you if you don't stay out of it I swear . . ." He was babbling. He was terrified.

For a moment I stood confused. I ran my hand up through my hair. My hand came out covered with sweat. I considered staying, grabbing him, making him talk. I glanced at my watch. It was quarter to ten.

Just then the toy soldier came running around the far corner. He tore past the trains, holding his busby on his head.

"What's happening here?" he shouted.

"Trouble in Lego Land!" cried his blond colleague.

The toy soldier spotted me. He pointed as he ran. "That's the guy who made fun of my uniform!"

"Oh my God, somebody get him!" shouted the Lego man.

"Wells!" the punk screamed hoarsely. "Wells, I'm warning you!"

That did it. It was unanimous. I bolted for the escalator. It was thick with shoppers. I shoved past them. Women cried out. Men cursed. Packages tumbled down. I hopped over the scattered boxes as I hit the ground floor.

There, at last, was the rear exit. Right next to an enormous Mickey Mouse marionette. I pushed out into the darkness of Madison. Gratefully I sucked in the winter air. It went down about halfway, then hit a wall of used nicotine. I started coughing.

Through tear-filled eyes I spotted a cab pulled to the curb. A man was getting out. A woman waited to get in. I hobbled to the cab's door, slipped behind the emerging man. I collapsed onto the backseat, gasping for breath.

"Hey!" shouted the woman.

"Drive," I said.

The hack headed uptown.

I looked over my shoulder as we pulled away from the curb. The woman stood there shaking her fist at me, but no one had followed me out of the toy store. I leaned back against the seat, wheezing quietly. Now I could go meet Paul without the pleasure of the punk's company.

Unless, of course, it had been Paul who'd sent him after me.

Had it been Paul?

I thought about it as the cab went along. I thought about it and I coughed. I coughed hard. I bucked against the seat as I coughed. Remnants of cigarettes I'd smoked in 1967 came up into my throat. I spit them out into a Kleenex. I coughed some more.

"You okay, buddy?" the driver asked me.

"Yeah," I gasped. "Take me to the natural history museum, will you? I'm gonna donate my lungs."

He laughed. We headed up toward Seventy-ninth Street. I watched the lights of Madison roll by. I coughed.

I coughed and I thought. I thought about Paul. According to Holloway, Colt had enlisted Paul's aid in getting Eleanora out of Sentu when the rebels took over. But Eleanora hadn't made it. Colt had thought she was dead. Until that night in the Press Club, he'd obviously thought Paul was dead as well. "You owe me an accounting," Colt had said. An accounting of what? Of what had happened to Eleanora? Of the fate of the woman he loved? Maybe Paul had had Colt killed to keep from answering his questions. Maybe he'd called me out tonight to have me killed as well.

But then why have me followed? He knew where I'd be. Why warn me off? I wondered who these two guys were, the assassin and the punk in Toyland. I wondered and I coughed. After a while, I just coughed.

By now the taxi was pushing across Central Park to the West Side. I looked out over the transverse wall. A gibbous moon had risen over the white wedge of the Citicorp Building to the east. Its light fell on rolling hills and curving pathways still covered with a thin patina of snow. The naked branches of the December trees stood out starkly.

We came through a tunnel, around a curve. The traffic light at the edge of the park came into view. It was red.

"I'll get out here," I said.

The cab pulled over at the corner of Central Park West. I tossed some money at the driver, stepped outside.

I stood across from the northern edge of the museum. I was about a block from the front door. It was about two minutes to ten. Cars and cabs raced up and down the avenue, but the sidewalk by the park was empty. The gray octagonal stones that paved it shone dimly under the streetlamps. The branches of the overarching trees swayed above. Benches sitting empty against the park wall seemed to shift and shudder in the moving shadows. Coughing lightly, I stuck a cigarette in my mouth. My heels sounded hollow on the stones as I walked beneath the streetlamp, from pool of light to darkness to pool of light.

I moved along the sidewalk until I was directly opposite the museum entrance. I stood still there. A wind blew down from Harlem, and I hunched my shoulders at it. I cupped my hands around a match, held it to the cigarette.

Across the street, a sweep of white steps led up to the museum. Stone walls curled gracefully in toward the massive pillars flanking the doors. Atop the steps, before the doors, was a massive bronze of Teddy Roosevelt on horseback. He peered grandly over my head and into the blackness of the park behind me.

The blue Chevy pulled up to the curb suddenly. It was a big old hunkering jalop. Its spark plugs fired the way a bad chorus line kicks. I could hear the whine of its fan belt. I could smell its thick exhaust.

The Chevy's door swung open. The toplight did not go on. All I could see of the driver was his shape behind the wheel.

"Get in," he said.

I stepped forward, crouched over, slid into the car.

I shut the door as the Chevy pulled away. I turned to the man beside me. When we passed under a light, I caught a glimpse of his craggy cheeks, his scarred mouth. It was the man who had tangled with Colt in the Press Club.

The Chevy went north slowly. Lester Paul spoke in his deep, slightly foreign voice.

"You have come alone?"

"Yeah," I said. "Someone tried to follow me, but I think I ditched him."

He turned to me quickly when I spoke. "Are you sure?"

"Pretty sure."

He was silent. Then he said heavily: "We had better not be disturbed."

We went uptown a few blocks. At the corner of another entrance into the park, we stopped at a red light. Now I could make out the thick black hair that crowned Paul's head. I could see the brooding expression in his sunken eyes. His eyes glittered. They were black. They looked dead, like marbles.

I saw them shift up to the rearview mirror. Paul tensed beside me.

I glanced back and saw a cop car. It had stopped at the red light a block back.

Our light turned green. Paul swung the wheel over. The Chevy turned the corner, into the park. He moved away from CPW slowly. He did not relax until he saw the police cruiser pass by the park entrance without turning.

There wasn't much traffic on the park drive. Cabs mostly. They shot by us at high speeds. Paul kept the Chevy in the right lane and moved slowly. He said nothing as he drove.

All at once, Paul reached for the dash, hit a button. The headlights died. There were no other cars around us. He pulled the Chevy sharply into the left lane. There was a little walkway there. It climbed out of sight up a steep hill. Paul yanked the wheel over. I bounced in my seat as the car bumped over a curb. Paul drove up the footpath, over the hill, out of sight of the road below. He killed the rattling engine. Quiet settled in around us. We could hear the whisper of the cars passing on the drive below.

I smoked my cigarette. Paul sat, still silent, surveying the scene through the windshield. Beyond his profile, I saw a long flat playing field. It was white with snow and moonlight. It was bordered by a black stand of trees. When I glanced out my window, I saw the high walls of an outdoor theater blotting out the sky. There were golden statues before it: an old man, his beard blown by the wind, shielding a young girl with his cape. A man and woman embracing.

When I faced Paul, he was looking past me.

"Shakespeare," he said. "*The Tempest*. 'What seest thou else in the dark backward and abysm of time?' "

I shrugged. "I don't come to the park too often."

"No, I don't suppose you do."

"Look," I said, "I'd love to discuss the classics with you, but first I'd like to know who cut Tim Colt's heart out."

Paul had a dull, flat laugh. It was hardly a laugh at all. "A Sentuan murder-man, I imagine."

"Right. Great. What's that?"

"It's a cult," said Paul. "It used to have quite a following in Sentu. It was already dying out when I was there. Not something the ordinary Westerner would even hear of. I'm sure the new government has quashed it by now."

I took a pull of my cigarette. I stared out at the darkened field. I shuddered as if someone had walked over my grave.

"They were something like the thugs of India," Paul said. "Religious highwaymen, more or less. Trained from earliest youth to commit murder and robbery in the name of the gods. By cutting into the hearts of their victims, they somehow connected with the source of life."

"I'll say."

"The little ceremonial knife you described so accurately in your story on Colt's death," said Paul. "That was their weapon of choice."

There was silence a moment.

"Sentu," I said then.

"Yes," Paul answered in the same tone. "Sentu."

I glared at him. His sunken eyes were circles of darkness. The eyes of a skull.

"Did you kill him?" I said.

He laughed his mirthless laugh again. "Is that what you think?"

"It's what the cops think."

"Yes, I know. One of them was so kind as to visit me at my hotel and tell me I was wanted for questioning in the case. But, of course, I knew that already from reading your newspaper."

"So you shot him," I said.

He hesitated. "Yes, I shot him."

"How'd you beat the raid?"

"While he called for help, I disguised myself as one of my many indigent neighbors. Before the other officers arrived outside, I climbed out the window and onto the nearest ledge. I made so bold as to go through that window into the next apartment. For the price of ten dollars, the current occupant allowed me to share his quarters. When the police arrived to arrest Lester Paul, they evacuated me with the others to keep us from harm."

Paul's voice took on a slight undertone of pride as he recounted how he'd done it. I played to that, to keep him talking.

"That was pretty clever," I said.

"Not really. Your police are not exact—"

The words stopped as if cut off with a blade.

"What . . . ?"

He hissed at me. "Shut up." His body had gone taut, his head was cocked in an attitude of listening. "Below us. A car has stopped on the drive."

I glanced over my shoulder. "I didn't—"

"Shut up."

I turned to him. "Listen—" I shut up. He had a gun.

Its barrel was long and black. The bore peered at me lifelessly, like his eyes.

"You betrayed me," he said.

I could tell by the sound of his voice that he was going to kill me.

"Listen, Paul," I said. "I tried to drop them. It's those guys with the funny knives. I didn't—"

"Get out of the car."

He raised the gun. The bore was level with my eyes. I tried not to look at it. The sight made my guts roil.

"Get out now," he said.

"Hell, no. I want you to have to clean the blood off your upholstery."

He shoved the gun barrel up under my right nostril. "It's an old car, Wells," he said.

"There is that."

I opened the door. I figured I had half a chance in the open.

I could dodge, I could duck, I could run. Probably not, but it was something.

I moved fast. I curled myself up and went out the door in a ball. I hit the snowy grass at the edge of the path. The jolt knocked the air out of me. The snow crunched under me as I kept rolling. I waited for the gunshot, for the bullet that would burn through me. It seemed the seconds did not pass as I rolled.

I jumped to my feet. Lester Paul was leaning forward through the open door as if to get a better bead on me.

But he didn't fire. Instead he grabbed hold of the door. He pulled it shut with a bang.

The Chevy's engine roared. The headlights sprang on, blinding me. Tires screeching, the car jumped backward. It tore down the path to the drive.

I ran after it to the top of the hill. I looked down in time to see the big car bounding over the curb. The rubber squealed again as the Chevy spun around, righted itself, pointed downtown. With one great, throaty explosion, the car threw itself forward along the drive. It shot out of my sight like a cannonball.

I stood staring at the place where the car had been. There was a streetlamp there, at the corner of the footpath and the road. The lamp let down a circle of dim yellow.

The man who killed Timothy Colt stepped into that circle, pointed a pistol at me, and pulled the trigger.

He was a good man with a dagger, but he was not as expert with a gun. If he'd gone for my body, he'd have taken me down. There'd have been plenty of time to kill me. He tried for my head. A tougher shot. I felt the breath of the bullet in my ear as it went by.

He fired again, but by then I was running. I faked to the left, broke to the right. I heard the crack of the pistol but felt no pain. I ducked deep into the shadow of the Shakespearean theater.

I pressed against the wall, panting. A fresh bout of coughing worked in my throat. I gulped it back. I stared at the crest of the footpath.

The assassin came jogging over it. He wore black as he had the last time I saw him. A black jump-jacket this time, black jeans. His face still bore the scars I'd given him. In the moonlight, I saw his nose was bandaged. One of his cheeks was scarred.

The sight of him nearly stripped me of hope. I remembered our fight in the hotel. I was a reporter. He was an assassin. If we tangled again, I didn't think I'd survive.

He stood on the path. He scanned the ball field for me, the barrel of his gun following his gaze.

I crouched down quickly. I grabbed a fistful of snow. It was melting, icy. It stung my hands with cold. I packed it into a ball.

The assassin was turning slowly toward the theater. He stood now in profile to me, staring down the path.

I gave the snowball an overhand toss. The assassin turned to face me. I watched the little gray missile fly over his head into the moonlit night. The ice in it glittered.

The assassin started. He'd spotted the statues. At the same moment, the snowball hit the edge of the field behind him.

He whirled and fired. The gun cracked once in the quiet park. The barrel spat flame.

I took off, stretching my legs over the snow.

There was a path around the theater's curving wall. I took it, putting the building between us, blocking his shot. I stood still for a second. I tried to quiet my panting. I listened.

He was coming. Slowly. Warily.

I ran.

I stayed on the clear path so the field's brittle snow would not betray me. He was young and in good shape. I had no chance of outstripping him without the element of surprise.

I was around the theater now. I was sprinting by the edge of a small lake. The white light of the moon rippled on its surface. Some kind of castle peered down on it from above. My arms windmilled the air as I ran beside the water. My lungs heaved. My breath came in little cries.

Just ahead of me, the path curved away from the lake. It went up a small hill and disappeared behind some shrubbery. I did not look back. I poured it on. My head hung loose on my neck with exhaustion. I watched my feet flap against the pavement. I didn't have the energy to keep it quiet now.

I hauled myself up the hill, my breath rasping. I turned the corner into a circle of bushes.

A horse reared over me. A grim rider raised a sword.

I cried out. I stumbled back. I fell on my ass.

Another goddamn statue. A king on horseback. He peered down at me crossly.

I sat on the pavement under him. I cursed. I coughed. I fought for breath.

Around me the trees moved and rattled in a chill wind. Their branches made a lacework against the purple sky. Even here, the wind's whisper mingled with the whisper of cars passing. Otherwise the park was quiet, empty.

I bowed my head between my knees. I hacked hoarsely. I spat into the darkness beside me.

I heard the killer's footsteps coming up the hill. I raised my head a little. On the other side of the statue, the path continued. Down through the shrubs, out of sight. I stared at that exit. I was too tired to run anymore. If I fought with him, he'd kill me. I didn't know what to do.

With a breath that sounded like a squeaky door, I climbed painfully to my feet. I staggered to the statue. I hid behind the pedestal. I rested my head against it.

Around the edge of the concrete, I saw the assassin come into the little grove. With a cry, he swung his gun up at the mounted king. He lowered the gun. He cursed softly. He chuckled.

He stood there amid the bushes, a silhouette surrounded by the shaggy darkness of their branches. He surveyed the platform around the king. I forced myself to breathe through my nose.

I watched the gunman. For a moment he seemed bewildered. He looked around him again. He swept the bushes with the gun. Finally he settled on the pedestal. He came toward it slowly, circling wide, so I couldn't slug him when he came around.

I was out of choices. It was run or die. My legs felt wobbly. My chest felt like it was on fire. I gave one great push off the pedestal, like a swimmer pushing off the pool for another lap. The shove sent me half running, half reeling backward. In that single instant, there weren't fifteen feet between me and the guy who wanted me dead. The assassin saw his chance. He wheeled. He pulled the trigger.

I left my feet, diving for the way out. I heard two shots fired fast before I hit the ground.

I came down on pavement. It tore the skin off my forehead as I slid. Then I was going over and over in a somersault. I came up to my feet and stumbled on down the hill.

I was dazed. The side of my face was damp with blood. I careened this way and that, reaching out with my hands for purchase like a drunk. The shadow of the assassin crested the hill just above me. He raised his gun again.

There was a flash. I was blinded by it. There was an ex-

plosion of noise. It filled my ears. Confused, I saw the assassin
lower his pistol. A massive shape whipped by me, obscuring
the killer from my view.

It was gone. He lifted the gun again. Again, the light, the
wailing noise. The massive shape blocked his fire.

I was on the park's eastern drive. Cars were honking at me
as they slashed by. They blocked the killer's line of fire. He
couldn't get off a shot.

I made my way across the road. The cars passed. One,
then another, then another. I waved my hands at them. They
didn't even slow. The assassin was now making his way down
the hill after me. I jogged away from him, south along the
road.

At first, as I went, I looked back over my shoulder. I waved
at the passing cars. I was hoping for a cab.

A cab came. Its toplight was on. It was free. I spun in my
tracks and waved both arms over my head. The cars' headlights
dazzled me. The long honk of its horn peaked and died. The
cab whizzed by. It vanished around the corner. Unless you
happen to have a bazooka, the odds for getting a car to stop
in Central Park after nightfall are pretty slim.

So now we played cat and mouse. My friend the murder-
man had reached the snow at the edge of the road. I was jogging
away from him along the opposite curb. Car after car flashed
in between us as he followed after me, waiting for an opening
to get across.

Desperately, I sought for an opening of my own. A place
to run where I wouldn't have to test myself against his swiftness
and his youth. Next to me was the darkness. A darkness car-
peted by the eerily gleaming snow, roofed by the shifting halo
of the branches against the moon. Past that—not very far past
that—there was a low stone wall. On the other side, the pink-
whiteness of Fifth Avenue streetlamps flashed and vanished
behind thick clusters of sycamores. I was about ten blocks
from home.

I jogged slowly down the road. The killer jogged across
the street from me, a few steps behind. The cars kept passing.
I wondered whether I should go for the wall. Once I made my
move, I was committed. Without a long head start, he would
surely run me down—then shoot me down—before I gained
the Avenue.

I decided to go. Too late. The last car rushed by us. The assassin came dashing across the drive, his gun half-raised. Another group of cars had come whipping around a corner, bearing down on him. But he had it beat easy.

I crossed the other way. I ran out in front of the traffic. The glare of headlights washed over me. The horns, the screeching brakes bore down.

Then I was over. The wall of cars was again between me and my assailant. With all that was left of my energy, I ran along the roadway's snow-covered edge.

I ran on blindly. The cars kept going by. More pulled out ahead of me. There was an intersection. I plunged into it. Horns, lights, screaming brakes heralded my crossing.

With the cars from the intersection feeding into the drive, the traffic was heavier now. It was tougher for the murderman to make his way across. He sidled along the road, waiting for his moment. Somehow my legs kept carrying me forward. I was putting some distance between us.

I was on a path again. A stone wall rimmed it. The wall was topped with boulders and bushes. They peered down at me as I stumbled past.

The road turned. I came around it. For a few seconds, I was out of the hunter's sight. It was then I looked up. I stopped short. I nearly screamed.

This time it was a panther. A great black cat poised to pounce on the rocks two feet above me. It seemed to have just emerged from the bushes that surrounded it on either side. It was bent forward, its head jutting out, its eyes pinning me.

The thing was so real it took a long moment before I could completely convince myself it was just another statue. It took another moment still before I could break its hypnotic stare and move again. By then my mind was racing, grabbing at a possibility. With my wind gone and my legs close to giving, it was the only possibility left.

I jumped. I reached up. I grabbed the panther around its lowered neck. My feet found niches in the wall. I pulled myself upward. My hands scrabbled over the back of the beast. I crested the wall.

I moved behind the bushes. I took a step away from the panther, then another. I crouched down, inching toward the edge of the wall.

On the drive below me, car after car raced by. Then a break. The road was quiet. I heard the killer's footsteps padding across the pavement. He came around the corner. He came walking by the wall. I crouched down even lower, hiding behind the cat, peeking over at him.

He was coming on fast. His eyes were going over the path in front of him inch by inch. He'd lost me, but he knew I couldn't be far.

About a step before he came under the panther, he stopped. I could see him clearly. I could see his long, brown, youthful face. I could see his sharp, brown, ruthless eyes. He was thinking. It didn't make sense. I couldn't have vanished like that. I could almost hear his mind working. He was about to think of the wall, about to look up and spot me.

But before he did, he took another tentative step forward. He was directly under the panther.

I growled.

I did it deep in my throat. I let the hoarse rasp of my breath run through it. It came out harsh and real: the sound of an animal. A grinding sound under the sough of the traffic.

The assassin looked up. He saw the cat. He let out a high-pitched shriek, waving the gun but too scared to fire. I jumped off the wall, landing on the path beside him. He whipped around, his mouth still open on the scream. I slugged him.

It wasn't much of a punch. I didn't have much to put into it. It was an old-fashioned haymaker, though, and it came a long way before it scored. It crashed into his teeth. I felt one of them snap beneath my knuckles. I felt my knuckles sliced by the blow. I followed through, falling forward with the motion of the punch as he fell backward with the force of it. We both went down to the ground, several feet apart.

I wasn't happy. I'd been going for his nose. I figured it was hurt already, if I connected, it might put his lights out. As it was, I don't even know if he let go of the gun when he fell. I do know that by the time I fought my way to my feet, he had the pistol in his fist again. He was climbing to his knees, looking around for me. His chin was running with blood.

I could not cover the distance between us before he shot me. If I turned tail, though, there was a chance I might make it to the Fifth Avenue wall. It was a small chance. It was the only chance. The road was still empty in front of me. I ran into the darkness.

I was across the street in a moment. I was on the grass. I was on a flat plain of lacy snow, broken by the black, towering trunks of the oaks and sycamores. Branches danced and rattled above my head. My feet fell hard. The snow broke under them. The low wall bobbed before me as I ran, coming closer and closer. The lights of the Avenue flashed and bobbed beyond it.

I reached my hands out. I touched the wall. I grabbed it.

I do not know if he was close behind me. I don't know if he tried to shoot again. I vaulted that little wall as if West Berlin were on the other side of it. I went over the top, expecting bullets to bring me down.

I hit the ground. My momentum carried me out onto the sidewalk. I went to one knee. I sobbed for lack of breath, kneeling there on the gray octagonal stones, the same stones that paved the side of the park from which I'd come.

I lifted my eyes. There was the Avenue. A steady stream of Friday traffic passed south along it. On the sidewalk, two lovers were coming toward me from the north. They were arm in arm. A middle-aged man was walking his German shepherd up from the other direction. The eager dog strained at the leash, panting. On the opposite sidewalk, a band of young people were swaggering downtown. I could hear them calling to each other. Laughing.

I got to my feet and looked back at the wall. There was only darkness beyond it. That weird darkness, gleaming eerily with the moon and the snow.

I was out of the park.

I'd ducked the little son of a bitch again.

20

Then I got arrested.

I had stumbled out to the sidewalk's edge. I raised my hand to hail a cab. The headlights of another car started to pull over. It did not have a toplight. He's back, I thought. I edged away from the curb.

When the car was about fifteen yards away from me, its flashers popped on. Its siren blooped once and died. I squinted into the spinning red and white lights as the cruiser pulled up beside me. The cab I'd been trying to hail passed by and into the night.

A young patrolman jumped out through the driver's door into the street. An old patrolman grunted his way out on the passenger side. The old one rose up in front of me like a whale from the deep. I knew him. His name was Rankin. He was gutter dirt. Not smart enough for promotion, but shrewd enough for the take. Not tough enough for the big collar, but mean enough to shut off a perp's windpipe with the web of his hand. He was big, paunchy. He had an enormous head with tiny black eyes in it. Those eyes held me like a snake's eyes hold its prey. He towered over me.

The kid was a stranger. He was long and thick and muscular. He had a mustache to hide his big, soft Irish features. He had the dull, dangerous, openmouthed expression they teach at the academy.

I responded with a friendly—not to say shit-eating—grin.

"Who says there's never a cop around when you need one?" I said.

"Shut the fuck up, asshole," said Rankin. He was not, on the whole, my biggest fan. Every time I wrote about him, he seemed to get suspended. "Watts is looking for you. Get in the car."

My lungs were already collapsing. Now my heart sank. "Watts? What the hell does he want?"

Rankin licked his thin, white lips. They twisted into a smile. "Get in the car," he said almost dreamily. I didn't like the sound of it.

"There's a guy in the park with a gun," I said.

"That's funny," said Rankin. "Usually there's a lot more than one. I don't want to have to cuff you, Wells."

"He shot at me."

"No accounting for people's tastes. Get in the fucking car."

The young cop's eyes shifted between us nervously. The lovers walked by behind me. Then the guy with the dog. They walked around me carefully, as if I were a puddle. They rubbernecked to get a glance at me. Then they were gone on their own business.

"Aren't you going to do anything about it?" I said.

"I sympathize, Wells. I really do," said Rankin.

"How about reading me my rights?"

"You have the right to a Christian burial." He reached out and laid a big hammy hand on my shoulder. He squeezed. It hurt. The young cop's eyes shifted faster and faster. He leaned forward, as if he were about to interrupt.

"Open the door for Mr. Wells," said Rankin without looking at him.

The young cop jumped to it. He wanted this over, fast. He opened the cruiser's back door. Rankin gripped my arm, shoved me toward it.

"I want a lawyer," I said.

"Write to Santa Claus," said Rankin.

He tossed me inside. I had to duck fast not to hit my head. I went sprawling over the backseat. I dragged my feet in just as the door slammed. Good thing I was press or they might have mistreated me.

Rankin and the young cop got in front. Their doors slammed

in unison. Rankin flicked on the siren. The young cop took the cruiser away from the curb. They hurtled down Fifth at high speed, flashers spinning, sirens screaming. Just like real policemen.

The back of the car seemed very small, very cramped. It seemed far away from the rest of the city. It seemed like no one would hear me if I called for help. I thought about Holloway being taken to Imperial House. I thought about Tom Watts.

Tom Watts was not a good-news kind of guy. He was a lieutenant. He used to be a captain. He'd been a captain, in fact, right up to the very moment I did a series of stories on the precinct he commanded. It was a precinct in the Bronx with a heavy traffic in drugs. The traffic so heavy, rival dealers had to fight for the selling territory. At least, they did until Watts got there. Watts organized a permit system, sort of like the pretzel vendors use. The permits kept things organized, kept the hardworking dealers safe from unfair competition. They also kept them safe from the police. In fact, the police were selling the permits. And a goodly portion of the permit fees were channeled to former Captain now Lieutenant Thomas W. Watts.

Six patrolmen took the fall for that little scam, and two detectives. One cop even did some time. But as for Watts, the DA never got a thing on him, and the courts never tried him. This seemed to me a grievous oversight. So I tried him. I tried him in the *Star*. He was convicted in the city's corner taverns. When the people's verdict came in, the department finally had to bust him to lieutenant. It wasn't much; still, it seemed very small and cramped in the back of the car.

Rankin and his pal took me to midtown south. It's a square brick building set amid the towering warehouses of the garment district. Rankin kept his paw on my arm as he led me through the front door.

There was a woman crying in the broad lobby. She was crying to the desk sergeant. The desk sergeant was shaking his head. There was a man lying facedown on the floor. He was groaning or snoring, I'm not sure which. None of these people looked up at us. We weren't even an interruption. The desk sergeant simply reached out and pressed a button. A buzzer went off, and the young cop pushed open a door with heavy wire mesh on it. He went through. Rankin followed, dragging me with him.

I was escorted down a hall. Into an elevator. Down another hall. It was dismal there. One of the ceiling fluorescents had burned out. Another was giving off no more than a dull purple flicker. The shadowy figures of cops passed by us. They turned to the side to let me and Rankin go by. The young cop followed behind us.

At the end of the hall, Rankin reached out with his right hand and opened a door. He used his left hand to shove me through the door into a room.

"Have a seat," he said.

He left me there alone.

The room was small. A rectangle. Small and stark. The walls were lined with green tiles. The floor tiles were green, too. There was a spiral of fluorescent light on the ceiling. Parts of the curling tube gave off light, parts didn't. There was a window onto the alley next door, but the blinds were drawn. The room was only a little brighter than the hall.

There was a clock on the wall. It read 11:05. There was a table in the center of the room. There were plastic chairs around the table. I took off my overcoat, draped it over the back of a chair. I leaned against the edge of the table and crossed my arms. I tried to look like the prospect of being alone in here with Tom Watts didn't bother me a bit. I tried to look like it was my idea of a vacation. I couldn't quite get it. I tried lighting up a cigarette. I let it dangle from my mouth. I let the smoke curl up around my squinting eyes. I sneered. That was much better. I faced the door. I waited.

I kept waiting. Watts took his time. I sneaked a look at the clock. It was eleven-fifteen, then eleven-thirty. I went through two more cigarettes. My sneer got tired. My eyes started to tear.

Tom Watts came in. He had a cigarette pasted in his face, too. He also had a sneer, a pretty good one. He waved a hand at me.

"Knock it off, Wells," he said. "I know you're terrified."

"Okay," I told him, "but that doesn't mean you can push me around."

"Sit down and shut up," he said.

I pulled out a chair and sat down. I unplugged the cigarette.

I wiped my eyes with my hand. I massaged my lips. I sneered. I stuck the cigarette back in. I was ready for him.

Watts hovered over me. He jutted his chin at me. He had a good chin for jutting. It was one of those long, rounded, Kirk Douglas jobs with the hole in the middle. He had round cheeks, too, and a pug nose. A full head of auburn hair, perfectly coiffed. He was in his forties, medium height, well built in a well-tailored suit, a black two-piece. He was a good-looking character all in all, except for the green eyes where his soul showed through.

He pulled out a chair and propped his foot on it like a cop in the movies. I could see the pistol under his jacket. He plucked his cigarette from his lips. He carefully tapped an ash on the floor.

"Where were you tonight, Johnny?" he said.

"Oh, come on, Watts," I told him. "You're dirty but you're not stupid. There's a shield law in this state."

He studied the end of his cigarette intently. His rosy cheeks darkened. "Where were you, Wells?"

"I want a lawyer, pal."

Watts flicked his cigarette to one side with one hand. He grabbed the front of my shirt with the other. He dragged me out of my chair. He swiped at my face, knocking my cig out of my mouth.

My eyes were less than an inch from his clenched teeth. "Where were you, fuckhead?" he said.

Normally I don't hit cops, but this had been a bad night. I brought my right arm across my chest, knocking his hand off me. Then I snapped the fist back. It sledgehammered him in the chest.

The former captain fell two steps away from me. He stood there a moment. He wasn't hurt, but he was shocked I'd gone for him. Shocked and pissed. His eyes burned, his face was livid. His hand slid inside his coat.

I thought he was going to pull out his piece and blow me away. Instead he brought out his tin. He flashed it at me.

"You know what this is, you scumbag?" he screamed. Spittle flew from between his lips. "You know what this is? It's a shield. A *real* shield! You just hit an officer of the law, you asshole!"

I took out my wallet. I flashed it right back at him. "This

is a press card, Tommy boy," I said. "My job's protected by the goddamned Constitution. Yours isn't even mentioned."

We confronted each other like that for another second. Then Watts's hand fell to his side. He shook his head at me in wonder. He smiled a little. "You're meat, Wells," he said. "I'm standing here, I'm talking to you, and all the time, you're dead meat, you're Gaines Burger."

I put my wallet away. "Tell me about it. I'll have your badge for this."

Watts kept shaking his head. He approached me. I glared at him. He put his finger against my chest. "You'll have my badge?"

"That's right."

"You hit a cop, I'll have your fucking head."

"Keep talking. It's good copy."

His finger poked me. "You met with Lester Paul tonight. One of my boys saw you get in the car. He lost you in the park before he ran down the plates, but he saw enough to nail you for it."

"I met a source . . ."

"From the minute this case started, I knew you were in on something dirty, Wells. I knew it. I've been keeping an eye on you. I've been waiting just for this. Now nothing your little Yiddish friend can do is gonna protect you."

"I met a source . . ."

Watts's handsome pug face contorted and turned red. He started screaming. "He's a murderer!"

I screamed back. Our noses were almost touching. "I met a source!"

"A murderer at large! I had plenty of cause . . ."

"He was a source on a story!"

"You were in that room . . ."

"It's not even your case, Watts!"

"What do you know?"

"It's not even your case!"

"You tell me my case? You tell me my case? I'll tell you the case . . ."

"It's Gottlieb's . . ."

"I'll tell you. . . . You were in that room when Colt died, you're in on something, protecting . . . !"

"I got the shield and you better . . ."

"Gottlieb's protecting you and you're protecting . . ."

"Oh, horseshit, man! Even you can do better."

"You hit a cop tonight, boyo. I'm gonna put you away!"

"Subpoena me! I got a source . . . a shield, I mean. Subpoena me!"

"You hit a cop . . ." He grabbed the front of my shirt again. He twisted the knot of my tie, choking me. "That was real dumb," he sneered.

I knocked his hand off. "Fuck you."

His voice dropped suddenly. He spoke softly now, with that sense of wonder again. It was as if he couldn't completely believe his good luck. "I mean, you hit a cop, he's gotta defend himself," he said.

We stood toe-to-toe. Our eyes locked. "Why don't you put your badge down?" I said.

"Because it's more fun this way," said the former captain. And he sucker-punched me.

He came up low. A hard jolting shot below the belt. I grunted. I doubled over. My legs wobbled. I fell to my knees. He backhanded me. Hard. Blood squirted out of my nose. I keeled over sideways onto the floor. I lay like that, my cheek pressed to the linoleum. I clutched my belly. I groaned.

Watts stood over me. "You're meat," he said.

I forced out the words. "Your badge is mine, Tommy. Your fucking badge is mine."

The cop's lip curled. His eyes lifted—they nearly rolled —in his rage. He pointed the tip of his shoe at my face. He pulled his leg back. I waited for the kick.

The door snapped open. Watts lowered his foot to the floor. From somewhere above me, I heard a familiar voice.

"Eesh," it said.

I looked up from the floor. I saw Gottlieb standing in the doorway. He looked blurred to me. He seemed bathed in pink. I blinked. He came into focus. The pink remained. It was his shirt. It was pink with little black swirls on it. It was stretched tight across his big belly and shoulders. It was open at the neck. Black chest hair poured up out of it. It all went very nicely with his navy blue suit.

He looked at me. Then he looked at Watts. Watts faced him with defiance. Behind that defiance, I thought I saw a trace of fear. Gottlieb just looked worried as usual.

"So?" he said.

Watts gestured at me. He blurted: "Wells had a secret meeting with Lester Paul tonight."

"Oh? You're on the Colt case now?"

The former captain's arm fell limp. "You'd gone home for the day."

"I'll tell my wife to have a phone installed, next time you can call me."

"Listen . . ." That's as far as Watts got. He looked at Gottlieb and stopped cold.

"Come into my office," the burly detective said very quietly. "We'll sit, we'll talk." He glanced down at me. "Meantime, get off the floor, John. You'll catch cold."

He walked out. Watts watched him go, his hands clenched at his sides. He hesitated before following. He glared down at me. I had just finished working my way into a sitting position. I glared back.

He said: "Remember, Wells. You hit a cop tonight."

"Your badge is mine, Watts."

"You can't hide behind that bastard now, you hit a cop."

"Enjoy it while you got it, shithead. Because it's mine."

He hesitated another moment. I think he was trying to decide whether to finish that kick he'd started. He decided against it. He went out after Gottlieb.

Alone now, I took the opportunity to groan pitiably. I dragged my hand across my upper lip. It came away dark with blood. The blood ran down into my mouth. I tasted it. I didn't like the taste.

I grabbed hold of the top of a chair. I pulled myself up and slid onto it. I leaned forward on the table, my hands in front of me.

After a few minutes, Gottlieb came back in.

"A terrible situation. Just terrible," he said. He tossed me a washcloth damp with cold water. "Clean your nose, you don't bleed to death. You need a doctor?"

"I need a drink."

"You need a drink. You need a wife, you need a home, you need little John Wellses running around withholding information and hitting policemen."

I stared at the washcloth lying limp in my hands. I held it up to my nose. "Don't start on me," I said. "I've had a bad night."

Gottlieb sat down next to me. He folded his hands together on the tabletop. "Tell me something, my friend," he said. "Are you a schmuck, you hit a policeman?"

"He started it."

"No, no, no, no." Gottlieb waggled a finger at me. "You hit a cop, you started it."

"Hid badge id bine, Fwed, I'm tewwing you." My voice sounded funny with the cloth to my nose.

The detective leaned back in his chair. He sighed. He shook his head. The worried look returned. "A terrible situation. Who knows what'll happen?" he said.

"Tell me about it." With a wet sniffle of blood, I lowered the washcloth. I stuck a cigarette between my bloody lips. "I started today with a funeral. Colt's. Since then, I've been followed, threatened, forced out of a car at gunpoint, shot at, chased, arrested, and beaten up by a crooked cop." I lit the cigarette and blew a great haze of angry smoke all over the place. "Yeah," I said. "Yeah, I'd call that a terrible situation."

"Eesh."

"Yeah. That, too." I pointed the red tip of the cigarette at him. "But it'll be worth it, Fred, if I get that bastard's badge."

Slowly Gottlieb shook his dark head from side to side. "Well," he said. "I'll tell you. . . . This is something you should think about."

"I'll think about it, all right."

"I just convinced Watts not to bring charges against you for hitting a policeman in a room alone where no one sees you and knows what's what especially when you're a muckraking reporter."

"Fred . . ."

"I mean, you shouldn't get me wrong: personally, I enjoy your work. But there are more than a few city officials right now, some of whom, I shouldn't be surprised, are judges, who would like to see you buried like an onion with your head in the ground. If you write about Watts, Watts brings charges against you, I'm not sure Watts is the one who gets hurt. A word to the wise is all I'm saying."

I started to speak again, stopped. I sucked on my cigarette. Gottlieb hoisted his shoulders in a long shrug.

"Oh crap," I muttered. I hung my head.

"What can I say?" said Gottlieb.

"All right, all right. I'll lay off. But I'm gonna get him, Fred. Maybe not this time. But one of these days, he belongs to me."

"I believe you. Now let's talk Lester Paul and shootings and chasings."

"I'll tell you the same thing I told him: I met a source on a story tonight. I promised to protect him."

He lifted his hands to supplement his hoisted shoulders. "So protect. Tell me what you can."

"All right. I'll tell you this: I don't think Lester Paul had

Timothy Colt killed. If he was any kind of killer at all, I'd be dead by now. He had a gun on me tonight. He thought I'd betrayed him. But he didn't pull the trigger."

"He is, on the other hand, a smuggler and a fugitive," Gottlieb said. "Not to mention he shot at a cop at the Hotel Lincoln."

"At his feet. He shot through the door at his feet. You don't kill a man that way."

"Maybe. You should remember, if it was Paul, he didn't do the killing himself."

"I remember," I said. "Our friend with the knife chased me through the park tonight. This time he had a piece."

"Uh boy. But why is he chasing you through parks in the middle of the night? Because you know what he looks like?"

"I guess. Or maybe just because he wants me off the story. Someone does."

"And you're sure this is the same guy? The guy you haven't come in to look for in the mug shots like you promised?"

"Yeah, yeah, that's him," I said. I tossed my cigarette on the floor, stamped it out. Gottlieb glanced at the dead butt and clucked a little. "Anyway," I went on, "I don't think you're gonna find this guy in the mug shots. I'm told he's from Sentu."

"Again with Sentu. It's got a paragraph in the *Columbia Encyclopedia*. Now I know more about it than they do."

"Well, it figures in here somehow. The knife the killer used. Have you traced it?"

"No."

"I'm told it's a knife used by some kind of breed of assassin they used to have there. A kind of religious killer. I don't know. The point is: I think there's a connection between Colt's death and Sentu."

Gottlieb had his hands resting on his stomach now, the fingers laced. He twiddled the thumbs a minute. "There's a connection, but you're not going to tell me anything about Lester Paul, who was in Sentu at the same time and got in a fight with Colt the night before he died? You want to at least call me when the case is solved?"

I smiled. "I don't know where he is, Fred. I really don't."

"And if you did, you wouldn't tell me."

"What can I say? He's a source."

"Uy." He unraveled his hands, slapped them on the table. His chair scraped the floor as he pushed out of it and stood. "Okay," he said. "Go home. Go home and put your weary nose to bed."

I stood, too. I collected my overcoat. Gottlieb opened the door. I had started to walk past him when he said: "Let me ask you something, though."

I paused. "Ask."

"There's no one else who can cover this story when people are trying to kill you?"

I tilted my head. "Lansing's on it."

"Nice girl, Lansing."

"Good night, Fred."

"I'm sure she'd rather cover the story herself than have a nice man who could make her happy if he would stop being an idiot killed in Central Park for no reason at all."

I laughed. I stepped out the door.

"What I'm asking," he said. "Is there some reason why you can't just let this one go?"

I hesitated, turned to him. "It's good copy," I said. And left.

I took a cab home. I sat in the middle of the rear seat with my head thrown back and my eyes closed. I could sense the glares of streetlamps passing over me. I could sense the darkness that followed.

I thought about my conversation with Holloway that morning. It seemed like a very long time ago. I thought about Colt and Paul and Robert Collins going off together in an effort to rescue Eleanora and her underground network. What had happened to her? Had she been killed? Paul was the only one left alive who knew. And now he was missing again.

But then, what difference did it make? I wasn't covering Eleanora. I wasn't covering Sentu. I was covering Colt's murder, if I was covering anything. I wasn't even sure I was covering that.

Is there some reason why you can't just let this one go?

An ache of loneliness passed through me. For an instant, I thought of my late daughter. I thought of the day she learned to walk. It happened in the living room of the cottage we lived in then. I was reading the sports pages. Olivia was sort of crawling over my feet, grabbing my knee, hauling herself up. Suddenly, I felt her hand let go of me. I peeked around the paper to see if she'd gone down. I saw her take one step, then another, then another. One more and she toppled over. She looked at me, uncertain. She grinned.

I sat up in the cab, opened my eyes. I stopped thinking about it. I didn't even know why it had come to mind.

Because I love her that much.

My mind was wandering. That part of my life was long gone. I didn't love anyone. Not like that. Not anymore. That level of feeling is reserved for doting parents. Or for romantics like Colt. Or for madmen like Wilfred Campbell. Or maybe sometimes it's a gift you get from a woman. A woman like Eleanora.

Once again, I saw her in the empty air before me. Eleanora. I saw her face with its crown of golden hair, and then I saw the rest of her. She was gazing upward. She was lying on a bed and gazing upward. She was undressed. Her skin was white. White as Colt had said it was. Her white skin blushed everywhere as Colt had said it did. She panted. She cried out. She looked like a statue brought to life. Brought to life by the man who loved her. . . .

"This it?"

I looked up, startled. The cabby was watching me in his rearview mirror. I glanced out the window. We were in front of my apartment building. The brick facade looked stark and drab in the gaudy lights from the movie house.

"Yeah," I said. "Yeah. This is it."

I paid the man and went inside.

I took the elevator to the fourth floor. I was about halfway down the hall to my apartment when I stopped cold. Light was leaking out from under the door. My heart hammered. I felt faint with the force of the blood coursing through me. I did not think I could handle any more trouble tonight.

I came forward slowly now, step-by-step. I hewed to the wall. When I reached my door, I heard noises inside. A voice. A woman's voice.

"Shit," I said.

Chandler Burke. I'd totally forgotten she was due today.

Shaking my head, I fished my keys out of my pocket. I had a good excuse for being late anyway.

I opened the door. There she was, just coming out of the kitchen, carrying a steaming coffee mug. She seemed to have frozen at the sound of my entrance. She was standing as if in midstep, one foot beyond the other, her shoulders slightly forward, the mug extended.

Her stare, though, was not focused on me. It was riveted, instead, on the easy chair.

There, in the easy chair, was Lester Paul. He leveled his .38 at me.

22

I shut the door.

"Put that goddamn thing away, Paul," I said. "Anyone else tries to kill me tonight it just might make me mad."

For a moment the gun's black bore kept staring at me. I turned my back on it. I stripped off my overcoat and hung it in the closet. When I turned again, Paul was easing the pistol inside his jacket. He was smiling slightly. Chandler, watching his every move, waited until the gun was out of sight before she started breathing again. Slowly, the mug still out before her, she turned her eyes toward me.

She'd probably prepared herself for the sight of me. She'd known I wouldn't exactly look my best. I don't think, all in all, it was the scars from the old wounds that bothered her so much as the dried blood on my face, my general dishevelment. In any case, her pale cheeks went paler still at the sight. She hurried to the coffee table to set the mug down. Then she hurried over to me.

She came close to me. She smelled clean, like shampoo. Her hand came up to my face. She hesitated, as if I might knock it away. She touched me gently, her fingers on my forehead, then my mouth. I flinched. She studied me with her sad eyes.

I reached up and took her hand. "Sorry I'm late, kid," I said. "Hard day at the office."

She stood on tiptoe. Kissed me.

"Ouch," I said.

"Are . . . are you all right?"

"Yeah, I guess. How'd he get in?" I nodded at Paul.

Paul had taken the coffee mug from the table. He lifted it to me now in salute.

"Don't blame the lady," he said. "I was here when she arrived. I told her I was a friend of yours with the *Post*."

I shook my head at Chandler. "You know I don't have any friends at the *Post*."

She did her best to smile. "I'll try to remember."

"Do I need a gun to get a drink here?"

"I thought the doctor told you not to drink. I'll make you coffee."

With another wary glance at Paul, she returned to the kitchen.

Standing alone in the center of the room, I lit a cigarette. Paul sipped his coffee, watching me over the top of it.

I smiled. "Good coffee?"

He lifted out of it with a loud "Ah!" He touched his tongue to the roof of his mouth, considered. "No. Not really."

My smile widened to a grin. "If I'd known you were coming, I'd have poisoned it."

"Oh now," said Paul in his deep, foreign voice. "So unfriendly."

"Not at all. I just want to show my appreciation for your giving me a lift into Central Park, that's all. That Szechuan murder-fellow chased me way the hell over to Fifth Avenue. With a goddamned gun."

Paul tilted toward his mug again. "How unpleasant for you."

"Yeah. And I was spotted with you, too. I got picked up and given the third degree."

That got him. His lips had just touched the white mist floating atop the black surface of the coffee. He recoiled suddenly, as if scalded. "By the police?"

"They don't hand out third degrees in college, man."

"Did you . . . tell them anything?"

I took a long drag of smoke, let him sweat. "Nah," I said, the smoke rolling out of me. "I told them you were a source. They've got your plates, though."

"That is no longer a problem. I have gotten rid of the car."

One eyebrow raised, he cast me a shrewd glance out of those sunken eyes. "I take it you have come to the conclusion that I did not kill Timothy Colt," he said.

"Have I?"

"When I pointed my revolver at you just now, you did not seem quite as . . . what?—nervous?—as you did in the park."

"Why should I? You're the only person in town who hasn't tried to kill me this evening."

He lowered his face to his coffee. "The night is young," he said.

The scotch bottle and glass were on my desk. I went to them, poured myself a shot. I turned the desk chair around. I straddled it, the drink and cigarette dangling over the back.

"You're dropping ashes on the floor," said Chandler. She had come in, carrying another mug for me. She set it on the desk.

"Thanks," I said. I sipped my scotch.

"I thought the doctor told you not to smoke, too," she said softly.

"The doctor talks too much."

Chandler didn't answer. The butts have always been a sore point between us.

There was a hard wooden chair at the end of my desk. She moved to it, sat. She was wearing a long pleated green skirt and a white turtleneck sweater that showed off her figure. Paul eyed her as she arranged herself. She noticed it and flushed. She folded her hands in her lap, the fingers moving nervously. She sat silent, serious, prim, and erect. She listened, moving her eyes from one of us to the other.

"So," I said to Paul. "Aside from the chance to point your gun at me again, what brings you to these parts?"

He smiled charmingly. "In fact, Mr. Wells, as you have decided I am not a killer, I have decided you are not a traitor."

"Do tell."

"When I left the park unmolested by the police, I knew I had made a mistake in thinking you had alerted them to our meeting."

"So you retraced your steps and rescued me from the murder-man."

"So I wished you well in my heart," said Paul, "and came here to tell you my story in the event you returned alive."

"What a guy."

He smiled again, his scarred face wrinkling. No matter how he smiled, though, the haunted look in his deep eyes never left. He said, "My apologies, Mr. Wells. I am wanted in too many places to act carelessly, even in the aid of others. In one or two countries, I have even been sentenced to death in absentia, a fact which could make deportation very unpleasant."

"Okay. I forgive you. I'll name my children after you. But as you can see, I've made plans . . ."

"And may I say that it is really too bad of you to leave such a charming young lady waiting." He nodded at Chandler. She gave him nothing, an empty stare.

"Sure, you can say that," I said. "Or you can say what you have to say. Whatever you say, say it fast and get out."

He took a long swig of his coffee and, with a flourish, plunked the mug down on the table. He reached into his jacket. I tensed in my chair. He pulled out an elegant black cigarette case. He removed an unfiltered job and lit it with a silver lighter. The smoke drifted toward me. It smelled like perfume.

"A fair request," said Lester Paul. "I have detained you long enough." For another moment, he smoked and gathered his thoughts. Then, at last, he began: "I wanted to tell you about the source of the conflict between me and Timothy Colt. What accounted for the scene you witnessed in the Press Club. I cannot tell my story to the police—as I say, I am wanted already and prison would not agree with me at all. I had hoped that if you wrote about it . . ." He shrugged, his cigarette smoke tracing a spiral in the air. "Well, let's just say I am planning to leave your lovely country soon; when I do, I would like very much to be free of any suspicion of murder." The hand holding the cigarette kept moving. The tendrils of smoke unraveled along with his story. "There was, as you might suspect, a woman in the case. A woman named Eleanora."

Without thinking, I glanced at Chandler. She, of course, had not reacted to the name. I said quickly: "Yeah, the missionary. The underground worker. I've heard of her."

"You could not have heard everything," said Lester Paul. "You could not have heard everything she was. She was the most beautiful and courageous lady it has ever been my honor to meet. She had the face of an angel and the soul of one. She was . . ."

"You did meet her, then." I tried to keep the eagerness out of my voice. "You met her in person."

He inclined his head once gravely. "I did."

We both fell silent. There were plenty of things I wanted to ask him. I wanted to hear again about how she looked. About her golden hair, her high, proud cheeks, her graceful neck. More than that, I wanted him to describe how she moved, how she spoke, how she smelled. Had he touched her? That white skin that Colt had said looked like marble—did it feel like marble, too? Cold and smooth. Or did it soften at the touch and give off the heat of her? I wanted to ask a lot of things.

I glanced back at Chandler. She remained as she was: quiet, stiff, watchful. She was looking at me, waiting for me to speak.

"Go ahead," was all I said to Paul.

"Earlier this evening, we discussed Sentu and the murdermen. Do you know the country's history?"

"I know there was a revolution there. And the rebels won."

"Yes. It was during their final advance on the capital city of Mangrela that I first made the acquaintance of Timothy Colt. He had contacted me through a journalist of our mutual acquaintance. An Englishman by the name of Robert Collins. I liked Collins a good deal. He was . . . jolly. He knew how to wink at what was none of his business, how to do a favor for a friend. And at the same time, he was very dedicated to his profession. A serious journalist. And a brave one, as you will hear. When Collins came to me and asked me to talk to Colt, I was happy to oblige. We met in the bar of the Hotel Victoria, late at night. The rebel shells were falling closer and closer to the city limits, and already an exodus of civilians had begun. Collins introduced me to Colt and we sat together at a table. Colt was always, as you know, a charming and persuasive man. But just then, there was a fire burning in him just beneath the surface. I diagnosed it immediately as a fire of desperation. He spoke calmly enough, but the sweat rolled steadily down the crags in his cheeks and as he leaned toward me across the table, his eyes seemed to grow bigger and brighter with every passing moment."

Paul paused just a moment to let us appreciate his description. Like every great con artist I've ever met, he loved to hear his own voice creating a world. He went on: "I had heard of Eleanora, of course. She was legendary. So much so that I was somewhat surprised to learn she was real. But Colt assured

me she was real indeed, and he said she needed my help. With
the city near collapse, those who knew where to find her had
come to her and begged her to take their children, to insure
their escape even if the parents were killed. Eleanora declined.
Her network was collapsing. Everywhere, her people were
being captured and killed. Not only by the government, which
looked upon her as an arm of the rebellion, but by the rebels,
too, in those cities which had already fallen. The rebels, indeed,
were the fiercer enemy. Eleanora had given refuge to their
intended victims, too. And in the panic of the nation's fall,
those who hoped to buy their lives by betraying a friend's had
done irreparable damage to her. Those underground workers
who were not dead were making their escapes as best they
could. Eleanora could do nothing for the children of the refugees who came to her. But some would not take no for an
answer. They left their children on her doorstep, as it were,
and snuck away into the night.

"Now, Colt had fallen in love with Eleanora. And indeed,
she appeared to return that love, although perhaps she was only
using him for the help he could offer her noble cause, sacri-
ficing her own flesh, so to speak . . ."

His voice trailed off. He stared into the smoke that swirled
around him. I straightened a little in my chair. "Why do you
say that?" I said. I could not hide the tone of eagerness now.
"What proof have you got?"

"Hm?" Paul smiled at my hopeful expression. "Proof?
None at all. None at all, really. Perhaps it is just difficult for
me to believe that a woman like Eleanora could commit herself
to any man. Any *other* man." He cocked his head. He gave
me a long, speculative glance. "You know," he said, "I do
believe you understand me, Mr. Wells."

I snorted at him. I looked at the floor. "Keep going," I
told him.

Paul chuckled nastily. "Yes. Yes, well, at any rate, Colt
was desperate to get Eleanora out of the country before the
rebels descended. But the great lady herself—she would not
leave until she had found a way to get the children out of the
city to safety. That was where I came in. I am, as you know,
a . . . trader of sorts. Colt hoped I would be able to secure a
boat of some kind to transport the children up the coast, possibly as far as Morocco, and so out of harm's way. I agreed."

Chandler coughed. I had lit another cigarette by now. So had Paul. The whole room seemed to have sunk beneath the haze of smoke.

"Sorry," I said. I got up and opened the window behind my desk. The air rushed in with the rushing sounds of the night traffic. I poured myself another slug, replanted myself in the chair. "Why?" I said. "Why'd you agree to do it? Colt couldn't have paid you much."

Paul made a grand gesture with one hand. He was really enjoying himself now. "In the country of the blind, Mr. Wells," he said, "the one-eyed man is king. Exactly so, in a nation of corruption, not the official, not the soldier, not the populace, but the trader, the man who will deal in anything for a price, has the reins of power in his hand. If on occasion I chose to use that power for my own aesthetic reasons and without thought of gain . . . well, it was no one's business but mine."

I remembered how he had rescued Holloway from Imperial House. I nodded.

Paul continued: "I won't bore you with the details of how I managed to secure a small trawler in the midst of all that chaos. Suffice it to say that I did. I paid the captain to lie under anchor in the gulf on which the city sat. At a prearranged hour, he was to send a lifeboat into shore to meet with us. The children would be rowed out to the trawler and then taken out to the Atlantic and up the coast. Would you mind?"

He held out his mug to me. I grabbed my scotch bottle by the neck, dashed some of the liquor into the mug.

"Thank you," he said. He took a sip. He nodded, satisfied. "I met with Colt and Collins at a prearranged hour. They took me to a small, unprepossessing house in the suburbs of the city. There, I found Eleanora. . . ." He took another shot, shivered as it went through him. "She was surrounded by children when I saw her first. The house was full of them. Maybe thirty of them, one-year-olds, near-adolescents. All of them looking up at her. All of them trusting her to see them to safety. Well . . ."

He waved away the image. I didn't ask him to go on. I clenched my jaw so I wouldn't ask him.

"I suppose," he said, "I was most impressed with her calm, brisk, businesslike manner. It was heroic, but there was not a touch of charade about it. It was very unaffected and real. Very

British, too. She described to us the route we would travel—a route designed to help us avoid both the soldiers and the panicked populace. And a route, clearly, which she had made use of many times before. She insisted on coming with us, on leading the way. Nothing either Colt or I could say would dissuade her. As midnight came, we set out into the darkness. The muffled thud of the rebel shells was close enough now to make the ground beneath our feet tremble. The flare of the explosions lit the night sky red. All around us in the blackness was the sound of weeping as refugees prepared to begin the trek out of the city. Eleanora led us creeping along alleyways, through windows into cellars with holes smashed in their walls, through these holes into the next cellar and the next, out finally onto some byway until we reached a fire escape, up the escape to run, bent over, across the city's rooftops.''

I could picture them: a string of children punctuated by the adults who shepherded them, all of them silhouetted against the purple sky.

"More than once, we had to plaster ourselves against a wall as the soldiers rushed past, as they fired into the panicked crowds in their own panic. More than once, the cry of a toddler or the complaint of a child threatened to betray us. But in the end, we reached the gulf shore unmolested. The boat was there as planned, and the children were loaded aboard and taken out to the trawler. It took three trips to get them all. When the last child was gone, the boat came back one more time. For Colt and Eleanora.''

He paused. For dramatic effect, I guess. But I already knew what was coming. "She wouldn't go," I said.

"She was shocked at the thought. There was still business to be done, she said. Documents, codes, other evidence that had to be destroyed. The lives of those who had risked everything to help her hung in the balance. She would not compromise their safety for her own. She sent the boat back empty.''

Despite the open window, the perfumed smell of Paul's cigarettes was now thick in the room. He lit another one. He waved it around.

"That was how she lived," he said.

I nodded. I said nothing.

"Now," said Paul, "I will tell you how she died."

23

"This, I suppose, is the part of the story that concerns you most. That will explain my meeting with Colt in the Press Club the night before he was murdered."

Paul now knocked the rest of his scotch back as if to brace himself. I did the same. Chandler, hands folded in her lap, just looked on.

"Colt, of course, begged her to go," Paul said. "But she—she bowed her head quietly under the onslaught of his argument and would not budge from her position. In her simple, straightforward fashion, she explained that the final responsibility for this network belonged to her. She surely wanted to escape, but she would not leave disaster in her wake. If it had been another woman, I do believe Colt would have physically forced her into the boat. But that was not the sort of thing one did to Eleanora.

"Instead, we returned to the safe house by the same circuitous way we'd come. We made coffee and toasted the success of our mission. When we'd done, Eleanora went to a rolltop desk in the living room and opened it. When Robert Collins saw what was inside, he let out a long whistle of delight. He was looking at a ham radio."

I shook my head. "So?"

"Well, by then, you see, the city was entirely cut off from the outside."

"Yeah, Holloway told me about that."

"Collins—who, as I say, was a serious and ambitious reporter—realized he was looking at what possibly was the last means of filing dispatches out of the city. That realization cost him his life."

The smoke—all the smoke—drifted between us now. It was a single gray-yellow mass. I saw Paul floating in it where he sat as if from a distance. He seemed insubstantial, like a figure in a dream. Like the smoke, his voice drifted on.

"At any rate, Eleanora used the radio to contact one of her safe houses in Jacobo, a city nearby, a major center of her operations. She was told that the situation there was dire. Desperate refugees were gathering in the hopes she would appear, and no one else was left who could help them. She believed that if she could get through the rebel lines to Jacobo, she could give what aid there was to give and possibly arrange her own escape as well. Colt declared it was too dangerous. He demanded she let him get her out in the American airlift. But Eleanora was adamant. It was left finally to me to propose a more sensible . . ." Paul stopped. We exchanged a glance through the perfumed smoke. He smiled. "But there is no point in trying to deceive you, Wells, is there? The prospect of aiding Eleanora's escape, of acting as her hero, earning her gratitude and admiration—such a prospect was as appealing to me as it was to Colt. I suggested that, with my contacts on both sides of the affair, I could guide her safely and easily to Jacobo provided she had a passport under a false name. To my surprise, Eleanora had taken no precautions to secure her own escape from the country. She had no valid passport at all, and the conditions in the city being what they were, it would be difficult to procure one.

"So we hit upon an idea which allowed all of us to display our gallantry. Colt rendered up his identification papers, Collins photographed Eleanora, and I used my small talents to doctor Colt's passport to look like hers."

"Which meant," I said slowly, "that Colt couldn't travel with you. That only you and Collins could escort her to Jacobo."

Paul laughed without much pleasure. "Collins was not interested in the enterprise. He had asked Eleanora—as payment for his help in rescuing the children—to allow him to use her radio to send out his dispatches on the fall of the capital.

It was a stupid thing to do. A shell hit the house not long after we left, I'm told, and Collins was killed. None of his dispatches reached the public.''

The air from the open window chilled the back of my neck. It dried the sweat that had been running down my back, dampening my shirt. There was a chill inside me, too. My left hand clenched and unclenched. My right hand raised my cigarette to my lips again and again. The end of the story was near. I didn't want to hear it.

I didn't want her to die.

I stood up. Paul's voice ceased for a moment at the scraping of my chair. Chandler looked up at me, surprised. I felt embarrassed in front of her.

I turned my back on both of them. I stood at the window. I peered out on the bright lights of the movie theater below. I smoked. Paul went on. His voice had taken on a slightly mocking tone. He seemed to enjoy what I was feeling. Misery loves company.

"I don't have to explain to you," he said, "how I felt as I watched Colt kiss her good-bye. As I watched her lay her head against his chest, whisper plans for their reunion. As I say, perhaps she had only been using him for the good he could do her network. . . .''

"You know damn well she wouldn't have done that," I said, without turning around.

"Perhaps," was all Paul said in answer. "At any rate, we helped Eleanora destroy her papers, uproot her communication lines, give warnings to contacts, and so on. Then Colt went back to the heart of the city to join the airlift, Collins stayed behind, and Eleanora and I set off for Jacobo.''

He paused. I watched my reflection on the windowpane. I imagined her form floating in the night beyond it. I imagined her looking in on me as I looked out at her. Have pity, Eleanora, I thought, on those of us still stuck in the world.

"Travel is part of a trader's business," Paul said. "I knew the ropes, as they say. Even under the circumstances, the trip to Jacobo was not eventful. We were stopped on the road no more than four times. Each time, my name—and, of course, my money—saw us through. However, the going was circuitous and slow. It took us three days to reach Jacobo. By the time we had, the capital had gone under. The nation belonged to the rebels. In Jacobo, rebels and rebel sympathizers had risen up and set the city on fire. We managed to reach Eleanora's safe house but found there a scene depressingly similar to the one we'd just finished with. Here, again, were the refugees, children and adults—about twenty of them—who'd made their way here in hopes of finding one last chance of escape. When they saw Eleanora, they were overjoyed. And the great woman set about the effort of getting them out of the country in small groups of two or three. One of the journalists you mentioned in your article—Donald Wexler—he helped with that.''

I turned sharply from the window. ''He was there?''

''Yes.''

''He met Eleanora?''

''Why, yes. They spoke together for some time, in fact.''

''He never told me that,'' I murmured.

''Ah, well, my friend,'' said Paul in that mocking tone again, ''she was not an easy woman to share.''

I nodded. ''Go on,'' I said. I watched him now through the smoke.

''Then again,'' said Paul, ''perhaps he was just too modest to tell you of his heroic exploits. As I recall, he had a jeep which he used to drive some of the refugees through enemy lines to safety. That was the last I saw of him. Soon after that, anyway, the end came. . . .''

This time, when he paused, he stared sadly at his black cigarette case. Mournfully, he lifted a new butt to his lips.

I couldn't stand it anymore. ''Why don't you tell it?'' I said sharply. ''Why don't you quit stalling, and tell the end?''

''John.'' It was Chandler. She spoke quietly from her chair. I could hear the surprise and agitation in her voice. I didn't look at her.

Paul made a small bow her way. ''No, no,'' he said. ''Your friend is quite right. I am too much enamored of melodrama. A lifelong weakness.''

''Just tell the story, Paul,'' I said.

The smuggler pinned me with his sunken eyes. ''They raided the house,'' he said without expression. ''Rebel soldiers. They descended on us out of nowhere one night, circled the place, calling her name, calling for Eleanora. I was in a bedroom upstairs at the time. She was in the room beside me.

I could have gone to her, I could have tried to save her. I could have died defending her.'' He gestured with his cigarette again. Now there was too much smoke everywhere to follow a single trail. ''I made one of my . . . famous escapes,'' Paul said. ''Onto the roof, down a drainpipe . . . into the night. I turned back and saw the soldiers close in on the house. I heard the sound of splintering wood. I heard Eleanora call for me.''

''All right,'' I said.

''And then I heard her scream.''

''Knock it off.''

''I heard her scream again and then again.''

Without thinking, I went at him. Hurling my cigarette to one side, I reached down and grabbed him by his jacket lapels.

Chandler leapt up. ''John!'' she cried.

I dragged the bastard to his feet. I pulled him up to me until we were nose to nose.

''What did you do?'' I screamed into his face. ''You son of a bitch, what the fuck did you do?''

Paul smiled sadly. Mockingly. ''I left her there,'' he said. ''I left her there.''

For another moment, I held him. I peered in rage into that scarred, miserable face. I wanted to smash him. I wanted to knock him to the floor and beat him till he said it wasn't true. Till he admitted he'd gone back for her, saved her. . . .

''I ran for my life,'' he said, ''and left her there to die.''

My clenched hands opened. Paul dropped back into his chair. His head sunk on his breast. I turned away. I wandered toward my desk. As I went, I came across the cigarette I had tossed away. It lay on the brown wood of the floor. The smoke drifted up from it in a thin stream. Beneath it a small circle of char began to spread.

I stepped on the cigarette. Ground it under the toe of my shoe. The smoke faltered, died.

I heard the door open and shut behind me. When I turned, Paul was gone.

24

I stared at the dead cigarette. I ran my fingers up through my hair. Chandler came up beside me.

"What is it?" she said. "What is going on? Tell me. I don't understand."

I smiled at the floor. "Just another fun weekend with Wellsey," I told her.

She put her hands on my shoulders. "Talk to me, John. You've locked me out for too long. This Eleanora—is she someone you knew?"

I looked up into her round, tired, serious face. Her eyes were still nervous, even fearful. But they were patient, too. She waited for me to come to her. My hands remembered the fullness of her flesh. How warm she was. I remembered how sweet she tasted, and all the passion in her.

When did you see her last, Wells?

Tim Colt had asked me that the night he died. But he was really asking me something else. *Do you love her? Do you love anyone? Do you know how to love? Have you ever loved the way I have? The way I love Eleanora? Do you think you ever will?*

Suddenly, without thinking, I reached for Chandler. I gripped her by the shoulders. I pulled her to me. I kissed her, hard, and her mouth opened to let me in. My hands went over her, over her waist, her breasts, up to hold her face while I kissed her and kissed her.

That night, I made love as I hadn't in years. The rhythms of it were fierce, almost primal. The heat of it coursed through me like a river of blood. Chandler cried out to me again and again, and again and again I came into her with a fever I'd almost forgotten.

I ached when I woke up the next morning. Saturday morning. I ached all over. My legs hurt from running in the park. My gut hurt from where Watts had slugged me. My nose and forehead stung. When I breathed deeply, my lungs felt like there were pins in them.

I ached, too, with the deep, pleasurable ache of last night's love. But when I reached out for Chandler, she wasn't there. The other side of the bed was empty.

I made a low, guttural sound of pain as I forced myself to roll out from under the covers. I fit my legs into my pants and pulled the waistband up around me. Gingerly, stiffly, I walked into the other room.

She was there. She was curled up on the easy chair, where Paul had sat last night. She was wrapped in my bathrobe. It billowed around her. She stared into space, sipping occasionally from a mug of coffee.

We'd left the window open. There was only a faint smell of stale smoke under the fresh, dry chill of the air that filled the room.

Chandler barely glanced up at me when I came in. I remembered the thoughts that had gone through my mind as we'd clung to each other in the dark last night. I felt guilty, as if she knew what I'd been thinking. I avoided looking at her and went into the kitchen.

She'd left the coffee on for me. I poured some into a mug. McKay had given me the mug for my last birthday, my forty-sixth. It was black, with the words SHUT UP in white letters on the side.

I walked to the kitchen doorway, leaned against the jamb. Chandler sat there, still staring into space. I watched her.

"What did you think of me before we . . . before we were lovers?" she said softly. She sipped her coffee, staring into space. I didn't answer. She said: "You must have thought was a terrible old spinster woman. Prim and nervous and living alone with my cat.''

"No," I lied. "I didn't think that. That's dumb."

She paid no attention. "I suppose I had . . . turned into that. An old maid, I mean. I guess I was all . . . shut up in myself. I guess I still am."

"I'm no better," I said.

"Maybe." Chandler stared off thoughtfully. "Maybe we have too much in common in a way. Do you know what I mean?"

"No."

"I mean, ever since I lost my parents . . . my mother, really . . . ever since she died . . . it's been very . . . very hard for me to . . . to be close . . . close to anyone."

I nodded. "Yeah. I know."

"And you . . . since your daughter died . . ."

"I know," I said.

Finally she raised her eyes to me. Those sad eyes with so many people's sad stories in them. She listened to them well at her suicide hot line. She listened as people on the brink reached out to her. She and her volunteers listened as people wandered through the caverns of themselves, searching for their long-buried reasons to live. She had traveled through all those other people's caverns, and that's not an easy thing to do. But it's easier than some things. It's easier than traveling through your own.

"Sometimes," she said, still softly, "when you wouldn't call . . . all those weeks when you wouldn't call, I would feel . . . relieved. Sometimes . . . Do you understand? Can you understand that?"

A pack of cigarettes lay on the desk. I went to it. Set my mug down, hoisted a butt, lit it. I hacked on the first tug of smoke, but I fought to keep the next one down.

"I would feel relieved," said Chandler. "Because it's . . . it's hard. Trying to . . . get close, be close. It's hard, and it's . . . painful. For a while, there at the beginning, it looked like we were going to make it, didn't it? It looked like . . ." Her voice trailed off.

"Yes," I said. "It did."

"But now . . ."

"Since that night. Since that night I had that dream."

The words seemed to startle her, as if I'd stolen them directly from her mind. "We just can't. Can we, John? We just can't do it. Be close, I mean. Either of us. Maybe that's why we picked each other. Maybe we recognized that somehow from the start."

I studied the floor. "Maybe," I said.

"You know . . ." For the first time, I heard a trace of tears in her voice. Under her voice, where it would not give her away. "You know, I think you're one of the most remarkable people I've ever met."

I made a noise at her. I was thinking: Colt. Colt knew. Colt knew me from the beginning. He must've taken one look at me—one look heightened maybe by the liquor. Heightened by his annoyance at striking out with Lansing, his jealousy . . . But he must've taken that one look at me and pegged me dead to rights. He must've been some reporter if he could see that deep that fast. What could he have told me about the others? About Holloway and Wexler and Paul and Robert Collins? About the way they felt about Eleanora? About the way *she* felt? Surely she must have been the key to it somehow. The way she affected all of them. Otherwise, why hadn't Wexler told me about seeing her? Or had Paul lied about it? I didn't know. What would Colt have been able to tell me if he could talk to me still as he had that night in his hotel?

While I considered it, Chandler was saying: "You really are remarkable. You're . . . brave is the only word I can think of. I mean, I look at you, at the way you are, and I think . . . I think you must hurt terribly sometimes . . . that you must hurt so that you can barely stand it. But then you just . . . you just keep on . . . you keep on doing whatever it is you're doing . . . getting your story, doing your job, or whatever. And sometimes . . . I mean, sometimes, I look at you—I look at you doing that—and I think: there's something . . . something just not quite nice about this man. Something . . . But then maybe it takes that . . . that distance. For you to do your job every day. I don't know."

I was only half listening. My mind was elsewhere. I was wondering—trying to imagine—what Colt could have told me about Eleanora. And then, as Chandler spoke, I thought of the one person who might be able to answer that. I thought of the one person who might be able to speak for Colt even now.

That's what I was thinking up until then. Up until Chandler spoke those last words: "I don't know." That's when she started to cry.

I had never seen her cry before. Not for herself anyway. She wasn't very good at it. She didn't just open up and let go of it the way some women can. It chugged out of her painfully. She coughed, trying to fight it back. The tears barely crested her cheeks before she wiped them away as if they angered her.

I took a step toward her. She looked up at me. I stopped.

"Last night . . ." she said. "Last night, when we were making love . . . over and over when we were making love . . ." She buried her face in her hands and cried: "You called me Eleanora."

25

I stood at the window and watched her go. She hailed a cab at the curb. I kept watching as the cab carried her off into the light stream of Saturday morning traffic. I watched the people passing back and forth on the sidewalk with their newspapers under their arms.

The air coming in from the window was as clean as it gets in Manhattan. I could even smell Christmas in it, the scent of the oncoming cold. I plucked my latest cigarette from my lips and jammed it out in the ashtray on my desk. I felt empty inside. I did not think I would see Chandler Burke again.

I decided to stop thinking about it. I decided not to think at all. I made a couple of phone calls, then climbed into a clean suit and went downstairs. I walked to the donut store on the corner of Lexington. I bought myself some breakfast in a bag and carried it to the local garage. There, I had the attendants exhume my old maroon Dart, the Artful Dodge.

I munched my donut as I left town. I tore a hole in the cap of my coffee cup and sipped from it, steering with one hand. The Dodge and I rolled over the bridge and out of the borough. We headed down to the Long Island Expressway. I kept not thinking. I kept the radio on.

I turned off the L.I.E. and headed into the little brick neighborhoods of Queens. Small trees lined the roads here. Two-story, two-family houses stood close together behind the trees. They were squat brick structures with white curtains shifting at the windows. When I turned a corner, I could see small, square backyards fenced in with chain link behind them. I could see laundry fluttering back there.

Valerie Colt's house was no different from the others. Two stories of brick. A concrete walk out front. A square of grass out back. As I came up the walk, I could see the blue light of the television flickering behind the white curtains. I could hear bangs and sharp voices and canned laughter. The kids were watching Saturday morning cartoons.

Mrs. Colt opened the door for me. I'd called to let her know I was coming. She was dressed for the occasion in jeans and a pink blouse that set off her red hair. She still wore too much makeup where the wrinkles gathered at her mouth and eyes.

She let me in and led me through a modest kitchen. I glimpsed the kids through a doorway on the right. A boy and a girl, stretched out on their bellies, chins in hands, eyes on tube. Mrs. Colt took me down a hall into a cramped living room. On one wall, glass doors looked out on the backyard. The grass was dead out there. The lone tree was bare and gray. There wasn't much light coming in. The room seemed dank and shadowy.

She pointed me to a wooden chair. She took the sofa. She folded her hands between her knees. She leaned forward, watched me with her sharp, bright eyes. "You said on the phone you had some questions you wanted to ask."

"Yes," I said. I hesitated. I wasn't really sure now why I had come. "I thought maybe you could give me some . . . some idea, some insight into the way your husband thought."

Mrs. Colt leaned forward a little more. "Thought about what?"

I ran a hand up over my head. "Mrs. Colt, I've been looking into your husband's murder," I said. "And the more I find out, the more I become convinced it had something to do with the time he spent in Sentu."

She was too smart for that. The corner of her lips curled. "That's not what you mean, is it? Not really. You don't mean something to do with Sentu. You mean something to do with Eleanora. Don't you?"

I didn't answer. I didn't have to.

Then she startled me with a quick peal of laughter. The

sound ran up the scale and drifted away like the last chord of a song. When she laughed like that, I could imagine her as a young girl. An easy, spirited kind of girl who could do things to you with a backward glance. I could see the girl that Colt had fallen for.

"I need to know more about her," I said. "Are you sure she's dead? Was there anyone else who . . . who felt about her the way your husband did? Anyone who might have fought with him for her? Do you know if she . . . if she . . . ?"

"If she loved Tim back?" said Mrs. Colt. The laugh was still in her voice.

I nodded. "Yes."

Mrs. Colt smiled wryly at me. She stood up. "Mr. Wells, as it just so happens, I can give you everything you want." In one corner, there was a small writing desk. It was covered with papers. They lay loose all over the surface, disorganized. But the one she wanted was right on top.

She handed it to me. A crumpled piece of blue stationery. Cheap paper but elegant somehow, womanly. The handwriting was a woman's, too. Neat and swift and small. A schoolgirl hand. The ink was faded. At the edges of the letter, there were white patches blotting out some of the words. Constant fingering had worn away the surface of the paper.

I glanced up. Mrs. Colt was walking away from me slowly. Her hips swung haughtily as she walked. She turned smartly and settled on the sofa again. She propped her elbows on her knees, folded her hands under her chin. She watched me, smiling. That wry, bitter smile.

For a long time, I could not look at the page in my hand. I knew what it was. I suppose it was what I'd come to find. But I could not look at it. I felt the paper under my fingers. I imagined her touching it, holding it like I was. I lowered my eyes and read.

My dearest love,
    Tonight, I think the end is very near. In a week, certainly no more than two, the rebels will be upon us, and so will the holocaust. The city will be put to the torch, the people put to the sword. My small enterprise—which has thrived amidst the day-to-day corruption of the government—will no doubt be among the first "reforms" of the new regime. I, who have

seen and survived such reforms before, feel somehow certain that I shall not survive to see another.

I have been wondering—on this warm summer's night to which you have so unchivalrously left me—I have been wondering why I should feel my fate so heavily. The scrape is similar to others I've been in, the odds of escape the same. Why should I feel doomed this time of all others? Why no hope from your ever-hopeful Eleanora?

But of course, that is the answer. It is that I am *your* Eleanora now. Yours and always yours and yours alone, my darling, my darling . . .

I looked up. "You found this," I said. I had to say something. I was embarrassed by the letter, by the passion of it.

Mrs. Colt's smile had faded. All that was left was a trace of irony at the corner of her lips. Irony and pain. "The police gave it to me," she said. "They gave me the papers Tim was carrying when he died. The ones they didn't think they'd be using in their investigation."

I nodded. I kept nodding as, irresistibly, my eyes were drawn back to the page. The letter went on:

There are now, for me, so many ways to die. That's the rub of it. Before, there was only the danger of losing my own life. But now—now, you might lose your life and make mine useless, worse than death. Or we might be separated forever somehow so that death would be a comfort. I never feared imprisonment before, but that also would be dying now because it would keep me away from you. I never feared torture before or all the cruelties they devise for people like me. But what if I were disfigured or disabled, rendered, I mean, incapable of giving myself to you? Which is all I want to do always. What good would life be to me then?

Last night, you said that you could not go on living if I died. That, too, murdered me a little. If I knew you would be safe and well, maybe I would not fear this onrushing catastrophe. I wish I could tell you that I do not love you—or even that I hate you—so that you would forget me. But would you believe me? How could you? Say you would not. Say you never could.

Do you know what I think? I think that only people who love each other as much as we do really know the face of death, because only we really know the face of life. And if this fear, this certainty of the end . . . if this intimacy with death is what we have to pay for our intimacy with living and each other, then I wanted to tell you tonight, my darling, that your smallest kindness to me was worth it, that your whispered word was worth it, that the briefest sight of you was worth it as nothing else could be, and that no matter what happens, I am

Yours, yours, yours,
Eleanora

My love, I thought. *Eleanora, my love, my love.*

Mrs. Colt's green eyes were glistening when I looked up now. I saw the pain there, the pain she lived with day by day.

"You see, Mr. Wells," Mrs. Colt said. Her hands were still tucked under her chin. "You see, you didn't come here to find out about Tim's death, did you? You came here to find out about her. All your questions—Is she really dead? Did she really love Tim? I half knew—right from the day I came to your office—I was almost sure that you would come to me like this."

"I don't understand."

"I looked at you and I thought: He's one of hers, just like Timmy. Just like Timmy: he belongs to her."

I stared down at the letter. I shook my head, uncomprehending.

Mrs. Colt lifted her chin off her hands. Her back straightened. She gazed at me with towering hurt and pride.

"What is it you *want* anyway?" she asked me. "What is it men like you *want* from us?" She smiled quizzically. She really wanted to know. "I was a good wife to Tim, Mr. Wells. I was a wonderful wife."

I murmured, "I'm sure. I . . ."

"I was everything he could have asked for." She gestured at the wrinkled blue page in my hand. "Everything except an illusion."

My fingers rubbed the paper in my hand, as if to reassure myself that it was real.

But she went on: "She wasn't like that: all courage and beauty. No one is like that. Not all the time, not day after day. Tim had a romance with her for a few weeks in a dangerous place and it was special. I understand that. But she's dead now.

She's dead and it's over and . . . and I was here. I couldn't afford to be an illusion, Mr. Wells. I was here day after day."

I stood up. I walked to the desk with the papers on it. I held Eleanora's letter for another moment. Then I placed it on top of the pile.

"I know what you're thinking," Mrs. Colt said behind me. "You're thinking that I chose what I have, that I'm kidding myself."

I faced her a moment. I felt tired. Very tired. Too tired to think. "It doesn't matter," I said.

She didn't care what I said. "Maybe I am," she continued. "But you're kidding yourself, too. You fooled yourself into thinking Tim's murder had to do with Eleanora, but it's just you . . . it's just the way you feel . . . it's . . ."

The words were choked off. She shivered. She hugged her shoulders and turned her head so I couldn't see her face.

I stood where I was, near the desk. I stared at her. I was shaken by what she'd said. I had known it was true, deep down. I had known it was true all along. But when she said it aloud, it suddenly struck me with full force: Colt's murder was not about Eleanora. It never had been.

Everything seemed to change the moment I acknowledged that. It was as if I'd been sitting in a room while twilight came. As if I hadn't really noticed it was getting dark. It was as if Mrs. Colt had come in then and said simply, "Why are you sitting in the dark like this?" and hit the light switch. All at once, everything seemed clear.

All at once, I knew who had killed Tim Colt.

26

There was only a shadow staff in the city room. The white maze of cubicles stood silent, mysterious. Tom Cochran was at the desk. A young guy. Handsome prep-school kid. Short brown hair, three-piece suits. He had his feet up, his hands behind his head. He was chatting up Sally Giles. She was a pretty young redhead Cambridge was grooming for the night desk. Cochran lifted a hand to me as I came in. Sally smiled.

I sat down next to them at the long table.

"Listen," I said. "I've got something." I told them what I had.

Tom Cochran's feet came down to the floor with a thud. His circular face went pale. He ran his palm up over the well-combed hair on his brilliant head.

"Well, has there . . . I mean . . . has there been an arrest?"

"No. Not yet. But there will be after I call Gottlieb."

"Yeah, but I mean . . . should I call Cambridge? Maybe I should call Cambridge?"

"You do, and I'll quit and peddle this to *Reader's Digest*," I said.

"Yeah, but . . ."

"Let him read about it in the newspaper."

I pushed away from the desk.

"Oh hey," Sally said. She had a soft voice, a whisper. She smiled again when I glanced back at her. She had a dazzling white smile. It lifted her freckled cheeks. "Someone's been calling for you. A guy. Wouldn't leave his name."

"Yeah? Okay, pump it back to me if he calls again."

She smiled some more. She had blue eyes. There was something vague about them.

I started down the corridor to my desk. As I went, I noticed Alex, the copyboy, hovering over the printers. I began to wonder if Alex had a home.

My desk was buried under papers. I grabbed handfuls of them and dumped them in the trash. I pushed some others aside until I uncovered a coffee mug. It was black with the words SCREW OFF in white letters on it. McKay had given it to me last Christmas. I picked it up, peered in at the bottom. A crust of coffee about an inch thick had hardened there.

I peeked my head up out of my cubicle. I shouted, "Yo, Alex!"

The kid looked up. His arms were full of the hard copy he'd been tearing. I hurled the mug at him across the room.

"Yaagh," he remarked. The copy went flying up in the air. His hands clapped together like a seal's flippers. He managed to catch the mug. The copy fluttered down around him. A sheet of it folded gently over his head.

"You ever see a copyboy fly?" I called to him.

He shook his head no. The copy slid off him and drifted to the ground.

"Right," I said. "So keep that mug filled or I'll toss you out the goddamned window."

"Sure thing, Pops," said Alex.

I felt no remorse.

I went to work. I stuck a sheet of paper in the Olympia. I stuck another cigarette in my mouth. I stuck the phone's handset under my chin. I dialed a number. The phone started to ring. I started to type.

I battered out my lead. A woman spoke in my ear.

"Manhattan South. Sergeant Harrison," she said.

"How ya doin', Harry? This is Wells at the *Star*."

"Hi, Wells at the *Star*, nothing's happening."

"Yeah, it is, you just don't know it yet."

"Ooh, that's not what we like to hear from you, Wells."

"Is Gottlieb there?"

"No. It's Saturday, darling."

"Oh yeah. Damn. Well, listen, it doesn't matter. I need him. Call him at home, tell him I need him."

"Oh, thanks a lot."

"No, no. He'll thank you for it. Really. He'll want all of this one."

"Okay, Wells," she said dubiously. "Only for you."

I hung up. I went back to the typewriter. I battered away. The clacking rose up out of my cubicle. It floated away over the broad, silent, white-lighted room.

Alex brought me my coffee.

"You clean the crud out of it?" I said, typing.

"Yeah, sure, Pops," the kid said.

"Good. I'll recommend your promotion to underling."

"It'll be an improvement over slave." He sighed. And he was gone.

The pages rolled up in front of me. The story rolled out with them. It seemed a simple story now. Just a slight shift of emphasis had made it seem simple. I had most of the pieces. They fit together. The fit was tight.

The phone rang next to me. I snatched it up. Jammed it onto my shoulder. I kept typing.

"Fred."

It was not Fred.

"John? John, is that you?"

"Chandler," I said. I stopped typing. I grabbed the handset, shifted it to my other ear. "Chandler, what's . . ."

I heard her gulp once. I heard her breath come fast. Her words came faster. "John, there's a man . . . he says he's going to . . ." She gave a little gasp. She was gone.

I straighted in my chair. "Chandler?"

Another voice came on the line. A man's voice. It was light and quick as a knife blade. It had the slightest touch of an accent.

"I have her, Mr. Wells," it said softly. "I have her here I have her and I will kill her if you don't come to me."

"One hair, shit-for-brains. Hurt one hair on her head and they'll bury you in a fucking water glass."

"I know a way to kill her that she will not like," he answered. "No, no, sir, she will not like it at all."

I controlled my breath so I wouldn't sound scared. "What do you want?"

"I want you here. I want you here within half an hour. Then we will negotiate."

"Listen, how do I know . . ."

"You know if you are not here I will kill her. I will kill her in my not-very-pretty way."

"Where are you?"

He gave me an address way downtown on Crosby Street. It was a lane of old lofts and abandoned factories.

"Too far," I said. "Gimme an hour."

There was a pause. "Until twelve," he said. "And then I will kill her. If there are police, I will kill her. If you are not alone, I will kill her, too."

I looked at my watch. It was 11:05.

"By noon," I said. "I'll be there."

A dial tone answered me.

I nearly tipped my chair over as I jumped to my feet. I clutched at the pages I'd been writing, bunched them together in my fist. I grabbed a pen, dropped it, grabbed it again. I scrawled the address I was headed for on a message note. I ran out down the aisle to the copydesk.

"Cochran!" I screamed.

Tom had been walking toward the coffee machine. He swiveled and came running back to me. I jabbed my story into his hands.

"Call Sergeant Harrison at Manhattan South. Read her the first two graphs of this story, then tell her to get some manpower to this address."

I shoved the message sheet at him. Cochran didn't even look up at it. He was staring at the top graphs of my story. He was wide-eyed.

"Holy shit, Wells!" he said. "I mean, holy shit!"

"Just tell her!" I screamed.

I stuffed the address into his hand and went racing for the door.

I had fifty-two minutes left.

27

The Artful Dodge was waiting at the curb. I jumped in. I peeled away into the traffic with an explosion of black exhaust. I turned the corner, leaving rubber on the road behind me. I ran the lights until I hit Madison Avenue, going uptown.

The avenue stretched away before me in the clear blue day. The buses crowded the right lane, coughing their way from stop to stop. Cars and taxis wove up the left lane. Not many. Just the first of the morning's Christmas shoppers.

I set my palm at the center of the car's wheel, ready to lean on the horn. I hit the gas. The Artful Dodge roared and groaned its way up to forty. Cars—cabs mostly—bunched around me, then fell away. More bunched around me. We raced and swerved together in a little clot for about a block or so. I swung the wheel this way and that, going for the daylight between the yellow cabs. I spat ahead of the pack again. Cars dropped back on either side of me. The office towers and shops with their wreaths and lights and trees all melded in a colorful blur.

Intersections came and went. I leaned on the horn. I made it wail as I rocketed under red lights and in front of oncoming cars. I left a trail of screeching brakes and shrieked curses behind me.

All that time, I waited for the sound of a siren. I kept glancing in my rearview mirror, hoping for the sight of a flasher. Hoping for some enterprising patrolman to come after me for reckless driving. I saw the green street signs rushing past me. I saw the numbers on them rise into the sixties, into the seventies. Not a patrol car in sight. Not even a traffic agent to pull me over. This is a very dangerous city.

The posh shops of the eighties streamed by. The traffic seemed to dissipate. Eighty-fifth Street. The Artful Dodge shot forward like a bullet, her old engine straining. Eighty-seventh, Eighty-eighth. I had my eyes glued to the black and battered Manhattan pavement. Ninetieth.

I wrenched the wheel.

It was a one-way street in the wrong direction. I didn't even look. I hauled the wheel over like I was turning a great schooner in the middle of an empty sea. The world spun at the windows. The old car turned so fast under me it seemed to lift into the air. For a moment I was certain the spinning world would roll and I'd be spilled out into a roaring, tumbling, shattering explosion.

But she held the road, the old Dart. She held the road for dear life. Her rear tires flew wide. I fought with the wheel, muscled them straight. The Dodge righted herself onto Ninetieth as a little red BMW swung around the corner of Fifth Avenue and headed toward me. The BMW screeched. It lurched toward the line of parked cars to the left. It halted. I kept barreling toward it. I had a quick glimpse of a young executive type sitting behind the windshield. I saw him scream like the girl in a Dracula movie and throw his arms up in front of his face.

I hit the brake. The Dodge didn't even slow down. It skated over the road toward the BMW. About ten yards from the screaming exec, my faithful jalopy touched down with a sound like an elephant sliding over a chalkboard. I threw the wheel and slid just past the BMW to the right. Came to a stop right beside it, in the center of the road.

I looked at my watch. It was 11:17. I had forty-three minutes. And then that son of a bitch down on Crosby Street would start killing in his not-very-pretty way.

I snapped the Dodge's door open. It slammed into the side of the BMW, chipping the paint. I slid out fast.

Young Mr. Executive started to come out after me.

"What the fuck's the matter . . ."

I slammed his door, forcing him back inside.

"Shut up," I said.

I went around the Dodge, leapt onto the sidewalk, and headed up the steps to Wexler's town house.

He was waiting for me. He must have known—or feared—that this was one of the ways it could go.

As I reached the top of the stoop, the maid in the black uniform opened the door for me. I nearly knocked her down as I pushed past her into the front hall.

In the shadow of the staircase that wound grandly to the second floor, Wexler stood alone. He was wearing a trim, elegant, three-piece suit. One of his hands was perched in its vest pocket. The other dangled down easily at his side. His legs were slightly akimbo so that one of his feet fell on a black marble tile and the other fell on a white one. The pouches of his cheeks turned upward with a slight, welcoming smile. His watery eyes glinted warmly with it. He looked the perfect host.

He started speaking the second I entered. "Well, John," he said, a little too quickly. "I was rather hoping you hadn't yet gotten quite this far."

I wasn't listening. I was striding toward him over the marble. Almost before he finished, my fingers were curling around his expensive lapels.

"I filed the story, Wexler. Call him off," I said.

He swiped at my hands. I held on to him. "Let go of me," he said. There was an edge of panic in his voice. He fought it down, steadied himself. He looked me in the eye. This time it was a threat: "Let go of me."

I thought of slugging him. Then I thought of Chandler. My

hands unclenched. His lapels slipped from them. He dropped away a step.

He dabbed at his suit with his fingers.

I lowered over him like a storm. "You only took her to get to me," I said. "But it's too late, man. The story's in. 'The editor of the popular newsweekly *Globe* may have had a motive for the murder of Timothy Colt.' That's my lede. Like it?"

He took a breath, drew himself up a bit. The panic was still there, just beneath his damp glare, but he held it at bay. "Very nice," he said. " 'May have had.' Very responsible of you."

"I figured if you were in custody for the late editions I could change it."

"Another scoop for John Wells, boy reporter." He sniffed at me. He waved a hand at the maid. "That will be all, Terry," he said.

Terry was saucer-eyed. For a moment she didn't react at all. Then her body lowered a little in a sort of curtsy. She backed out of the room.

Wexler gave his full attention back to me. "If you run that story," he said simply, "your friend will die."

"What's the point of that?" I said. "What's the point of that anymore? It's over, man. It was all for nothing. It'll be in the bulldog for everyone to see."

Donald Wexler turned his back on me. He took two paces away and turned. A rainbow from one of the crystals in the chandelier above us danced on his forehead. It settled. It trembled. So did he.

There was a grandfather clock in the hall's far corner. I heard it ticking toward the half hour. "I always knew it would happen, you know," he said. "I never thought I could keep it hidden even as long as this. I even thought . . . .it shows how silly you can be, really. I even thought I would take it gracefully when the end came. Go quietly into obscurity and poverty . . . even death, if it came to that . . . and just be thankful for what I'd had."

"It might never have happened. They might never have figured it out."

He smiled. Wistfully, I thought. "Oh, but they would have. Colt would have, anyway. You don't know what he was like."

He cocked his head to one side. "Or perhaps you do, John. You're really so much like him." He swiveled his profile to me. He paced away from the winding stairs, turned, paced back. "And when I saw that it had come, at last, when Paul showed up in the tavern and I realized that the day of reckoning had actually arrived, well, I wasn't willing to go quite as quietly—to lose all"—he waved vaguely at the grandeur of the place—"to lose all this as serenely as I'd imagined." He stopped, raised his eyes to me in a speculative glance. "I wonder if you would believe me if I told you that it wasn't the money. Well, it was: the money, the position, all of that. But mostly . . . mostly it was Anne. Mostly, it was the thought of losing my wife Anne. I do love her, you know. When Colt and Paul got in that fight . . . the situation seemed to be tailor-made. I thought the police would just naturally gravitate toward Paul as the suspect." He shrugged. It was a strangely frivolous gesture. "You know, it probably would have gone just right, too, if you hadn't happened to be there. I couldn't have known about that, of course. Even then, if you had just stopped . . . stopped worrying at it, John. Or if Geoffrey had killed you in the park. Or if you'd figured it out tomorrow instead of today. Then you'd have gone after Miss Burke, wouldn't you, and . . . well, everything would be all right."

I nodded. I didn't give a damn. I despised him. It wasn't a pleasant sensation. I didn't hate him for having Colt killed. I wasn't angry at him for holding Chandler. I didn't even condemn him for trying to murder me. I just despised him—despised him for being weak and making other people suffer for it. Colt, Chandler, me. Eleanora. I thought of her screaming, dying for Wexler's weakness. I felt nothing for him but disdain.

Because he was weak, he had lied. Even before Sentu, he had filed that phony story, pretended to infiltrate a cult when he hadn't. He'd gotten himself fired, disgraced. He'd had to go to Sentu to redeem himself. But no matter how far he went, he was still the same. When the rebels had broken through the army lines, when they'd headed for the city of Mangrela, Wexler had been in Jacobo with Colt. They'd both planned to return to Mangrela, Colt to rescue Eleanora, Wexler to cover the city's downfall. Colt returned. He'd been terrified, he'd nearly been killed, but he returned. Wexler had said he would follow. But when Paul arrived in Jacobo with Eleanora a week later, Wexler was still there. By that time, the passage between the two cities was slow and dangerous even for someone with Paul's connections. Wexler could not have made it to Mangrela and back in such a short time. He must never have returned to the capital.

He must have decided not to risk his life for the story. And that was fine. No one expected him to. No one would have held it against him.

But then he filed the story anyway. He had won the Pulitzer Prize for his series on the fall of Mangrela. He had won the Pulitzer and regained his reputation and come back to a fine job and a marriage to a socialite and the inheritance of millions because he had filed on the fall of Mangrela. Another faked story, like the one on the cult. Only this time, he'd gotten away with it. He'd gotten away with it because, in a way, it wasn't really faked at all. When Wexler, too frightened to go to Mangrela, got caught in Jacobo, he made his way to Eleanora's safe house, desperate to escape. There, he found her radio. He heard Robert Collins filing from the falling capital. He promised to pass the dispatches on and took them down. Collins must have kept filing until he died. Wexler must have heard him die. . . .

And, when Collins was dead, Wexler must have begun to think about what he had.

He had a story. A good story. The last dispatches from Mangrela. Filed long after the airlift, long after the other Western journalists had fled. They were all his, no one knew he had them. Now all he had to do was get the hell out of there and file them himself.

That's when Paul showed up with Eleanora. The minute Wexler heard her name, he must have realized he had a ticket to ride. He went to the rebels who had now taken over the city. He promised to tell them the whereabouts of the leader of the underground in exchange for his freedom. They went for the deal. That's why they came for her in the dead of night. Wexler had sold her out . . . and gone free.

He'd gone free, and he'd taken a couple of refugees with him. A couple of the children. It was his excuse for leaving the others at the safe house, but maybe one of those—the one he'd called Geoffrey—was a fledgling assassin, the kind of

murder-man Paul described. Maybe Wexler liked the idea of
having a kid like that indebted to him for his life. Anyway,
he'd brought them home and they'd become his servants. Maybe
one of them was the chauffeur I'd missed at Colt's funeral.
Whatever. He'd saved their lives and they were forever grateful
to him. They were willing to do anything for him.

Including kill Tim Colt.

Once Paul showed up, Colt had to die. At least one of
them did—Colt or Paul, it didn't matter which. The only thing
that mattered to Wexler was that if the two got together, if
they talked, if they realized they'd each seen Wexler in Jacobo,
then both of them would have discovered what neither of them
knew alone: Wexler could not possibly have written the stories
that had won him the Pulitzer.

Wexler would have been disgraced again. Colt would have
made sure of that. He would have been disgraced, and with a
lot more to lose than the last time. The job, the wife, the
money, the reputation. And, if Colt had kept thinking, he might
have realized what Wexler had done to Eleanora, too. And
then, Wexler might even have lost his life.

So he had to kill one of them. He didn't know where Paul
was. He had to kill one of them, so he sent his faithful servant
after Colt, hoping Paul would catch the blame for it.

But I'd gotten drunk and passed out on the sofa. And I
became a witness. And now I was more than that.

I fought to keep the disdain out of my voice. "Call him
off, Wexler," I said again. "I filed the story before I left.
What have you got to gain now?"

"Time," he answered immediately. "I still need time."
He faced me fully again. He stood with his hands clasped
behind his back. He stood very erect. "Whatever happens now,
I will lose everything. I will lose Anne, when she finds out
the truth, and very little else matters. But if I can somehow
persuade you to hold the story for one day, one single day,
Wells, I will have time to gather whatever . . . liquid assets
are available to me, and make my way out of the country. If
I must live in exile, I would like to live comfortably. That's
not too much to ask."

"If I hold the story, you'll let Chandler go."

He nodded. "Correct."

"Right now."

"Of course not. If you hold the story, I will call Geoffrey and tell him not to kill her. When I am safely out of the country, he will release her."

I glanced at my watch. Thirty-five minutes left.

"It's done," I said. "Call him."

"I have your word."

"Yes. Call him."

Wexler seemed to consider this for a moment. Then he nodded once. He gestured at me to follow and headed toward the draped entranceway that led to the living room.

He ducked under the drape. I followed. I saw the walls of gilded mirrors reflecting the marble statues back and forth at one another. Wexler was moving among the sofas and chairs with their scrolled legs and arms. Moving toward a little oaken table on which sat an antique telephone. I took two steps toward him and stopped.

Someone had come up behind me and placed a gun barrel against the base of my skull.

29

I raised my hands. It seemed like the thing to do. Wexler stopped and turned to me. He looked surprised, as if he'd just remembered something.

"Oh . . . William," he said. "No, no, there's no need for that. Mr. Wells and I have come to an understanding."

"Yeah, William," I said. "An understanding."

The gun barrel was pulled away from my head. William came sidling around me into view. He turned out to be the guy who had chased me through F.A.O. Schwarz. He looked jumpy as a moth on a light bulb.

Wexler stood by the phone table waiting for him. William came up beside him. Wexler extended his hand, palm up. William gave him the gun.

"Thank you," Wexler said. And to me: "I'm sorry. When I saw you coming, I didn't have much time to prepare. I thought it best to have William in reserve. You understand?"

"Most natural thing in the world," I said.

Wexler smiled thinly. He turned to the phone. He picked up the handset. I put my hands down. The grandfather clock chimed. Eleven-thirty.

Wexler stuck his dialing finger in the rotator.

The doorbell rang. Wexler tilted his head like a bird trying to get a look at something.

Goddamn it! Goddamn it, I thought. *Not now*.

It was the cops. I'd told Cochran to send them, and maybe

I should have waited for them to show up. But now the timing was all wrong. They were the last thing I wanted. The last thing in the world.

"Who on earth is *that*?" Wexler murmured. Absently he began to replace the handset.

"Listen, would you call first," I said.

"What?" He looked up at me, dazed.

That was all the time it took. The maid was at the door. Good old efficient Terry. I heard the latch click. I heard Gottlieb's voice, flat and hard and sharp as a knife blade: "Police!"

Wexler heard it, too. For a moment, he seemed not to comprehend. In another, it seemed to wash over him in a great red wave of understanding and anger. He stared at the drapery that hid the hall. He turned and stared at me. Back at the drapery again. And then he panicked.

That, after all, was Wexler's way: he panicked. He always had. He'd panicked when he faked a story because he thought he might not make it on the up-and-up. He panicked when he was faced with traveling through rebel lines. He panicked when he robbed Collins and sold out Eleanora. And he panicked when he saw Paul and ordered the killing of Colt. That was who he was, that was what he did. He was weak and he panicked. He panicked now.

The drapery was thrown aside. Gottlieb came charging through at the head of a wedge of patrolmen. He was resplendent in his mustard-colored jacket and peach shirt, his stocky shoulders squared, two cops striding on either side of him.

Wexler—his watery eyes wide—raised his pistol at him.

The wedge of cops exploded in all directions. The patrolmen dove for cover. Two dropped to the floor. One went skidding under a sofa. One went flying over a chair, went headfirst into a statue of a young man. The statue began to totter.

Gottlieb stayed on his feet. He stepped to one side, shoving me out of the way with his shoulder. At the same time, his hand shot inside his mustard-colored coat.

Wexler waved the big gun wildly. He fired it. It bucked in his hand. Gottlieb yanked out his detective's special.

I stumbled against a chair, one of my knees planted in the seat cushion. Beside me, the statue tilted this way and that.

Wexler brought his gun under control. He leveled it at Gottlieb. The detective took aim.

I held my hands up. I screamed crazily. "Don't fire, don't fire, don't fire!"

Gottlieb fired first. A black hole appeared at the dead center of Wexler's forehead. The rest of his brow seemed to cave into that hole from either side. Wexler skidded back across the floor on his heels. Then he fell over stiffly. He bounced on the floor stiffly. He was dead.

There was a second of silence. It seemed to go on forever. Wexler's body seemed to rock, head to toe, as it settled endlessly. William's mouth seemed to open and open and open on a cry of mourning, but the cry never seemed to come. The tottering statue finally fell with a crash. William cried out. The statue's head broke off and it rolled across the floor: *burrump burrump burrump*.

Gottlieb shook his head. "Ooh, I hate things like this," he said.

"Oh Christ," I said. "Chandler."

I started running for the hall.

"John, wait!" Gottlieb shouted.

I couldn't wait. It was twenty-five minutes to noon.

f there are police, I will kill her.

My old friend, the murder-man. He was out there now, on his own.

I will kill her in my not-very-pretty way.

Without Wexler to call him off, I'd have to go after him alone. One sight of the police and he'd tear her to pieces. He'd said so, and I believed him. I'd seen the man at work.

I was out the town house door. I skittered down the front steps. The street was blocked with cop cars. It would take me fifteen minutes just to get the Dodge out of it.

I started running. Toward Fifth Avenue. Dimly, at my back, I heard a shout: "There he is, Officers! There he is! That's the man who dented my BMW!" I did not slow down.

I could see as I approached the Avenue that there were cabs everywhere. They were heading downtown toward that gathering mass of Christmas-shopping fares. That mass that would soon have traffic on lower Fifth at a standstill. I reached the corner and held out my hand. Luck was with me. A cab pulled over at once.

I leaned in at the driver's window desperately.

"Can you speak English?" I cried.

He poked his round, mustachioed face at me. "Jes. A leetle."

"Can you get me to Crosby Street in fifteen minutes?"

His eyes widened.

"For twenty bucks," I said.

His eyes widened some more. "I weel try, my freng."

I jumped in the back. There were twenty-three minutes left.

It took him twenty. I don't know how he did it. Down Fifth awhile. Over to Park. Around Grand Central. On down into the jumbled streets and squares below Twenty-third. He never sped up much, he never slowed down. I think he hit every light. I think he won every tug-of-war for street space with the other cabs. In the Village, where the roads narrowed to single lanes crushed between cafés, I think he invented empty byroads, then took us down them.

They were twenty excruciating minutes, all the same. Helpless, I sat in the back, my eyes shooting from my watch to the street signs. I told myself that Geoffrey would not kill her at the stroke of noon. He would phone in first, try to reach Wexler. He would find out something was wrong. Maybe he would abandon plan A and move to another. Maybe a lot of things.

I lit a cigarette, took a drag. It felt fine. I leaned back with my head against the seat. I thought of Wexler's brow caving in around the black spot in the center. I thought of his body rocking on the floor. I thought I had never tasted a better cigarette than this. I did not know anything could taste so good.

I sat up with a start. I had lost track of myself. Drifted off in my own thoughts. For a second I felt panic rising in me as I wondered what time it was. I looked at my watch. Seventeen of. Thirty seconds had passed since I'd looked last. It had seemed like an hour.

And the driver kept to his course.

We hit the spot with three whole minutes to spare. Three whole minutes for Chandler to keep living. The driver left me off on the corner of Crosby and Spring. I handed my last thirty dollars across the seat to him.

"You're a genius," I said, and jumped out of the car.

Even at noon, Crosby Street looked dark. The heavy walls of the old loft buildings leaned close to each other from either side of the warped cobbled lane. The air, when you looked down the road, seemed overhung with shadows. There was no one in sight. No cars. No signs of life at all.

The address Geoffrey had given me belonged to a loft building that sat right on the corner. Six stories of concrete.

A heavy, rounded cornice rimmed the flat top. Rows of pilasters marked every floor.

On the side facing Spring, a rusting fire escape zigzagged down from between some of the windows. On Crosby Street, there were only the windows. Huge windows. Great blank screens staring out on either side. They were pivot-hung, the kind that swivel on a pivot in the center. They were the same kind as the ones in Colt's room. The ones through which Geoffrey had vanished after nearly killing me. The blank stare of those windows made the building look abandoned.

I jogged a few steps down Crosby until I reached the building's front door. It was a heavy wooden door with black paint chipping off it. There was a For Rent plaque screwed into the wall beside it. I didn't recognize the realtor's name, but it was a good guess the building belonged to Wexler.

I pushed through the door into a gray, shabby vestibule. My feet scraped over the curling floor tiles. There were mailboxes on one wall. There were no names on any of them. There were buzzer buttons in a line beside a speaker. The buttons were unmarked also, but Geoffrey had told me to hit the one for the third floor.

Somewhere, outside, I heard a church bell ringing. I reached for the button. Chandler started to scream.

I heard her only dimly. A thin cry from inside, beyond the door. I jammed my finger against the button. I hit it again and again. I heard the screaming stop.

I looked at my watch. It was twelve on the money.

"Jesus!" I hissed to myself. "You asshole! Jesus!"

The speaker crackled at my left shoulder. Geoffrey's voice followed.

"Mr. Wells," he said. "Good of you to come."

The buzzer sounded. I pushed the door open. I let it swing shut again. I turned and sprinted out of the vestibule onto the street.

I had figured from the beginning that he meant to kill us both. He had let Chandler see his face, after all. And though Wexler's motive for getting rid of us vanished when I got wise to him and wrote my story, Geoffrey still had a good enough reason to want the two of us out of the way.

I did not plan to lumber up the stairs while he waited for me. I did not plan to have him meet me at the front door.

I hurried around back to Spring Street instead. I stood under the building's fire escape. The ladder was in the up position. It dangled about two feet above my head. I jumped. I felt a muscle in my armpit tear. I grabbed hold of the ladder. For a second I dangled in the air. I felt a muscle in my shoulder tear. Then the ladder came loose and rattled down.

Wincing with pain, I climbed up to the first landing. I went quietly from there. I ran up the stairs on the balls of my feet. All the same, the metal steps rattled below me. My own breathing seemed to roar. I went by the first-floor window. It was about a foot from the stairs. I could peek in at the huge expanse of loft behind the glass. I glimpsed the door of it. It was on the opposite wall, where I thought it would be. That's where I hoped Geoffrey was standing now. Peering out into the hall. Waiting.

I kept climbing. Up past the rows of pilasters. Up to the second-story window. Here I noticed that the window was shut. For a second, I was afraid that Geoffrey's would be locked. But I did not think it would be. I think he had a penchant for open windows, for potential avenues of escape. I think it was the first thing they taught him at Murder-Man U.

And on to the third floor. I kept my back bent. I kept my head low. I came up onto the third-floor landing. I was on my knees. I leaned out over the railing to look inside.

Geoffrey was there. He was at the door across the long expanse of the loft. The door was open. He was leaning out into the hall. I could only see his back. He was where I wanted him.

I reached for the window. I touched it. The huge pane swung. The glass swung in on my side, out on the other. It swung in silence. A beautiful silence. The figure at the door didn't turn. A small opening appeared between the glass and the wall.

I stepped over the edge of the fire escape right onto the windowsill. I grabbed hold of the window's jamb and hoisted my other leg around. I slid into the loft that smoothly, that easily. My feet came down on the floor with hardly a sound.

Now I was standing in the long, empty room. I could smell the fresh paint on the white walls, see the patina of paint dust covering the floor. Networks of exposed piping ran overhead. They'd been painted lavender by way of decoration.

Geoffrey's back was to me still. He was maybe fifteen running steps away.

I took one of those steps before he turned, smiling, and leveled the .22 at me.

He did not look the same as when we'd met in Colt's hotel. I don't suppose I did either. That meeting had taken its toll on both of us. I could feel it in me. I could see it in him. His nose was an ugly, scabby mess. His brow was crisscrossed with scars. The dark lines that made him seem older than his twenty-odd years were still there. But some of them were darker still. Some of them were jagged from where I'd ripped at them with my fingers.

His eyes, too, were different now. When he'd killed Colt, they had been cold, impassive. Now, as he got ready to kill me, they were like the gray ash covering a red-hot coal. He was smoldering with rage.

He smiled. It was a cold, black smile, like a gash cut in granite. He closed the door quietly. I stood frozen beside the partly open window.

"Mr. Wells," Geoffrey said. That light, swift sound. "That was very close to intelligent."

I shrugged. "I'm a brainy guy. Where is she?"

He puffed some air through his lips by way of laughing. "This is not the thing that should worry you most right now, I think."

"Listen, my friend," I said. I pointed at him. I thought it would make me look tough. "Wexler's dead."

His face went impassive. Only his eyes stayed hot, alive.

"The cops shot him fifteen minutes ago. That'll be on the radio now, if you don't believe me. Everything else'll be in the *Star* tomorrow."

The fire of his anger had spread now from his eyes. I watched it. It made him quiver like a plucked string. When he spoke next, his voice had lost its lightness. It had become the rasp of a knife cutting bone.

"Why . . . Why did you . . . *pursue* this?"

"Same reason you kill without thinking, pal. It's what I'm trained for." He stared at me blankly. He did not seem to understand what I was saying. I said: "The point is: it's over. The cops have got your friend William. He strikes me as the nervous type. He's probably talking right now. Probably telling them all about you. If I were you, my friend, I'd head for the hills. At least let the woman go, you don't . . .''

In the wildness of his fury, Geoffrey was looking around him. He looked at the floor, at the ceiling. He seemed to be searching heaven and hell for help. Finally he looked down at the gun in his hand.

He looked up at me. ''The woman?'' he said. ''You were too late to save the woman. You were fifteen seconds too late.'' He smiled again. He giggled. Hee hee hee. A high-pitched, childish sound.

I felt something inside me turn to dust.

''You fuck,'' I said. It was barely audible.

He giggled some more. Hee hee hee. He looked at my face and fought to control himself. He frowned in mock sympathy. ''Oh, so grim, Mr. Wells. Do you hurt a little? A little bit like I hurt? I am so sorry. So sorry. I can hardly bear myself. Here . . . shoot me.''

He tossed the gun onto the floor between us.

I did not move. I stared at the gun. It lay in the white paint dust. I looked up. Geoffrey gestured to it with his left hand.

''Go ahead,'' he said simply. With his right hand, he drew a small black cylinder out of his pocket. There was a click. I saw the silver switchblade flick out into the open. I guess he was out of ceremonial knives. This would do, though. It gleamed in the light. ''I have hoped for this since our meeting in the hotel,'' he said. ''I had hoped for the chance to do this unpleasant thing to you that I know. Now . . . now that you have Mr. Wexler's blood on your hands . . . now it will be all the sweeter. Go ahead, Mr. Wells. Pick up the gun.''

I held my breath. I could not stop staring at that gun. It was smack between us. I'd never killed anyone before. I don't even know much about handling guns. But it didn't matter. I wanted my hands on that revolver. I wanted my finger on the trigger. I wanted the barrel trained on his skull. I wanted this guy. I wanted to kill him.

I jumped forward. It was a feint. I went with the top half of my body, but brought my right foot forward and braced myself, pulled up short. That was all it took. Geoffrey sailed into the air, across the room. He landed with his feet astride the pistol, the knife poised, ready to cut my throat. If I had really gone for it, I wouldn't have had a chance.

I straightened. Geoffrey grinned. He came forward. I didn't even have time to go out the window. Not the way he moved. I stood there. I waited.

He came forward another step. He slashed the air in front of him with his knife. He raised his eyebrows as if to ask me: How do you like it? He flipped the knife up in the air. It twirled end over end. He caught it cleanly by the handle. He giggled. If he took another step, he'd have me.

He took another step.

I grabbed the edge of the window and slung it at him. It came whistling around on its pivot like a revolving wall. For a single frozen instant, Geoffrey seemed to flash and waver behind the glass. He was still grinning when the thing hit him.

The heavy sill struck him just below the waist. His upper body snapped forward. His head smashed through the glass, and it shattered all around him. There was a cascade of sprinkling shards amid a pink spray of blood. I came wheeling back around and clubbed him with my fist on the side of the head.

That was the only time he screamed. The blow sent his face into the jagged shards still protruding from the frame. The scream became a gurgling sound as his face seemed to dissolve in a gout of blood.

Geoffrey sagged. He dangled over the bottom of the frame, dripping blood. Slowly he began to slide backward. His arms slid over the frame, pulling off pieces of glass as they went. He cleared it, finally. He fell to the floor. He lay there on his back. There was a single gleam of white in his bloody face where one of his eyes stared up at the ceiling. There was a round black hole in the red blood too. It was his mouth, still drawing breath. His chest rose and fell heavily.

Other than that, he was motionless.

"Chandler," I said.

I went through the loft, shouting her name. I shouted again and again. My voice grew more frantic with every second.

After what seemed a very long time, she called back to me. It was a weary, forlorn sound, full of tears. I followed it down a little hall. There was a bathroom there. She was lying on the floor, handcuffed to the pipe beneath the sink.

He'd cut her. The front of her dress was torn open. It was soggy with blood. He'd cut her just under the arm, just where the swell of her breast began. He'd cut her deep. Her head

slumped on her shoulder. She was fading from the loss of
blood and from the pain.

I went back in the big room. Geoffrey was still lying there,
gasping like a fish. There was a phone on the floor. I called
the cops. Then I dug into Geoffrey's pockets until I found his
keys.

When I set Chandler free, she started to cry. Her mouth
opened and closed once or twice as she looked at me. Her
cheeks were streaked with mascara. Her nose ran. She laid her
hands together on her outstretched legs. She rubbed her wrists
together. She cried. I put my arm around her shoulder. She
shrugged me off. I tried again. She gave a short, shrieking
sound and pulled free.

"Leave me alone," she said, crying.

I sat with her till the police showed up.

It rained the day Lester Paul left the country. It was January then. It was cold in that damp way that eats into your bones. The rain fell steadily. You could not see it fall. It was just an opaque sheet lowered from a gray sky, a sky that seemed like it had never been any color but gray.

I drove out to Kennedy in the rain. I parked and walked through the rain to the main departures terminal. Paul had called me at the *Star* at noon, not three hours before. He'd told me to meet him here quickly if I wanted to say good-bye.

I stood by the long window in the departures building. I smoked a cigarette and watched the planes taxi down the runway. I watched them gather speed, bolt into the air, and fly away.

I felt a hand on my shoulder. I turned and saw a young soldier standing before me. He was a pimply-faced kid, from the Midwest it looked like. His blond hair was cut short on the side. On top it was covered by an olive garrison cap.

It took me a moment before I recognized him. Then I laughed and shook my head.

"Ssh," he said.

"What am I supposed to do?" I said. "Salute?"

He smiled. "Disguise may not be dignified, but for me, it's the only way to travel." He even spoke in a flat midwestern twang.

I laughed again, nodded. He popped one of his perfumed

cigarettes between his lips, bent toward the match I offered
him. We walked together slowly beside the window.

"I have not had a chance to congratulate you on your fine
stories," he said. "You made quite a sensation there for a day
or so."

"Thanks," I said. It was true enough. For a day or so,
even the cops had been reading us for information. I was the
only one who had the whole story on Wexler and Sentu.

"I liked the way you wrote about *her* especially," Paul
went on. "If I did not know better, I would have thought you
had actually met her."

We walked for a few moments without speaking. Beyond
the pane of glass, the airplanes taxied, lifted, flew into the gray
sky.

"It was easy," I said finally.

And that was also true. It had been easy to write about
Eleanora. For a couple of hours, sitting there at my Olympia,
I had felt she was with me. I had seen her cool white figure,
her golden hair piled high, her sleek neck showing. I had seen
her passing among the refugees, offering them solace, working
for their escape. I had seen her the way she was when she
refused to leave Mangrela with the children. I had seen her
with her chin uptilted in defiance. I had seen her eyes alight
and alive. I had imagined them looking into mine.

More than anything, I had seen her as the woman who
wrote that letter. That letter Mrs. Colt had shown me.

*If this intimacy with death is what we have to pay for our
intimacy with living and each other, then I wanted to tell you
tonight, my darling, that your smallest kindness to me was
worth it, that your whispered word was worth it, that the
briefest sight of you was worth it as nothing else could be. . . .*

And when you made love to her, she was like a statue of
white marble suddenly suffused with life. I had seen her that
way, too.

It had been easy to write about her, all right. It had been
hard to stop.

"And the charming Miss Burke," Paul said. I looked up
out of the memory, startled. "I trust she's well."

"Fine, fine," I said. "As far as I know, anyway."

"Ah."

I shrugged. "She got a little tired of the company I keep."

"My condolences."

I shrugged again.

I had not heard from her since she had gone home. I had called her once. When she answered, I told her who it was. She began to speak, then hesitated. A long silence followed. Finally she hung up quietly. I had not called again.

"I trust," said Lester Paul, "that your acquaintance with someone so . . . unsavory as myself didn't contribute to your problems. With Miss Burke, I mean." He gave me his half-mocking smile. It looked strangely cosmopolitan on the young army recruit.

I tossed my cigarette to the floor. The butt lay smoking amid a dozen dead ones. "Don't flatter yourself," I said.

We both stopped walking at once. We faced each other. Paul swept his cap off, tucked it under his arm. "You know, Wells," he said. His midwestern twang was gone suddenly. I heard that trace of an accent in his voice again. Was it German? I wasn't sure. "You know, you are a very smart man. My question is: how smart?"

"Just smart enough not to be dumb," I said.

"Your stories in the newspaper were quite good, as I say, but it seemed to me that they were stories without a beginning. It seemed to me that when last we met, you neglected to ask me the one question that should have troubled you most of all."

I nodded. "It slipped my mind in all the excitement."

"Or perhaps you did not want to know the answer."

"Yeah, perhaps," I said. "Anyway, that's why I'm here now."

He cocked an eyebrow at me, waiting.

"Why did you come to the Press Club, Paul?" I asked him. "What the hell were you doing there that night Colt came in? It couldn't have been coincidence?"

He laughed. "Smart enough. For a while I was afraid I had overestimated you." He reached up and stroked his acne-covered cheeks with his fingers. It was a gentle motion: an actor checking his makeup. Satisfied, he looked out through the window at the runway. He sighed. "No, it was not coincidence. I was there because my sources had told me that Tim Colt would be passing through New York. And, on arriving, I learned that the Press Club was one of his favorite taverns."

"You were looking for him, then."

"Of course."

"Why?"

"Because she's alive."

It was the answer I was waiting for. The minute he said it, my pulse rose and pounded. I fought it down again. I shot a new cigarette into my mouth, stalling. I raised a match to it. "Go ahead," I said from behind the flame.

Paul didn't turn from the window. "It's just a rumor," he said. "But I've heard it more than once."

I waved out my match. I let out a deep breath of smoke. "And you believe it."

His shoulders lifted. "I maintain an open mind."

"Okay. What's the source?"

"Several weeks ago, I had reason to be in Lebanon," he said. "My business took me there. I had dealings with certain . . . political groups . . . and I heard them discussing . . ."

I tossed the match away. I watched it arc through the air, fall amid the litter on the floor.

"A woman," Paul said.

I gazed at the match where it lay. I said nothing.

"They say she is running an underground railway," Paul went on. "An escape route for Muslim and Christians alike . . ." He turned from the window. His voice became low, tense, urgent. "An escape route for both sides, Wells. Do you understand me? For all sides . . . And something else."

I looked up into his sunken eyes. They bore into me, sharp, intense.

Paul said: "I heard them talk about a love affair she'd had with a Western reporter. They said it happened in Beirut, but still . . ."

"Come on, Paul," I said. "She loved him. She loved Colt. I saw her letter to him. If she were alive, she'd have found him. Hell, he'd have found her. Somehow, they'd—"

"She's disfigured."

I stopped. "What?"

"They say she was kidnapped at some point by a renegade group of terrorists, but maybe . . . maybe it happened after she was captured in Sentu. At any rate, according to the story, she was raped, tortured. Her face and body mutilated. They say when they let her go, she felt too . . . ashamed . . ."

Sweat beaded on Paul's forehead. He cursed, dropped his cigarette, ground it out beneath his heel. He set his cap back on his head, fixed it at a jaunty angle. With an effort, he gave me a wan smile. "I came back," he said more slowly, "because I felt I owed Colt that much. After I abandoned her at Jacobo, I felt the least I could do was to tell him this. But when I saw him in the Press Club that night, I realized that if I told him face-to-face . . . well, it might have been an uncomfortable situation. I decided to wait outside and trail him to his hotel. I would have called him there . . . if I had gotten out before he saw me."

We looked at each other for a long time. "Or maybe you just balked at the thought of giving her back to him."

His smile widened. "Yeah, perhaps," he said in his flat American twang again. He stopped smiling. "You don't believe it, do you? You don't believe it is possible?"

My lips parted. I thought of Chandler Burke. I thought of the sound of her silence on the other end of the phone line. Already, I realized, that silence was beginning to seem more real to me than Eleanora. I began to speak.

But Paul raised a finger at me. He cocked his head, listening. A voice over the loudspeaker announced a flight to Israel.

"Ah," he said. "A pity." He stuck his hand out to me. "I must go."

I stared at the hand a second, surprised. Then I took hold of it, shook it. "You're going back," I said.

"Yes," he said. "I am going back."

"Paul . . ."

"I have business there."

I let his hand drop away. "Business," I said.

"It is risky business, I suppose. But it is my business now." He studied me for a second as passengers hurried by on either side of us. "You know, I would not consider it an imposition if . . . if you wished to come along? In a free market, there is always room for competition."

I looked into his eyes. I saw the ghosts in there that haunted him. "Thanks," I said quietly. "But I have business here. I have business in the city."

"Of course. Well . . ."

"Good luck, Paul."

"Good-bye, my friend."

He turned and started walking toward the gates. But then he turned again and faced me, walking backward. He forced a smile. He called to me: "But you do believe the enterprise is possible? Don't you?"

"Anything is possible," I lied.

He seemed reassured. He waved. He turned once more, still walking. I watched him go through the security check. Then I headed for the door in the opposite direction.

It was still early. Three-thirty or so. I still had time to get some work done. I was doing a story about the city finance department. I had a line on an assessor who might be taking big-time bribes.

I was grateful for that story. Grateful it was waiting for me. It meant I didn't have to think about going home for a while. It meant I didn't have to think about the empty apartment with the lights from the movie marquee glaring through the window. Glaring on the pictures that hid the cracks on the wall.

The terminal's electric doors slid open. I stepped outside. I tossed my cigarette into a puddle and started walking for my car. I flipped up the collar of my overcoat. I stuck my hands in my pockets. I eyed the sky and cursed.

The rain was beginning to turn to snow. It was going to be a long drive back to the city.